Tears in God's Own Country

A Novel

CLIFF ANTHONY

AMC Publications LLC

Jacket cover artwork:
Medha Karandikar
https:Medhaonline.com

Acknowledgments

I cannot thank those who provided me abundant fuel during my seven years of journey to complete *Tears in God's Own Country*.

My heartfelt gratitude goes, not in any particular order, to the members of the Fiction Writing Workshop at the South Euclid-Lyndhurst library, Ohio, for their suggestions; the workshop's coach Sarah Willis, author of *Some Things That Stay* and other novels, for her invaluable guidance; and Laurie Kincer, Writing Specialist at William N. Skirball Writers' Center at the library, for her encouragement and finding office space so I could string words without distraction.

My gratitude to Pulitzer finalist Bruce Weigl for his gentle nudges when I needed them the most; Sharon Smutak for her eagle eye and edits; and Abby Collette, author of *A Deadly Inside Scoop* and other novels.

My special thanks to my long-time friend and artist, Medha Karandikar, for creating a stunning jacket cover.

I'm grateful to *chenda* maestro Satish Kumar, of Trivandrum, now known as Thiruvananthapuram, Kerala, for explaining the nuances of playing the kettledrum and letting me practice the percussion; and to the partners of Surabhilam Homestay in Kovalam beach—Ram Balasubramanian and Arif Khan—for their hospitality, which helped me jumpstart one of my rewrites as the nearby Arabian Sea sang the songs of inspiration.

Last but not least, I'm indebted to my wife Mary and my daughter Anna Marie for their patience and for letting me wander in the fictional Alumaram Village while pretending to be watching TV with them. I'll be amiss if I don't acknowledge that my daughter was the main driving force behind this venture.

Jayge, Kerala

This novel is dedicated

to my parents in heaven

S. Pichiya and Muthulekshmi Ammal

We must have an innate respect for other religions as we have for our own. Mind you, not mutual tolerance, but mutual respect.

Mahatma Gandhi

I have a dream that my four little children will one day live in a nation where they will not be judged by the color of their skin but by the content of their character.

Dr. Martin Luther King Jr.

1

CROSS-TOED AMMU was the first to notice Chenda's body. Initially, the strange object on the northwest bank of the Alumaram River looked like a buffalo carcass.

She saw the dark object during her obsessive spitting from the bridge onto the river on her way to the market at the Alumaram Village junction to sell vegetables. She ignored it because it was not unusual for the river to dump tree branches, debris, and animal carcasses on its banks. But the continuous loud barking of a stray dog at the object prompted her to look again. Confused, she screwed up her eyes, studied it closely, and still couldn't figure it out. She pointed out the object to her niece Kamala, who accompanied her to the market, and asked, "Edi, what is that? A buffalo?"

"No. It definitely is not a buffalo," Kamala replied. "It's difficult to see clearly from here. But I'm sure it's not a buffalo."

So, they slowly walked from the bridge down the slope to the riverbank to check it out. Their bare toes provided a firm grip, like a bird's claws on the steep slope, preventing them from slipping and rolling into the river.

"Ayyo, Dhyvamey! Pretam. A dead body," screamed Cross-toed Ammu as soon as she had a closer view of the object. She trembled with trepidation and grabbed her niece for support. Kamala covered her mouth with her hand in horror. They looked closer.

"This is our Chenda!" Cross-toed Ammu screamed again.

"Oh, my God! Oh, my Amman Devi!" Kamala whimpered and held Cross-toed Ammu's hand tightly for support.

"We've to tell Big-legged Appu and astrologer Guru," she told Kamala.

They rushed from the riverbank onto the bridge and then to the junction, the heart of Alumaram Village. Driven by adrenalin and gripped by fear and confusion, they walked the one-mile unpaved street within half the time it would otherwise take to reach her destination. On the way, in trembling voices, they told whomever they met about their gruesome discovery.

"Our Chenda is dead. His body is under the bridge," Cross-toed Ammu told Appu.

He listened carefully, but suspiciously, and asked, "Are you sure it was Chenda? Our Chenda?"

"I swear it was our Chenda," she asserted, annoyed at Appu for doubting her. "I'm going to astrologer Guru's house to tell him. He should know this."

"Tell Guru I'm on my way to the river," Appu said. His hands and the scissors worked feverishly to finish clipping a customer's hair, he told a waiting customer to come later, and closed the barber shop. He took his bicycle, made sure the pedal didn't chafe his right leg with elephantiasis, and rode like a maniac to the Alumaram River.

ON THEIR way to the make-shift market at the junction, the duo took a detour to Guru's house. They gave him a rapid-fire description of what they saw. Guru sat dazed on his verandah as if he had been hit by lightning. He wiped his face with his hands, put on a white shirt, and told loudly to his wife Leela in the kitchen, "I'm going out. I heard that something had happened to Chenda. Please light the oil lamp in the pooja room and say prayers." He took a deep breath, tucked his umbrella under his armpit, and left before his wife could come out of the kitchen and ask for details. With a combination of running and walking, Guru went to the river.

By then, the news of Chenda's death had spread like the monsoon waters. Customers at the Brahminal Hotel and the Military Hotel at the junction gobbled up their food and hurried to the river. As soon as they left, Kuttan, owner of the Brahminal Hotel, and Kader, who owns the Military Hotel, half-shuttered their eateries and set toward the river. And tailor Gopi followed them. The Amman Devi temple and the Juma Masjid were deserted as the worshippers had already left to see Chenda's body. The make-shift market at the junction, which bustled with vendors, haggling customers, and crows, was deafeningly silent.

"Edi, there's not even a single soul to buy vegetables," Cross-toed Ammu told Kamala. "I think the whole village is at the river. I feel sad. Depressed. Scared. Let's go there."

Young men ran, middle-aged men and women walked in haste, and some rode their bicycles. They passed by huts and shops charred from the fire set off by rioters a week earlier.

Sivan, who was on his way in his bullock cart to see the body, didn't mind when a couple of teenagers jumped on the cart for the free ride. It was like going to a carnival; they didn't want to be late.

A crowd had already formed around Chenda. The crowd was big, much bigger than Comrade Doctor Vijayan's first election rally. Cross-toed Ammu and Kamala squeezed through the crowd for an unobstructed view of the body, like teenagers vying for front-row seats.

Thick, sad monsoon clouds hovered over the village like a huge gray umbrella.

APPU LOOKED aghast at the body and trembled and waited for Guru. Chewing a paan, Guru came a few minutes later, stared at Chenda in horror, and chewed the paan vigorously.

The body under the bridge was an anomaly, like a splotch of paint that slipped from an artist's brush onto the canvas while capturing the mesmerizing landscape of the Alumaram River. Chenda's face was turned sideways, half submerged as if trying to hide in the water. His right leg was still on the riverbank, reluctant to leave the village. A hand-woven, checkered red lungi was wrapped around his waist. Visible through the wet lungi was his blue underwear that had ballooned with water and air.

"This is shocking," Appu said.

Guru nodded his head in affirmation and exclaimed, "Unbelievable! My God!"

"Is he really dead?" asked Appu, folding his mundu up from his knee, exposing his swelled right leg, and entered the water and gently nudged the body with a twig. "Eda Chenda, wake up. Wake up! This is not funny!"

The body didn't move. It was like poking at a cold, wet tree trunk.

Guru also folded his mundu from the knee up, entered the water, and gasped, "Oh, my God! There's a big gash in his stomach. Look here, Appu. There's a stab wound. Somebody stabbed him."

Appu studied the spot pointed out by Guru, nodded in affirmation, and said, "There's another gash. He had been stabbed several times. Who will do such a horrendous thing to him?"

Confused, Guru looked at Appu, chewed the paan, and coarsely spat the red paan juice in a vain attempt to hide his quivering lips. The paan spit landed on the riverbank like a splatter of coagulated blood.

"I didn't know this was going to happen to him," Guru mumbled. "I offered a special pooja to Amman Devi for his safety."

"Did you say something, Guru?"

"No, I didn't say anything," Guru said and continued, "He always talked about going to America. Look at him. There are cuts and bumps on his head. Did he get into fights?"

"You know him. He never gets into fights," Appu said and wiped the tears with the back of his hand. "I gave him a haircut yesterday. Just yesterday! He seemed fine. He didn't complain about any threats or enemies."

The crowd of onlookers grew as nearby villagers poured into a stream, like ants traversing to and from their colony.

Kamala was the first to sob. Initially, in hushed sobs, gradually, they became loud and uncontrollable, even though she covered her mouth with her hands. Soon, a few other women wept and covered their mouths with the tip of their sari. When a woman's sobs died down, another would burst out sobbing, then another, taking turns to mourn in waves.

Men sat on the embankment as if waiting for the curtain to rise in an open-air theater. Hungry crows perched on trees and cawed loudly, eyeing Chenda's body, hoping for a sumptuous non-vegetarian buffet.

Appu and Guru moved closer to the body, guarding it against the crowd. Murmurs of rumors percolated. An old man, who wore a blue-checkered lungi and a handloom towel wrapped around his head, said, "Chenda may have been killed at some other place and dumped here by Muslims."

Another man disagreed. "He's not a Hindu; he is a Muslim. I'm sure Hindu extremists might have tossed him from the bridge."

The old man took a deep puff from his beedi and interjected, "Thrown off the bridge? It can't be because his head is intact like a coconut. It would have been shattered into pieces if he had been thrown from the bridge."

An eerie calm descended. The water lugged by the undercurrent in the middle of the river made rippling noise, like the muffled wails of a grieving mother.

The old man took another puff from his beedi and said, "He must have been killed by the CIA. The Criminal Instigators of America. He often talked about playing *chenda* music at Carnegie Hall. I know the CIA doesn't want him there. Who wants a parayan? That's why we need the support of the Kind Government Bureau. The KGB. We need the Soviet Union's KGB."

There was no empathy or grief in the conversation. Annoyed, Appu hollered, "Will you people shut up? We've to notify Chenda's relatives. Does anyone know his amma or achan? His brothers or sisters? Cousins?"

No one replied.

While Appu was concerned about locating Chenda's relatives, Guru was worried about whether to cremate or bury the body. "I gave him the name Narayanan after the Hindu God. So we can cremate him," Guru said. "What if his parents showed up, and they turned out to be Muslims or Christians?"

"Don't worry about it now. Perhaps, our MLA Comrade Doctor Vijayan might know Chenda's parents," Appu said.

Cross-toed Ammu, wiping her tears, said, "He may be related to Patti-Amma. He lives on her back porch."

"I don't think he is related to Patti-Amma," Appu replied. "Patti-Amma is a Brahmin. If Chenda were a Brahmin, he would have finished high school or gone to college. And he would be working as a clerk in a government office or a bank, not chopping firewood. Perhaps he may be related to Mani, the bootlegger."

Meanwhile, Guru, unconvinced that Chenda was dead, was about to put his finger near Chenda's nostrils to check whether he was still breathing.

"Don't touch him," Appu said as Guru moved toward the body. "This is a police case. We shouldn't tamper with the body."

"Yes, you're correct," Guru said quietly. He wanted to scream and wail, *Why Chenda? First, Sita died. Now him. Why?*

2

"WILL SOMEONE inform the police and Comrade Doctor Vijayan about Chenda's death? Please?" Appu asked the crowd. "You can borrow my bicycle."

No one came forward because they simply didn't want to miss if, by a miracle, Chenda got up and played the kettledrum. Appu told Guru that he couldn't ride long distances. "The strain will aggravate the pain in my swollen right leg. I hope someone else would report it to the police," he said.

Guru responded he never rode a bicycle and asked for volunteers from the crowd.

Appu looked around and, not seeing anyone coming forward, jumped on his bicycle and set out on the seven-mile ride to the police station at East Fort. Shards of glass, stones, and debris were still littered on M.G. Road near the banyan tree at the junction. Numerous stones, pelted by the rioting mob, were strewn among broken tiled and a thatched roof. The acrid smell of smoke from burned houses made Appu cough a few times as he rode the bicycle.

Sweating, Appu found himself standing in front of the police station—a brick edifice with urine stains on the rear wall and a medieval arched entrance, a remnant of the British Raj. Until then, he didn't realize he could ride the bicycle as fast as a scooter. Inside the police station, a few constables with cone-shaped khaki turbans, which resembled the tip of match sticks, stared at Appu. One of them puckered his eyebrows, questioning the purpose of his visit.

"There's a dead body under the bridge," Appu said. "Under the Alumaram River bridge."

The constable gestured Appu toward a Sub-Inspector who was busy rearranging a stack of documents on his teak table with coffee stains.

"What's the problem?" the Sub-Inspector asked, still rearranging the documents, without looking at Appu. What the Sub-Inspector meant was, "*Why are you bothering me?*"

Appu repeated what he told the constable.

"We already heard something about it," the Sub-Inspector said. The news of deaths travels faster than the news of births. Yet, no constable or Sub-Inspector showed up to investigate.

"Your name?" the Sub-Inspector asked and took a blank police complaint form from his desk drawer. In bold letters, the top section of the form boasted "Main Police Station, Trivandrum, Kerala (God's Own Country), India."

The Sub-Inspector didn't ask Appu to sit, though two wooden chairs were in front of his table. Finally, the Sub-Inspector raised his head, looked at Appu, and said, "We need the person's name reporting the case."

"Appu."

The Sub-Inspector wrote it down with a blue fountain pen on the form and asked, "Appu? No initials?"

"No initials. Just Appu."

"Your profession?"

"Mine?"

"Yes. We need to include the details of the person filing the report."

"Barber."

The Sub-Inspector looked at Appu for the first time, then at his right leg. Unlike other men in the village, Appu never folded his mundu from the knee up and let it down to hide the bulge in the right leg. "I carry my worries on my right leg, not on my head," he would say and chuckle. But he was not always successful, like trying to brush off the residues of the clipped hair of customers that clung to his shirt.

Pointing to the swollen leg, the Sub-Inspector asked, "When did you get elephantiasis?"

"When I was young, saar. Sometimes, it is painful. Very painful."

"Sorry about it," the Sub-Inspector said and wrote in the First Information Report form:

Complainant: *Barber Appu (Big leg).*

"Are you the dead person's relative?"

"No, saar. We are not related. He was a great help to me. I cut his hair. For free."

"Your address?"

"AV 23 Alumaram Village."

"What's his name?"

Appu hesitated.

"The dead man's name?" the Sub-Inspector repeated.

"Chenda," Appu replied.

The Sub-Inspector stared at Appu and said, "Chenda? Kettledrum? Is this a joke?"

"No, saar. I'm not joking. That's his name. Everyone in the village called him Chenda because he loved to play the kettledrum," Appu explained and scratched his head as if apologizing for not knowing Chenda's real name.

"No initials? No surname?"

"I don't know, Inspector."

The Sub Inspector's demeanor changed from a business-like attitude into a friendly one when Appu addressed him "Inspector." A promotion. He gestured for Appu to sit on a chair in front of his desk.

"His address?"

"I don't know, Inspector. He doesn't have a permanent home."

Noticing the confusion of the Sub-Inspector, Appu clarified: "Most of the time, he is near the banyan tree, playing the *chenda* music."

"No address? Did he fall from the sky or what?" the Sub-Inspector asked. He tapped his finger on the table, wrote "*Alumaram Village*" in the address column in the FIR, and fired another question, "Do you know his age?"

"I think he is twenty-six."

"Good! At least you know something," the Sub-Inspector said and filled out the age column in the FIR. "Any birthmarks? A mole on his face, forehead, or anything like that?"

"We couldn't see the pretam's face. When Chenda was alive, I never paid special attention to his appearance. He was a strong man. He delivered and chopped firewood to homes. And played the *chenda*. A terrific *chenda* musician."

"I think I have heard about him," the Sub-Inspector said as he took down the report. "What's his religion?"

"I don't know."

The Sub-Inspector marked a dash in that column and continued, "Caste?"

"I don't know, Inspector."

The Sub Inspector slammed the pen on the desk, stared at Appu, and raised his voice, "All you are saying is 'I don't know, I don't know.' What's this? How can we prepare an FIR, that too a death report, if we don't have the basic details?" He took the pen, drew a dash in the Caste column in the form, and asked, "What else do you know? What's his complexion? His skin color?"

"Dark. Black."

The Sub-Inspector wrote *"Black"* in the color column, then paused for a second, crossed twice the dash he drew in the Caste column, and wrote: *Harijan/Parayan.* Then he underlined the sentence so others would know that Chenda was at the rock bottom of the caste totem pole.

"Is there any wound or blood?"

"There are gashes in his stomach, on the right side. I didn't see any blood. And a few cuts and bumps in his head."

"Did he get into fights?"

"No, Inspector. He wouldn't hurt even a mosquito. He is harmless."

"Do you have any suspects?"

"If we had any suspects, we would have dragged them out of their homes, beaten them to the pulp, and have brought them here," Appu said. "Maybe you might catch them during your investigation. You should do it soon, before they erase the evidence."

The Sub-Inspector stared at Appu, presumably not pleased with his insinuation that the police should quickly probe Chenda's death.

"We have a long backlog of cases," the Sub-Inspector said as a matter of fact. "These parayans are real headaches. They beat up and kill each other. Trouble makers. We have other important pending cases to investigate. We are understaffed, and I need more constables."

But Appu tried to infuse a sense of urgency. "Inspector, his body is still there. Under the bridge. He was a good man, and the villagers loved him. He was always helpful."

The Sub-Inspector appeared agitated, like a teenager who was given an additional house chore. "I'll send a constable whenever one is free," he told tersely, signed the FIR, underlined his signature, put two dots next to it, and wrote the date:16-4-1965.

Appu gently bowed, thanked the Sub-Inspector, and left the police station perplexed over his lackadaisical attitude. To make up for the time wasted there, Appu jumped on the bicycle, carefully placed his swollen right leg on the pedal, and pushed it as fast as he could to the Secretariat, the Statehouse of Kerala, to inform Comrade Doctor Vijayan about Chenda.

The bicycle ride to the Secretariat would have been easier for Appu but for his depleted energy and gradually increasing pain in his right leg. His initial surge of vigor was sucked out of him by the Sub-Inspector's indifference. The bicycle didn't move fast, as if the air had leaked out of its tires. His every push to the pedal became laborious. The bicycle wobbled like Chenda's struggles to get an Indian passport and a U.S. visa.

CHENDA DIDN'T need liquor to unleash his imagination and draw vivid pictures of Carnegie Hall and the Empire State Building in the air. However, a few gulps of the illicit arrack sold by Mani near the marshland on a narrow lane, five streets north of the junction, or a glass of rasayanam from Krishnan Good Health Herbal Medical Store didn't hurt either. The liquor kicked his creativity to full throttle like the heavy monsoon downpour. His description of New York would become sprightly, like the music on the *chenda* he played with passion.

"The buildings in America are huge and tall. Very tall," Chenda would describe to anyone who had a minute to listen. "The Empire State Building is the tallest in the world. It's in New York City, the biggest city on the whole wide planet. The building is so tall that if we stacked all the thatched huts and homes with tiled roofs in our village on top of each other, we wouldn't reach half of its height. It has one hundred and two floors. Can you believe it?" Chenda would fold his blue checkered lungi and wrap it around his waist as if he was preparing to climb the one hundred and two floors. He would point toward an imaginary tower of the Empire State Building in the air for a visual clue. "It is that tall. If you stood on top of it, you could touch the clouds. When I go to New York, I'll climb the Empire State Building and touch the clouds. Maybe I could touch the moon and the stars." Then, with bare hands, he would animatedly tap the kettledrum to add a special sound effect to his description of New York City.

3

EVERY MORNING, Chenda delivered firewood in a handcart from the lumber yard to homes and chopped them. A few taps on the kettledrum, which he carried along with the firewood, alerted the housewives about his arrival. The "dum…dum…" taps attracted the children from the house with a tiled roof where he delivered firewood. They squatted on the cement verandah at a safe distance from Chenda to watch him chop firewood as if it was live entertainment—a welcome change from catching tadpoles from the pond at the marshland.

Often children from neighboring homes with thatched roofs and dried mud-verandahs joined the spectators.

Children eagerly waited for the show to begin. Chenda took off his white banian, exposing his broad chest, folded his blue checkered lungi from the knee up, and tucked it around his waist. He took the red hand towel from his shoulder, wrapped it around his head, and stood straight on his bare feet, their soles thick with a white coating of leathery callus gifted by gravel streets. Then, he lifted the twenty-pound ax high above his head, stretched his body as much as possible, and struck the firewood with a heavy thud. In the impact, the lumber broke into two pieces. He chopped the two pieces into four, four into eight, eight into sixteen until they were thin enough to fit in small clay stoves.

"Look at his muscles. Huge!" A boy, wearing a navy-blue knicker and no shirt, whispered to a girl sitting next to him. "Watch, when he lifts the ax, his biceps bulge as if bunnies were hiding in them. His abdomen is strong. If you punch him there, nothing will happen to him. You will break your fist."

The girl, in a frock with floral designs, agreed. "You'll have to eat a lot of mutton. This much mutton to build such strong muscles," she said and stretched her hands wide for emphasis.

The boy nodded and said, "When I grow big, I'll have strong muscles like his. I'll eat a ton of mutton, eggs, fish, and chicken."

The girl whispered to the boy, "He is strong, but he is dark. Black. I don't want to be black. My mother says no one will marry a black girl."

The boy looked at her and whispered back, "I know. I won't get a job if I'm black. My mother would yell at me if I played in the sun because it would make me dark. Then, people will think I'm a parayan like him. That's why my mother gives him water in a tin cup, not in a steel tumbler."

Chenda, without paying attention to the children's chatter, focused on chopping the firewood. After finishing his work, he removed the red towel from his head and wiped the sweat on his chest, shoulder, armpit, and back. Looking at his little admirers, he asked, "Want to play the *chenda*?"

They smiled and coyly nodded as if saying, "Yes, we would love to play the instrument." They took turns tapping the kettledrum with their tender fingers. They giggled and laughed with the exhilaration of making their own music. However, it lived only for a fleeting moment.

"I played better than you," the boy claimed.

"Mine was louder," the girl argued.

"All of you are talented musicians," Chenda complimented them.

Hearing the drumbeat, an elderly woman came out of the house to see what was happening. When she smiled, her lips pursed—a vestige of the woman's lost teeth and lost youth.

She asked Chenda the same question she and other elderly women and men had asked him, "Eda, how old are you?"

"Twenty-four."

"Why aren't you married? You are young and strong. Should I find a bride for you? A pretty girl?"

"No ammachi. Who will marry me?" He would repeat the same reply. Then, he would explain, "First, I want to go to America and play the *chenda* music at Carnegie Hall. It's an enormous hall...bigger than our village. It has special lights and sound system, a thousand times better than our Stephen's Lucky Sounds and Lighting. Let's see what God has planned for me."

Women and children would look at him, fascinated by the description of his dreamland. Like a painter touching up his art frequently, Chenda embellished every time he boasted about the Carnegie Hall, the Empire State Building, and Times Square. "Times Square is on a triangular corner, like our village junction. Times Square has a huge screen for advertisements. Bigger than the thirty-five-millimeter screen at Sree Kumar movie theater in Trivandrum City," he said and shook his head slowly in wonder.

"Isn't it far beyond the Seven Seas?"

"Yes! America is far, far away. Ten thousand miles away from our village," he said, pointing his hand toward the west.

Once enthralled them with his description of the Big Apple, he returned to the lumber yard, loaded firewood, and delivered it to another house with a tiled roof. Rarely did he receive business from those with thatched roofs. They collected broken tree branches and twigs. Even if they purchased firewood from the lumber yard, they would transport and chop it themselves.

Between delivering firewood to homes, he would hastily eat dosa and vada, wash them down with chai at Brahminal Hotel that sat on the southwest corner of the junction or eat parotta and egg curry at the Military Hotel at the northeast corner of the junction on Mahatma Gandhi Road. M.G. Road for short.

CHENDA WORKED only until late afternoon so he could get ready for his solo *chenda* concert in the evenings at the junction. If he was late, he would chop firewood just enough for cooking for the day and tell the lady of the house, "I'll be back early morning tomorrow to finish chopping the rest of the firewood. You pay me then."

He would rush to the Alumaram River for a bath, past huts with a thatched roof and mud walls plastered with cow dung hand-spread like a second coating of thick, round pastel designs on a canvas. On the way to the river, he would buy a slice of red Lifebuoy soap for ten paise from the grocery store, the only one in the village.

"Are you going to play the *chenda* today?" the grocery store owner asked daily and gave him a spoon of free coconut oil.

"Of course! You know I never miss a day unless there's heavy rain," Chenda said while applying the coconut oil to his hair.

"Play ugran music as usual. OK?"

"OK," Chenda said and went to the river. One had to climb down about a dozen steps from the street to get into the water.

From the top step, Chenda would admire the river that gently snaked through the lush green flora interspersed with tall switchgrass, papaya, banana, jackfruit, and coconut trees. The water was blue and clean, not murky as the first wash of the monsoon. The middle of the river flowed fast, drawn by the undercurrent, and the water near the banks made lazy waves as if singing a lullaby. Some sections on the banks flaunted clean brown sand-like imported American wheat. In the east section, adults took dips, and teenagers splashed water at each other. The men's area was near the two giant concrete pillars that supported the Alumaram River Bridge. About two hundred feet northeast was an exclusive section for women. They would discreetly remove their blouses, cover their bodies with a mundu and take dips in the water. And curious teenage boys, who slyly swam toward the women's section to ogle at them, were yelled at and chased to retreat to the men's section. If these peeping Toms were caught red-handed by men, they would knock their heads, yell profanities, and send them home.

Further northwest, on an elevated plateau, the Amman Devi temple sat as if protecting the river and the bridge. On the other side of the river bank was a designated area for dhobis who washed their customers' clothes by whipping them on rock slabs and rinsing the soapy laundry in the river. Not far from there, Balan threw water on his elephant that sat cooling off in the water. Then, Balan meticulously scrubbed its thick belly, wrinkled trunk, and yellow tusks with a coconut husk as if giving a bath to a child—a reward for lugging logs that helped Balan feed his wife, three young children, and his mother.

Chenda tapped the kettledrum twice loudly as if greeting Balan on the other side of the river bank. Balan looked at Chenda and acknowledged him by waving his hands. And the elephant raised its trunk and twirled it, feeling the tender vibrations of the musical notes. Chenda smiled at the elephant's gesture, carefully kept the kettledrum on a lower step, went behind a wall of switchgrass, took off his lungi and underwear, and wrapped his waist with the red towel he had on his head. He washed the lungi and the underwear in the river with the piece of the Lifebuoy soap and spread the clothes on the river bank for drying. He kept rocks on the four corners of his clothes so they were not blown away in the wind. He washed his body with whatever was left of the red Lifebuoy soap. By the time he finished his bath, the lungi and the underwear had dried in the scorching heat. He took the dried clothes, went behind the switchgrass, and put them on. In the humidity, Chenda's body was wet with sweat again, as if he had stepped back into a sauna. He wiped the sweat on his armpit, shoulder, and back with the red hand towel.

His next stop was Patti-Amma's back porch in Brahmin's cluster. He never entered her house from the front door.

"Come through the door from the back street," Patti-Amma had told him in her meek voice many monsoons ago when she offered her back porch to call his home. "Be discreet when you come and go. Other Brahmins will say bad things for letting you in my house. They are narrow-minded. I don't want any trouble. You know what I mean?"

"Yes, Patti-Amma."

"Are you really a parayan? A low caste?" she had asked.

"I don't know. But I know people think I'm a parayan because I'm black."

"What do you mean 'I don't know?' How about your parents? Mother and father? You should know at least their castes and names."

"All I remember is that my father brought me from a far-away village on a bicycle. He dropped me at the junction, gave me twenty paise to buy candy, and told me he would be back soon to take me to the beach. I never saw him again. I was little. Very little. It was a long time ago. I remember that we lived in a thatched hut with a mud floor. My mother made rice and wheat porridge in the mud kitchen on the floor. We ate only once a day. And drank a lot of water. Now I know why my mother cried when he took me on his bicycle. I wouldn't recognize them if they stood in front of me."

Patti-Amma's eyes swelled with tears, and she wiped them with the tip of her sari. She went inside for a couple of minutes and returned, swooshing her sari on the cement floor.

"Drink this," she had said, extending a steel tumbler of chai.

"You don't have to do this," he had said and continued, "Please leave the tumbler on the floor. I'll take it from there."

"Paravayillai," she said in Tamil. Her voice was firm. It was like an order. "Don't worry. Take the tumbler from my hand. Take it before the chai becomes cold."

Hesitantly, he took the steel tumbler from Patti-Amma's hand, which shook under its weight. Green veins on her hands protruded from the sagging yellow, pale skin of her hands like the exposed frayed roots of the banyan tree. The wrinkles on her face could tell stories of decades of sorrow. Her hair was gray and thin with age, wisdom, and fortitude.

Chenda raised the tumbler above his lips and tilted it so that his lips wouldn't touch the tumbler when he drank the chai.

"What's your real name? Do you remember at least your name?" Patti-Amma had asked.

"Kunju Mon."

"Kunju Mon? Baby Boy?" she had said. "Endearing name. But it is not a proper name."

"I think that's what my parents called me."

"Poor soul," Patti-Amma had said and wiped her tears again with the tip of her sari. "You can stay here as long as you want."

"Free?"

"Yes, for free."

"I cannot live here for free. I should do some work. Help you out with something."

Patti-Amma thought for a few seconds and said, "If I make papadams, could you sell them at stores? Every week, you can deliver them and collect money. An extra income for me. My Mister is bedridden with vaatham. Stroke. His pension is not much. You take a ten percent commission."

"Please, no commission for me, Patti-Amma. I'll deliver the papadams. Free accommodation is more than enough. Now I've got a place to sleep. And I'll chop firewood free for you."

Chenda also took upon himself another task. He would draw water from the well on the back porch in an aluminum bucket and fill in a big brass jar for Patti-Amma to wash dishes and clothes.

"Good boy!" she had said.

HEARING THE grating of the wooden gate opening, Patti-Amma ambled, her sari gently swooshing on the floor toward the back porch, and asked, "Eda Chenda, is it you?"

He had heard this question a hundred times. "Yes, Patti-Amma. Don't worry. It is me."

If he hadn't heard the whoosh of Patti-Amma's sari, Chenda would look inside the house and shout, "Patti-Amma, is everything alright? Your Mister Iyer is OK?"

"Yes. We are fine. I'm tired. That's all. My Mister made all sorts of noise at night. That kept me awake. Did you eat anything?"

"I ate at the hotel. Sorry about your Mister."

"He has good days and bad days. It is all providence. In God's hands. What can we do?"

This brief question-and-answer routine was like telepathy, assuring each other's safety and well-being.

Chenda kept his prized possession at the corner of the back porch: a green, rusty metal trunk without locks. In it were a pair of meticulously folded underwear, a handloom towel, a white mundu, a white shirt that he wore only on special occasions, and a tale of mystery. On top of the tangible items were a mirror with a metal handle, a broken black comb, and a can of Cuticura Talcum Powder. At the bottom of the clothes were a stack of newspaper clippings of the Carnegie Hall, Empire State Building, Times Square, and the Statue of Liberty. Neatly placed on top of the metal trunk were a small pillow without a pillowcase and a straw mat. The pillow had become brown with dust. Chenda combed his hair, applied Cuticura Talcum Powder on his face, and looked in the mirror. The powder didn't lighten his dark face. He put on another coating of Cuticura and looked again in the mirror, straight and sideways. His skin hue remained the same. He shrugged and set out through the back street to the junction to play the *chenda* at the foot of the fifty-foot tall banyan tree. Alumaram in Malayalam. Like an elderly sage watching over her children, grandchildren, and great-grandchildren, the banyan tree stood tall at the junction.

4

IN THE MORNING, the corner of the junction at the M.G. Road-split would transform into a market where Cross-toed Ammu, her niece Kamala, and other women with sun-burned faces sold vegetables and fish.

"Arthritis," Cross-toed Ammu would explain if you asked why her left toes crisscrossed on top of each other.

If you bargained, she would toss in a couple of beans or brinjal.

Adjacent to these vegetable vendors was Hassan's make-shift butcher shop. You could buy mutton or beef from Hassan, who cut the meat on his butcher's table: an enormous tree trunk with a round surface red with the stains of dried blood. Hassan closed his butcher's shop by noon and sold flowers in the evening in a wooden cart.

Hungry crows would stealthily hop around the market to steal a fish or a piece of meat and flee to the banyan tree with their loot, triggering a turf war with the bats that had already established a colony in there.

BY THE TIME Chenda set out to play the *chenda* at the junction, the sun would be ready to stroll to the West and give way to the moon. The Kerala State Regional Transport Corporation bus would have brought back men, exhausted and aggravated, from the city. After a long day's work, men hung around the junction to relax by watching the goings-on and listening to the All India Radio at the Brahminal Hotel. Women, dressed in saris with intricate flowery patterns, sauntered through the junction, their children in tow, to visit friends or attend the evening pooja at the Amman Devi temple. Teenage boys played cricket with the stumps and bats made by the lumber yard owner, and a tennis ball became their cricket ball. They would interrupt the game, an inheritance from the British, to let bicycles, handcarts, and stray cows pass by. Teenage girls beautified their already beautiful faces with talcum powder, bedecked their long braided lush hair with a string of flowers, and coyly strutted with friends.

Like a grand old lady, the banyan tree lorded over the junction, proudly overseeing the village with a web of narrow, dirt streets and lanes that grew around her.

In anticipation of Chenda's music, a small crowd would assemble. Among the regulars were Appu and Guru, who always carried an umbrella and massaged his beard often.

"Here he comes," Appu said, seeing Chenda with the kettledrum clinging onto his shoulder.

"Good," Guru said. "I read an awful horoscope today. Depressing. I need to uplift my mood."

"Same here. I had a busy day. It's tiresome to stand all day," he said, massaging his right hand to assuage the carpal tunnel. "I had to do a dozen haircuts, seven or nine shaves. And they want me to shave their armpits, too. Stupid idiots!"

Guru chuckled and said, "We can ask Chenda to play a little extra. He never says no to music."

They watched Chenda prime the kettledrum. He removed the red towel he had wrapped around his head, put it on the shoulder for cushioning effect, and hung the kettledrum's cotton strap on top of it. Out of respect for the music and the instrument, he unfolded his lungi that stretched from his waist to his toes. He closed his eyes, said a silent prayer, gently tapped the percussion with one bare hand and a drum stick in the other, like a singer warming up his vocal cord. As the music progressed, he used drum sticks in both hands. He sprinkled the music with special effects by grating the curved end of the drum sticks.

For a better music-playing posture, Chenda slightly drooped his shoulders. As the tempo of the drumbeat grew and reached a crescendo, his two drum sticks appeared to transform into four drum sticks, then to six, to eight, and to twelve. It was like a flock of birds fluttering and dancing on the kettledrum's tanned leather surface—a feast for the eyes and the ears. Chenda's head and hip swayed in tandem as if he was waltzing in abandon with an invisible angel of music. The waves of the music floated in the wind and caressed the village. The bats and the crows on the banyan tree spread their wings and pranced in the air. They made fervent flights and flapped their wings like an ensemble to the music. The cricket players on M.G.Road stopped their game to watch Chenda. Men chewed paan and smoked beedis and nodded their heads to the rhythm of the *chenda*. Its music created euphoria like a cool breeze on a sultry day and permeated exuberance at the junction. And the villagers knew that Chenda's kettledrum was singing the song of joy.

At the end of the free concert, either the owner of the Brahminal Hotel that served only vegetarian dishes, or the owner of the Military Hotel that sold beef, mutton, and fish curries, rewarded Chenda with a meal.

Appu applauded Chenda, "Sabash! Great music as usual."

"Excellent! You have the God-given talent," Guru said and pointed toward his heart.

Pleased with the compliments, Chenda nodded his head in acknowledgment and said, "When I go to America, I'll play at Carnegie Hall. Maybe President Kennedy will come."

"You are a very ambitious man," Appu said and massaged his right hand that held scissors from dawn to dusk.

Chenda noticed Appu's reaction and asked, "You think I'm crazy or something, don't you?"

"No… no… no," Appu replied. "I never said you're crazy. It is good to be ambitious. To have a dream. Without ambition, life is meaningless. But you should be realistic. First, you must get a passport, then an American visa and a plane ticket, etcetera. It will cost you lakhs and lakhs of rupees. It is a long process."

In between chewing paan, Guru interjected, "Why don't you join a local music group? You will be a famous *chenda* player in Kerala. Maybe in entire India."

Chenda's face became sallow, and his voice cracked when he said, "Do you know how many times I've begged the local groups to give me a chance to play with them? They won't include me, Guru saar. They won't tell me why. But I know why. They don't want a parayan in their group."

Guru was caught off guard, and his forehead puckered by Chenda's unvarnished reply. All Guru could say was, "People are beginning to ignore caste and religion. Things are improving, but slowly. Eda, you are an excellent musician. A natural. The local groups are foolish not to include you."

"Thank you, Guru saar. But they don't think as you do. Look at me... look at me," Chenda said, showing his hands. "I'm dark. Black. They are light-skinned. Brown. Who wants to play the *chenda* with a dark man?"

On an impulse, Appu and Guru discreetly looked at their hands. They were brown—neither dark as Chenda nor fair, like the sandalwood hue of Brahmins, Namboothiris, Menons, and Nairs.

Chenda pretended as if he didn't notice their self-inspection. He revered Appu because he gave him free haircuts, respected others, and expected reciprocity. Appu wouldn't mind if elderly people called him Big-legged Appu or barber Appu. He would insist people younger than him call him Appu Chettan. Big Brother Appu.

Similarly, Chenda didn't care if older people called him Chenda because he played the *chenda*. They identified him with the musical instrument. But, if anyone younger than him called him Chenda, he would yell obscenities at them.

"Who do you think you are?" he would scream in Malayalam. "Since when did you become older than me? I'm twenty-four. How old are you? Twenty-two? Didn't your Amma and Achan teach you to respect older people? What kind of stupid mother and father are they? You should call me Chettan. Big brother. Is that clear?"

The terrified youngsters in Alumaram Village would say "yes" to avoid being called an idiot, stupid, or a rascal. So, they added Chettan to his nickname Chenda. Chenda Chettan. Big Brother Chenda! It was a win-win solution. He smiled whenever they greeted him Chenda Chettan because he got the respect he demanded. The youngsters, especially the rich ones living in homes with electric lights and tiled roofs, were happy because the nickname Chenda neutralized the Chettan title. So were the Brahmin boys who didn't want to respect the untouchable.

AFTER PLAYING the music, Chenda would go to the medical store on the hub of M.G. Road, which boasted the largest sign in the village: Krishnan Good Health Herbal Medical Store, Alumaram Village, Kerala—God's Own Country, South India.

To attract customers, the medical store subscribed to three Malayalam dailies: *Kerala Kaumudi, Mathruboomi, and Malayala Manorama*. The only English publication subscribed was *The Blitz*—a Bombay-based English weekly with screaming red headlines on the front page and a color pinup of half-naked European girls on the back page. Vijayan didn't care about the spurt in visitors, especially testosterone-charged teenage boys, on Thursdays when *The Blitz* was delivered.

During the slow news days, these publications ran photos of American cities, especially New York City, as fillers. They featured tall buildings with dazzling lights and neon signs and competed for fame and domination. On the backdrop of the pictures were clean four-lane streets, large convertible cars of different colors and shapes, men in suits and boots, and women in flashy dresses, high heels, and hats. Chenda would study the pictures and, in amazement, would show them to Vijayan, the medical store's manager.

Awestruck by these pictures, Chenda would say, "Aren't these photos wonderful? There are no potholes. No gravel roads. No beggars. No mud huts. No hungry cows with their ribs sticking out. America is like heaven. I want to play the *chenda* there. Somehow, I'll go there. God will help me."

Vijayan would give him a glass of rasayanam, a black herbal potion—the poor man's rum.

By then, Appu and Guru would come to the store for their evening chat, which mostly focused on politics. It was their daily ritual, sort of. Often, tailor Gopi and Mashe would join the political discussion, which jumped from local to national to U.S.-USSR Cold War.

Chenda was the silent participant in the heated, boisterous debates. In between dispensing herbal potions and white sugary pills to patients, Vijayan argued that the Praja Socialist Party had been trying to improve Kerala. "Other parties, especially the RSP, are putting stumbling blocks. They won't let this state progress," he said and banged the store's desk with a hand in exasperation.

Appu interjected, "No party could surpass the Communist Party's manifesto. That's the best party in the world. Kerala should be a Communist state like West Bengal."

Not to be outdone, Guru chirped in, "We, Keralites, can do much better. We need a party that really cares about people."

Chenda, who stood at the right corner of the store while others sat in wooden chairs in the store, quietly took in the good, the bad, and the ugly in politics. The only comment he once made was, "Politicians come to the village during the election time, then they forget us. We need someone who will really do something for the village." Appu and others nodded in agreement.

Often, these discussions would get out of hand. They would become intense to the brink of assaulting each other.

"The Congress is the most corrupt party in the country. It is not the party of Mahatma Gandhi. Not anymore," Appu shouted.

Guru retorted, "The Communist Party is not any better. They don't know what communism is. They are capitalist to the core, but they talk about revolution, Marx and Lenin."

In the heat of the argument, they flailed their hands, thrust their fingers at each other's faces, and stared in contempt. After these emotionally-charged debates, they would go to the marshland where Mani sold arrack in thick glasses with round yellow stains at the bottom. They would gulp down a shot of the water-like pungent potion and eat oily spicy mango pickles with their fingers from the same jar. Mashe joined them only on the first day of every month when he received his pension. Unlike the rasayanam sold at the medical store, the potent liquor content in the arrack gave an instant temporary escape, like brief parole from their misery. And it was cheaper, too. Besides, Mani gave credit. Before pouring a glass of arrack and after, Mani would curl the tip of his thick mustache with fingers while his deep-set eyes surveilled the area for signs of the undercover police or the Flying Squad. When he folded his lungi up to the knee, the lower part of his long blue striped underwear peeked out. He kept the proceeds from the sales in the pocket in the underwear.

Some of Mani's regular customers would sneak into the narrow lane under the pretense of urinating, polish off the drinks in one swig, and leave quickly as if fleeing after shoplifting. The less adventurous ones bought rasayanam from the medical store under the guise of treating cold or indigestion. The state prohibition of liquor sales was a blessing for Proprietor Krishnan, who owned the medical store and two stores in other villages.

Mani gave Chenda free drinks, a reward for helping him hide jars of arrack in the marshland, and for being a lookout. Like a sentry, he alerted Mani when strangers showed up at the junction. They could be the members of the Flying Squad in plain clothes to raid illicit liquor businesses.

At the end of the business, after his customers had left discreetly as they came, Mani would send Chenda to buy parotta and mutton curry from the Military Hotel. While drinking arrack and eating dinner, Chenda entertained Mani with an elaborate description of the Empire State Building, Brooklyn Bridge, the Statue of Liberty, and the graffiti-ridden subway trains. Mani, marveled at Chenda's skills to draw pictures with words, would listen attentively and gently curl the tip of his thick mustache.

5

ON SLOW DAYS, when Chenda didn't have to chop firewood, he did errands. He guarded the barber shop when Appu went behind the bush on M.G. Road to urinate or take a quick dip at the Alumaram River. Often, Vijayan sought Chenda's help to unload crates of dark rasayanam bottles, green herbal oil bottles, packets of white sugary pills, and brown ginger powder delivered in a lorry from the store's headquarters in Kottayam where the owner Krishnan lived. The driver didn't load and unload the crates. "It is not my job," he would argue. "I'm a driver, not a laborer. Not a coolie."

Vijayan didn't load and unload them either because he thought the menial job was below the manager's status.

"Managers won't do any labor work. They manage. They are in charge of the store," he told Chenda while complaining about the lack of an assistant.

"I'll be your assistant," Chenda said. "I'll work hard. I'll sweep the dust, clean outside and inside the store, do the morning pooja, and load and unload bottles from the lorry. I can treat patients when you are busy."

Vijayan stopped rearranging the rasayanam bottles on the shelf, looked quizzically at him, and asked, "How can you treat patients unless I train you?"

Chenda gestured to the notebook hidden in a drawer in the desk and said, "I'll memorize the instructions in the book. I'll be the junior doctor, your assistant medicine-man."

He had seen Vijayan referring to the notebook and dispensing a small bottle of tiny white round sugary pills and a bottle of rasayanam. It brought levity to the brain and made the stomach rumble for food.

Some farmers called him Doctor Vijayan. He gave an extra ounce of rasayanam for free to those who called him a doctor. Vijayan would ask a customer, whom he called his patient, the symptoms of the ailment. Then, he would slyly peruse the notebook. It had a list of medications hand-written by one of his predecessors, like a grandmother's secret recipe. For a sprained arm or knee, Vijayan would give a green oil to apply that reeked of herb smell and make you gag. For nasal congestion and headache, he would give a packet of ground ginger powder to rub on your crown. A bottle of dark monkey-brand rasayanam was the magic potion for indigestion and insomnia.

"You should take one ounce of rasayanam, three times a day," he would say. "Once in the morning before breakfast, then before lunch and before dinner. Take a lot of bed rest and eat a lot of rice porridge."

A filled stomach and sound sleep were the prescriptions for curing all the illnesses of the world.

Vijayan looked at Chenda confused, and asked, "Eda, if I made you my assistant, what about your America trip?"

"I'll work for you until I get an Indian passport and an American visa. I've been saving money, little by little, for the plane ticket."

"You should have connections at high places to get a passport and a visa. Do you know any MLA or a party leader?"

Chenda scratched his head and lamented, "I don't know any MLA. Or the chief minister."

To cheer him up, Vijayan gave him a glass of rasayanam. Chenda gulped down the black potion as if it was water. Its unsavory taste didn't bother him. Over time, he had acquired a taste for rasayanam. He didn't reveal to Vijayan that he already had a swig of arrack from Mani. The mix of arrack and rasayanam was the perfect cocktail to send his brain on a tailspin. He enjoyed the tipsy feeling, even though it made him loopy. In this happy-yappy inebriated mood, Chenda told Vijayan to run for the Kerala Legislative Assembly. "Doctor Vijayan, you should become an MLA."

Vijayan lit a beedi, took a deep puff, and laughed at the suggestion.

"I'm serious," Chenda said. "I'll vote for you. The villagers will support you. They need someone reliable to bring pipe water, electricity, etc. Unlike the present MLA. I don't even know his name. Do you?"

"Not really. I think his name is Raghavan. But I'm not sure."

"See. You're also not sure of his name. He visits the village only during the election. Then disappears. Doctor Vijayan, you should run for election. I'll campaign for you. Once you become an MLA, you can get me an Indian passport and an American visa."

Vijayan poured himself a glass of rasayanam, pondered over Chenda's idea, and took another deep puff of the beedi.

"You will be Comrade Doctor MLA Vijayan," Chenda continued. "You'll make a lot of money. You don't have to worry about the dowry for your sister. You can hire servants to take care of your parents. You will have a big house with a tiled roof, electric lights, pipe water, and a telephone. Bigger than Mr. Arul's house."

"Eda, you are serious," Vijayan said, and chuckled. "I thought you were joking. We should discuss it with Appu and Guru." And he gave two rupees to Chenda to buy parotta and mutton curry from the Military Hotel.

By the time Chenda returned with food, Vijayan had already refilled the glasses. He didn't mind opening another bottle because he was discussing his future that might open the door to the golden vault with a large treasure of diamonds, jewelry, and stacks of rupees that he had frequently fantasized. He could always fill the empty bottles with water. The bottles' dark color offered a perfect camouflage, and Proprietor Krishnan wouldn't know whether these dark bottles contained rasayanam or water if he suddenly showed up to take inventory.

Vijayan took a sip of rasayanam, lit a beedi, and asked Chenda, "What party should I join?"

"Congress Party," Chenda replied. "I like its symbol. Two oxen and a tiller. Farmers will vote for you."

"How about PSP?"

"I like its symbol, too. It's a hut. Our villagers can relate to PSP. The poor live in huts with thatched roofs and mud walls plastered with cow dung. But you should join the Communist Party."

Vijayan took a deep puff of the beedi and exhaled. And the smoke hovered over his head as if emanating from his pondering brain. "The Communist Party is not bad," he said. "But I like the RSP. The Real Socialist Party. There should be socialism in this country. That's the only way to help the poor and the downtrodden."

"I agree, Doctor Vijayan," Chenda said. "You're already talking like an MLA. But, what is socialism?"

Vijayan explained, "Everyone gets the same amount of salary and benefits. There are no rich people and no poor people. All are equal. Either all are rich, or all are poor. All are government employees with a pension, sick leave, earned leave, and casual leave."

"That's wonderful. I'll be rich like Mr. Arul. I'll have a telephone, a car, a house with a tiled roof, electricity, cement walls, a coconut oil mill, and servants," Chenda said and took a sip from his glass. "Comrade, the RSP's symbol is a big red king cobra. It's easy to draw. And easy to make red paint. All we need to do is grind a few red bricks and mix them with water and red-ink tablets. We can make a lot of red paint without spending a lot of money. It is easy to draw a king cobra, difficult to draw other parties' symbols."

Vijayan sipped rasayanam and said, "In that case, the RSP, it is!"

"And, you will be Comrade MLA Vijayan."

"Midukkan. Smart!" Vijayan said, "When I win the election, I'll have contacts in high places. People will come to me begging for favors. I could easily get you an Indian passport and an American visa."

"Promise?"

"Yes, I promise."

Chenda tapped the kettledrum with his hands enthusiastically. Startled by the sudden burst of music, bats and crows in the banyan tree flew helter-skelter.

VIJAYAN COULDN'T wait to share his political aspirations with Appu and Guru the following evening. He anxiously waited for Chenda to finish his solo *chenda* concert at the foot of the banyan tree. He knew that Appu, Guru, and Chenda would come to the medical store after the free concert to talk politics. Appu walked slowly, dragging his right leg—a sign that the pain in his leg had flared up. During such periods, he would stand skewed by putting more weight on his left leg, which appeared thinner than its original size because of the bulging right leg.

Guru, an umbrella tucked in his armpit and a brown gunny shopping bag, always walked hastily as if chasing a missed fortune. The brown gunny shopping bag, given by a grocery store in Chala Bazaar, was his mobile library of astrology books with different charts and diagrams. The pouch in the bag contained betel leaves, chopped betel nuts, lime paste in a small aluminum container, and processed black tobacco.

Appu and Guru sat on the wooden chairs in the store while Chenda stood at his usual place on the right corner of the store. Vijayan told them in one breath, "I plan to run for MLA as an RSP candidate from this constituency because we need someone who can bring running city pipe water for all, build better roads, and create jobs. It was Chenda's plan. What do you think?"

They looked at each other with raised eyebrows.

"Are you serious?" Appu asked.

"Yes. I am."

"It is a great idea," Appu said after pondering for a few seconds. "We need a member of the Legislative Assembly from our village. We need our own man in the Assembly. The present MLA is a con man. He promised a city water pipeline and a tar-paved road long ago. You can't even walk on M.G. Road. Its gravels are like sharp pins. You are our man to fix it and improve the village. You should run on the Communist Party ticket."

Guru scoffed at that suggestion. "The Communist Party is a stooge of USSR and China. Vijayan, you made an excellent decision by choosing the RSP," he said. "Tell me your date of birth. The time. And the year."

Vijayan, after a pause, gave the details.

Guru drew a chart on the store's dusty floor. His fingers moved as if adding, dividing, multiplying, and subtracting the numbers in the air. His forehead puckered, and his eyes widened in surprise. "Huh! Sabash! Your stars are aligning well," he said. He gently chewed a paan. "Good," he continued, pleased with the tart taste of the red, raw paan juice. "Your time is good. Very good! Whatever you touch will turn into gold. Run for office without any fear. This is an auspicious time for you."

Vijayan smiled that stretched from ear to ear. So did Chenda. At last, Chenda found a pathway for his American journey, and he caressed the kettledrum. Vijayan filled three glasses with rasayanam and gave them to Appu, Guru, and Chenda. "Let's celebrate my entry into politics."

Encouraged by Vijayan's optimistic horoscope, Chenda asked Guru, "Could you please check my horoscope as well? When will I go to America?"

Guru looked at Chenda and said, "Eda, how many times have I asked you for the time of your birth, the date, and the year? And your real name?"

Chenda, hiding his embarrassment, shyly replied, "I don't remember them, Guru saar."

Guru shook his head and said, "Without these details, I cannot predict your future. Don't worry, whatever is destined for you will happen at the appropriate time. Have patience."

6

AS VIJAYAN rode his bicycle to the store in the morning, he was surprised to see large red slogans on the walls: "Elect Comrade Doctor Vijayan. Jobs for everyone. Free electricity. Free city pipe water. Free bus. Free! Free!! Free!!! Real Socialist Party Zindabad."

His eyes brightened with excitement that he had never felt before. His lips moved as he slowly read the slogans over and again. He lit a beedi and took a puff. Another one, and another. The continuous fervent puffs were filled with utter rapture. He read the slogans again, ostensibly trying to memorize them, and pedaled as fast as he could to the store.

Seeing Vijayan, Appu shouted from his barber shop, "Comrade, you got my vote. What a surprise! I'll tell my customers to vote for you."

Tailor Gopi waved and hollered, "I'll make huge banners for your campaign," and gestured that he would stop by the store later to talk about them.

Chenda was on his way to deliver firewood when he saw about a dozen people in front of the medical store. Piqued by the unusual sight in the morning, he came to check it out. They had been waiting to talk to Vijayan about his candidacy. Giddy like a child excited over a jar of orange candy, Vijayan told them he had decided to run for office. Then and there, the aspiring political leader gave a brief impromptu speech that the present Member of the Legislative Assembly didn't keep his election promise to the villagers, and he was a liar. After the address, he turned toward Chenda and asked, "Eda, Chenda! Who wrote these slogans on walls? Our barber Appu? Astrologer Guru?"

"Me," Chenda said and pointed the fingers at his chest and beamed with pride.

"You wrote them? You? You did? I didn't know you could write in English. Who taught you? Mashe? Our Ayyappan Nair?" The villagers used to call him English Master Ayyappan Nair because he taught English at the Boys High School in Thottam Village, a four-mile ride on his Hercules bicycle. Gradually, they dropped his name and called him English Master, which eventually morphed into English Mashe, and simply Mashe.

Even after retirement, Mashe continued to collect namastes as trophies for his low-wage profession.

"Yes," Chenda said and explained Mashe had given him old textbooks with large pictures to read. He also gave Chenda two-lined notebooks to practice writing Malayalam scripts and four-lined notebooks to practice writing the English alphabet. He read and wrote the alphabet every day. First, learn the alphabet, then string them into short phrases and short sentences, like learning to stand up, then walk and run.

"I can read *The Blitz*. Not fast like Mashe or Guru saar. But I can read slowly. Very slowly," he said. "With practice, reading and writing became easier, like playing the *chenda*."

"How much did you pay Mashe?"

"No charge, comrade. All free. But I chopped firewood for free for him."

Vijayan nodded his head as if he understood him. "When did you paint these slogans?" he asked despite noticing the dark circles around Chenda's eyes like a raccoon's.

"At night, after we left the store," he replied and looked at his fingers that were red with the residues of the paint. He explained to Vijayan that he made the paint by grinding red brick pieces from the street and mixing them with water in a rusty tin that he picked up from the garbage heap near the banyan tree. A dry coconut husk became the brush for his political artwork. And he wrote the slogans on walls until he ran out of the red water paint.

"I'm proud of you," Vijayan said. "You did a great job. You didn't tell me that you would paint the election slogans. I would have helped you."

"No problem, comrade. We cannot wait. Only six months left for the election," Chenda said.

The red slogans were written over the black "Stick no bills" signs on a few walls. It didn't bother Vijayan because his slogans were not the only ones to ignore the warning to keep the walls clean. Movie posters of *Arappavan* and *Ben-Hur* had already been plastered next to those "Stick no bills" signs. What bothered him was the "Doctor" title in his election slogans.

"You should make a minor change to the slogans," Vijayan said. "Scrap the doctor title."

"Why?"

"Others would be jealous that I am a doctor. I don't mind if people call me doctor, but don't mention it in our campaign signs," Vijayan said.

Chenda looked confused by Vijayan's request. "You are a vaidyan. A medicine man. That's why the farmers call you a doctor. You must be one because you read *The Blitz*, especially the back page."

Vijayan insisted with the authority of a newly minted MLA, "Don't use the doctor title, OK? I want to relate to the common man. The poor. The laborers. The farmers. The downtrodden. Not the rich people. Let's remove the doctor title as soon as possible."

"Yes. I'll do it tonight. Or, write something over it."

"Good."

Appu, dragging his leg, and Guru, an umbrella under his armpit, came smiling.

"Sabash," Appu said. "Who wrote those slogans?"

Vijayan gestured toward Chenda.

"Good. There are no spelling mistakes," Appu commented.

Guru raised his eyebrows in surprise. "Midukkan. A smart man," he said and spat the red paan juice on the side of the store.

Chenda beamed with pride.

VIJAYAN BEGAN his election campaign in earnest. His first step was to seek divine intervention from Gods of all religions by adding an evening pooja to his regular morning one in the store. If elected, he exhorted during the pooja ceremony that he would work tirelessly to improve Alumaram Village and the neighboring Marakana Village where he lived. He also prayed for more rasayanam sales and a good marriage alliance for his sister.

Chenda stood in reverence at his usual place in the shop and secretly prayed for world peace, an Indian passport, and an American visa.

Vijayan's elaborate pooja ritual included lighting two incense sticks that he placed in a wooden holder with tiny holes, lighting of a wick in a small brass oil lamp that he held in both hands. Then, he would wave the lamp thrice clockwise and counterclockwise around the framed pictures of an ornate Elephant God Ganeshan, Jesus Christ with a silver halo above the crown of thorns on the cross, and a black Kaba with a thick gold border. Vijayan placed his palms above the brass oil lamp as if scooping the blessings drawn from the framed pictures via the flickering brass oil lamp. Then, he touched his face and chest with his hands as if transferring the blessing onto his mind and heart. The oil lamp was passed on to Chenda so that he, too, could purify and enrich his mind and soul. No one questioned Vijayan why he worshipped Hindu, Christian, and Muslim divinities—all at the same time, side-by-side, and at the same altar of the store's wall. But then, Appu did the same in his barber shop. So did tailor Gopi; Stephen, owner of Lucky Sounds and Lighting; and Hassan, the village butcher in the morning and the florist in the evening. The villagers in God's Own Country worshipped all Gods, saints, and prophets. They celebrated all religious festivals as one people, which made Chenda smile and play the kettledrum every day.

MANY "Vote for Comrade Vijayan" slogans without the "doctor" title appeared on walls as the campaign slowly gained traction, like the initial pull of a locomotive train. The residues of the red paint became more pronounced in Chenda's hands. He spent more time at the medical store, drawing Vijayan's campaign slogans and the RSP's symbols. Images of large red king cobras sitting coiled with their menacing hoods ready to strike, which would scare the real cobras, appeared in every available space on walls. And housewives had to remind Chenda to deliver and chop firewood.

In the morning, Chenda would wait, the kettledrum still hanging from his shoulder, for Vijayan's arrival and help him open the store. It was another elaborate ritual: Chenda would take two crudely painted metal signs from the store and place them outside on either side. The sign on the left featured a smiling gorilla that displayed its sparkling white teeth. Above the gorilla's picture were the words "Brighten Your Teeth With Monkey Brand Tooth Powder." The sign on the store's right had a similar gaudy painting of a white bodybuilder who flexed his muscles. Its advertisement screamed: "Build Your Muscles With Black Monkey Vitality Jelly."

"Comrade Vijayan," Chenda asked, "is the vitality jelly made from real monkey parts? Does Proprietor Krishnan catch monkeys in the forest?"

Vijayan lit a beedi and looked at the bodybuilder's picture as though it had an answer. Then, he explained to Chenda, "Yes. Monkey parts are boiled, made into a stew, and mixed with herbs and other items. The ingredients for this jelly are a secret. A family secret. Proprietor Krishnan is the only one who knows it. The jelly will make you strong like the bodybuilder."

CHENDA WAS squatting on the floor, mixing red ink tablets and water in a large tin container in front of the medical store, when he was distracted by an intermittent honking from a distance. The honking became louder and louder. The source of the noise pollution was a black four-door Ford that appeared on the narrow, unpaved road from the east. The car rode up to the banyan tree, made a U-turn, whipped up dust, honked again, and stopped in front of the store. Chenda stopped mixing the red paint and stood up. Store owners craned their necks to see what was going on. And curious old men and teenagers milled around the car.

The driver, who looked like a security guard in a khaki shirt and sported a thick upward curly mustache and oily hair, stepped out first. Then, three men in white handloom shirts and mundu came out of the car and looked around, surveying the area.

Surprised by the arrival of the strangers, Vijayan whispered to Chenda, "Eda, are they our Proprietor Krishnan's auditors?"

"I'm not sure."

"Oh, God! I hope they don't check the petty cash and the stock. If they took an inventory of the rasayanam bottles, I would be in big trouble," Vijayan whispered. His lips moved as he secretly prayed to the Elephant God Ganeshan, Jesus Christ, and the Kaba on the wall that the auditors shouldn't open the bottles filled with water. *Proprietor will sack me. It will be a shame. I won't be able to set foot in the village again. I'm doomed,* he prayed.

By then, Chenda had hidden the aluminum tin, the coconut husk brush, and other paint-making paraphernalia near the bushes behind the store. He whispered, "Don't worry, comrade. First, let us find out who they are."

Then, Chenda asked the visitors, "Namaste. Can I help you?"

They didn't respond. Their eyes turned to Vijayan and stared at him like a cat sizing up a mouse before attacking it.

"Are you Vijayan?" the driver asked, raising his voice.

"Yes," Vijayan replied. "You are…?"

"We are from the RSP's District Headquarters," the driver said.

"I thought you were auditors," Vijayan said, took a deep breath, and let out a nervous laugh on the anticlimax to his anxiety.

"What is so funny?" The question in a booming voice came from a middle-aged man with a big belly that he didn't bother to hide. His eyes bulged like a frog's and were bloodshot as if he had a few drinks on his way to the store. "You know who I am?"

"No, saar. Namaste, saar," Vijayan greeted with clasped hands.

"Hmm. I'm the RSP's District President," the man said. He raised his head and shouted at Vijayan, "Who gave you the permission to run on the party's ticket?"

Chenda and Vijayan looked at each other for an answer.

The District President repeated, "Who gave you permission to campaign on the party's ticket?"

Vijayan's smile turned into a shock at the sudden volley of yelling like thunder and lightning before an onslaught of a monsoon.

"Please sit down. Let me explain, saar. Please have rasayanam," he said and took three glasses and filled them with the black potion.

The District President stepped inside the store and sat on a chair as if he owned the place. He was followed by a thin man, who introduced himself as the RSP's District Secretary. He took an aluminum foil packet from his shirt pocket, took a pinch of brown powder from it, and thrust it into his nostrils with his thumb. He snorted twice, took his handkerchief tucked behind his neck under his shirt collar, wiped his nostrils, folded the handkerchief, and put it back under the collar as it was before. The handkerchief had two functions: first, to absorb the shoulder sweat like a sponge and prevent the discoloration of the shirt's collar; second, to wipe his face, mouth, and nostrils. At times, he tucked the handkerchief under the rolled-up shirtsleeves, just below his armpit.

"Please try our rasayanam, President saar and Secretary saar," Vijayan said. "You won't find such a good rasayanam anywhere in Kerala." He offered a glass to the driver, who gestured that he would drink later.

The District President and the District Secretary didn't touch the glasses.

"Go ahead. Tell us who made you the RSP's candidate?" It was the District Secretary who asked in a steady, raspy voice that was more dreadful than the District President's loud shouting. The district leaders didn't show signs of drinking Vijayan's peace offering and looked at other bottles in the store.

Vijayan's forehead became moist with perspiration. He slowly moved behind the desk to hide his nervousness that had become a tremble. He took a beedi and was about to light it, but changed his mind and put it back in his shirt pocket.

"I want to… want to… um… improve the community… this village," Vijayan stammered. "I didn't know that… um… I had to get… get the District High Command's approval."

Again, the District President raised his voice like a teacher admonishing a student for missing the homework. "Of course, you need our approval. We decide the candidates. Are you an idiot not to know this? You stupid!"

Miffed by the name-calling, Vijayan didn't look at them or the villagers who came to admire the car. The shouting and yelling by the RSP honchos attracted more elderly men and teenagers who normally hung around the banyan tree. They came to the store looking for action—slapping, fist-fighting, or wrestling.

Vijayan wiped the sweat on his face with the back of his hand and nervously mumbled, "I wanted to come... to come... to the party's district headquarters. I didn't have the time because of the store... the store. I should be here from morning to night. From opening to closing. I'm glad you came here."

"Nonsense! Who do you think you are?" The District President barked, beaming with pride, and stared at Chenda and others as if showing them that he was a hotshot in the party hierarchy and had the power and the pull.

Vijayan looked on the floor like a mouse desperately searching for a hole to escape. So, he blamed Chenda for announcing his candidacy in large red letters on the walls.

"I was simply joking about running on the RSP's ticket. And Chenda, this man, the *chenda* player, thought I was serious and painted the campaign slogans on walls. Please believe me. It was a joke!"

The party honchos turned toward Chenda, shaking their heads in amusement. "This man? This coolie? You are contesting in the election because he painted slogans," the District President asked. "You, fool!"

Vijayan didn't respond. It was like a tacit admission. Confused, the District President stroked his beard; the District Secretary shook his head in amusement; the driver smirked and murmured, "Stupid idiot."

Chenda ignored their condescending remarks. He was busy devising a way to protect Vijayan from being assaulted by these shouting and yelling uninvited visitors. Chenda slowly walked across M.G. Road and looked for Mani. He was standing near the marshland, where he had a jar of arrack under a heap of leaves, waiting for customers. Chenda eyed him to come. Without any hesitation, smelling trouble, Mani rushed to the store. Mani's and Chenda's presence gave Vijayan a much-needed confidence and morale boost. He knew that Chenda and Mani would not stand impassive if he was assaulted. The two-man army of Chenda and Mani were the answer to Vijayan's desperate secret prayers for help. With the arrival of the backup, the mouse squealed a little louder. Vijayan cleared his throat and asserted, "I can win the election. I can defeat other parties, but I need the RSP's support. Your support. Chettan, I need your support."

The District President softened his voice as soon as Vijayan called him Chettan. Big brother. A sign of respect. A willingness to be subservient.

The District Secretary, his voice still steady and raspy, said, "Many people had given their lives to the party. They should be the first to run from this constituency. You didn't work even a single day for the party. You simply sprung up from nowhere. We cannot give you this seat."

"Chettan, I can win. People in this village and the neighboring villages will vote for me. Now, they all know about my campaign. The villagers would ridicule me if I backed out of the race. It is too late to change my mind. I need this seat."

The District President looked, raised his eyebrows, at the District Secretary as if transmitting a Morse Code. The

District Secretary took another pinch of the brown powder from the aluminum foil packet, snorted it, and took the handkerchief that was wedged between his shoulder and his shirt collar. The District Secretary wiped his nostrils with it, folded and tucked it back under his shirt collar. Then, he moved closer to Vijayan and whispered, "If you want the party's support, you should pay a small donation. As I told you, there are a lot of people who have given up their life for the party. They have seniority. We cannot give you preference."

"How much?"

The District Secretary wrote 10,000 on a piece of paper and showed it to the District President for his approval and then to Vijayan. "This is a special discounted rate for you. Don't tell anyone else," the District Secretary whispered. "Others will come up with a larger amount for this seat."

"But, I don't have that kind of money," Vijayan blurted out. "In fact, I have no money at all."

The District Secretary was nonchalant. "You will make tons and tons of rupees once you become an MLA. Do you know how government building and road repair bids are given? You know that, don't you? You should pay the party first," he continued. "After that you can make as much as you want. Be friends with contractors. Don't act as if you are innocent. To make money, you have to invest first. It's like planting a coconut tree. When it is fully grown, you can reap coconuts as long as you live. Do you understand?"

Vijayan's head stooped, and his voice reflected desperation. "Ten thousand rupees! It's a huge amount for me. Chettan, I would have arranged for my sister's wedding long ago if I had such an amount. She is twenty-two. I'm twenty-eight, and I am the only breadwinner in the family. My father is retired and has TB. My mother never worked in her life. I promise you, Chettan, once I become an MLA, I'll raise as much money as possible for the party. Please trust me."

The RSP district chiefs stared at Vijayan as if scrutinizing the limping beggar at East Fort bus station whether he was really crippled or a con man.

"Only fools will come up with such pathetic stories," the District Secretary said. "Let me tell you something: Politics is not for you if you couldn't come up with the money. Party tickets are not cheap. They are more valuable than gold."

Vijayan sighed and pleaded again, "I'm the only wage earner in my family. I don't have even five rupees with me. I've been taking money from the petty cash for my expenses. Chettan, I promise I would come up with large sums for the party after the election." Vijayan emphasized the "Chettan" salutation to make sure they heard it. Unfortunately, that ploy didn't work.

"We need the money upfront. It's an advance," the District Secretary demanded. "We need cash, or else you will face the consequences."

The District President took over the warning. He waved his finger at Vijayan and said, "Don't mess with us. We'll destroy your store, and we'll make sure that you never enter politics in your lifetime." He stared at Vijayan with contempt as if shooting fireballs with his eyes: a non-verbal parting shot to watch out.

"I'll send our men within two days for your response. Either cash or withdrawal from the election. If you decide to withdraw, all these slogans should be gone immediately. Tell the boy," the District President said, gesturing with his hand at Chenda, "to remove your stupid slogans. We need those spaces for our campaign." Then, the District President motioned with his head at the driver to start the engine.

The driver almost took a step forward, hoping to quickly grab a glass of rasayanam and gulp it down as if one for the road. He held back when he saw the District President and the District Secretary had already stepped out of the store without even touching the glass. The car took the brunt of the driver's frustration with missing out on free rasayanam. He loudly cranked up the black Ford and angrily honked several times, though no other vehicles were on the road. And the Ford lurched forward, kicking off a cloud of dust.

Soon after they left, Mani returned to the marshland to resume his clandestine moonshine business. And Vijayan took a long sip of rasayanam from a glass the visitors didn't touch and gave another drink to Chenda.

"Our campaign is over. It's doomed," Vijayan lamented and sat with his head on his cupped hand like a father grieving a stillborn child. "They need ten thousand rupees. Hmm! Where will I go for ten thousand rupees? I've to drop out of the election. I'm ashamed. What will I tell the villagers? I'm embarrassed."

Chenda sipped the rasayanam, mulled over the situation, and said calmly, "Remember what the astrologer Guru saar told you. Your future looks great. Whatever you touch will turn into gold. I think you should join the Congress Party, PSP, or the Communist Party."

"All parties are the same. Corrupt. They will demand thousands and thousands of rupees. I'm stuck at this store till I die. Broke. No escape from poverty."

7

THE NEWS of the RSP leaders' demand had spread throughout the village faster than the broadcast from All India Radio at Kuttan's Brahminal Hotel. Appu and Guru came early for their evening chat. They sat on chairs in the store while Chenda, the kettledrum hanging from his shoulder, stood at his usual place—the right corner of the store. They looked at each other awkwardly and didn't know what to say. Appu was the first to break the ice, "The RSP's demand is unreasonable. All these parties are greedy. Rascals!"

Guru agreed. "Now you know why I didn't enter politics. Anyway, Vijayan, I studied your horoscope again. Believe me, your zodiac sign aligns well with other zodiac houses. This is the most prosperous time of your life. You would find a way out of this predicament. Believe in God. Offer a special pooja for Amman Devi. Things will work out," he said.

Vijayan nodded as if heeding the astrologer's prediction and said, "I'll leave everything to fate. Providence. In Amman Devi's hands."

Chenda gently tapped the kettledrum, like the subconscious table-tapping while in deep thoughts. The tapping rose and stopped. "Comrade Doctor Vijayan," he asked as a matter of fact, "why do we need RSP's support? We can form our own group. RSP—Vijayan Faction. Or,

Congress Party—Vijayan Faction. Or, the Communist Party—Vijayan Faction. Or, start a new party. What is wrong with starting a new party?"

Vijayan couldn't believe what he had just heard. The stillborn child suddenly showed signs of life. It began to breathe, smile, and giggle.

The Gods in the picture frames on the store's walls had opened another path to the Kerala Legislative Assembly for Vijayan. Equally surprised were Appu and Guru.

"Eda, you are midukkan!" Vijayan said. "You are much smarter than I thought." Vijayan was relieved that he didn't have to come up with ten thousand rupees, and there was still optimism for his MLA dream. He couldn't hide his excitement over starting his own political party. He will be the party president, secretary, and candidate.

Appu shook his head in astonishment and said, "Eda Chenda, we don't give you enough credit. People who are against the RSP will vote for us. Those who are disappointed with other parties also will support us."

Guru patted Chenda on his back. "Sabash! You are brilliant. Full of surprises." Then he turned toward Vijayan and said, "Don't worry. Go for it. Start a political party. Start small, and slowly expand it, village-by-village, state-by-state, all over India."

"Thank you, Guru. Thank you, Appu. If you say so. If I've your blessing, I will start a new party. Let's celebrate," he said and opened two bottles of rasayanam and filled four glasses—one for him and the rest for them.

While sipping the drink, Guru said, "Now you must come up with a catchy name and a symbol. You know, something like the Communist Party's sickle and a corn head. Easy to relate to people."

Again, Chenda chirped in, "I have a great name for our party: People's Power Party. PPP. Triple-P."

Vijayan, Appu, and Guru looked at Chenda, admiring his spontaneous ingenuity. Noticing a slur in Chenda's speech, Vijayan said, "Eda, you come up with brilliant suggestions when you are drunk. People's Power Party. Hmm! What a great name."

Appu couldn't help commenting, "You're a genius, Chenda. Who knows? When you go to America, you might start a new party." They laughed at Appu's comments. Vijayan's laughter was the loudest, triggered by the relief from the need to give ten thousand rupees to the RSP, the anticipation of starting his own party, and the intoxication of the rasayanam.

Guru chewed his paan, spat the first tart juice, and said, "Now we should have an eye-catching symbol. Something easy for people to relate to the party." All of them turned toward Chenda for his response.

"How about a rocket as our symbol? The party should rise like a rocket. Up, up, up into the sky," Chenda said.

"I like the rocket symbol," Vijayan commented. "The party should take off as the Russian Sputnik. The PPP should soar up in popularity and support."

"It is easy to draw the rocket symbol," Chenda said. "We can paint it blue. The blue ink tablets are cheaper than the red ink tablets."

"Brilliant! You are more than a handcart-puller and a *chenda* musician. You're like a magician. You have a knack for coming up with great ideas," Vijayan said. After finishing their drinks, Appu and Guru left the store. Vijayan gave Chenda two rupees and asked him to buy parotta and chicken curry from the Military Hotel. When Chenda returned with food, Vijayan opened another bottle and filled two glasses.

Chenda emptied the glass in one gulp and sat silently as if reveling in a checkmate move he had just made in a political game. "We'll win the election," he continued. "We'll win."

Vijayan smiled. "When I win, I will first get you an Indian passport and an American visa."

And the kettledrum hummed the song of joy.

Vijayan closed the store earlier than the usual seven o'clock. Along with Chenda, he set out to change the campaign signs. They bought all blue ink tablets available from knick-knack shops in the village, crushed and mixed them with water in a big aluminum tin. Vijayan held the tin can with blue paint while Chenda made a brush out of a coconut husk and meticulously painted "People's Power Party" on top of the red RSP signs he had painted.

If there were a lack of space, he would paint the acronym "PPP" and a thin triangle with shooting flames underneath the rocket's image. It took a couple of hours to change the red slogans to blue.

"I'm tired. I didn't get enough sleep last night," Vijayan said. "Let's continue tomorrow."

"Comrade, you go home. You've got to ride your bicycle to Marakana Village. I'm pumped up, and I'll paint a few more slogans. I want to finish the rest of the paint in the tin."

THE NEXT morning, Chenda waited anxiously for Vijayan's arrival. On seeing Vijayan on the bicycle, he played a couple of loud notes on the kettledrum as if they were a welcoming drumbeat for a king.

"Comrade, did you see the new slogans? Come, I'll show them," Chenda said, and both went to see them. The red king cobra symbols had been meticulously replaced with blue rockets with shooting flames. The "People's Power Party" signs were drawn over the "Real Socialist Party" slogans.

"Midukkan. You're a hard worker, Chenda. You'll be successful in America," Vijayan said.

Chenda, though delighted, shyly shook his shoulder. "This is nothing. There's more to come," he said. "We want to win the election and prove that we, too, can start a party. And we care about our village."

"Yes, yes. We will prove to people that we can do better than other parties," Vijayan said as a matter of fact.

Noticing a lack of enthusiasm in Vijayan's voice, Chenda asked, "What happened, comrade? Don't you like the slogans?"

"No…no. There's nothing wrong with them," Vijayan said and scratched his head as if squeezing a family of lice hiding in his thick, black, oily hair. "Hmm…Guru said all those good things about my future just to make me happy. Did he mean what he said? Will I really win the election? Have a big house with a tiled roof, electricity, a telephone, servants, and a car like Arul's?"

"Of course, comrade. Why not? Guru is always accurate. Did you see how he tasted the paan before telling you that whatever you touched would turn into gold? A delicious paan was a good omen for him. You should believe him, comrade. Remember what happened to Preman? He didn't believe in astrology and paid for it dearly."

"What happened?"

"I thought you knew it," Chenda said and narrated Preman's story: Preman was stuck in his clerk's desk at State Bank of Travancore for fifteen years while his friends became assistant managers. More than him, his wife was concerned about his career prospects at the bank and pestered him to ask his manager why he wasn't promoted. She also badgered him to consult with Guru, who could explain the hold-up. Finally, under duress, Preman gave in.

Guru prepared Preman's horoscope and explained that his promotion was hampered by the alignment of adverse zodiac houses. "It is inauspicious. You should offer a special pooja to Lord Ganeshan to eliminate the ill effect." Then Guru dropped a bombshell, Chenda recalled.

"I'm glad you came to see me," Guru told Preman. "Assume that God had sent you to me. See, the inauspicious alignment of your zodiac houses is ominous. The next two weeks are bad for you. Very crucial. Something catastrophic might happen to you. We could avert it. All you need to do is offer another pooja. This one is for Amman Devi. It is for your safety. After the pooja, you should stay put at home. Don't go anywhere outside your home," Guru reiterated. "Your family needs you. If you went out, something bad would happen to you."

Preman told his wife about the astrologer's suggestion for two poojas: one for the promotion and the other for his safety. "I'm safe. No bad things will happen to us," Preman assured his wife and laughed. "I went to see astrologer Guru because you bugged me. Now he has scared the shit out of us. Look at me. I'm as strong and healthy as Dara Singh."

His wife would have nothing of it, and she insisted he stayed home. Confined, Preman bit his lips as his wife meticulously filled the cracks and crevices in the home. She also fervently prayed that he shouldn't suffer a stroke or a heart attack. And no snake or scorpion should slip inside the house. His wife wouldn't allow him even to sit on the verandah. Cooped up within the four walls like an orangutan in a zoo and with nothing else to do, Preman found a new game to kill time: Criticize his wife. He mocked how she combed her hair; complained that she put too much Cuticura talcum powder on her face; the fish curry was not spicy or lacked salt. On the thirteenth day of self-confinement, Preman convinced his wife that he was safe all along, and Guru had cooked up the scams to make money. To escape from his constant gripes, his wife yielded when Preman wanted to venture out to the corner store across the street and buy a packet of Panama cigarettes.

While returning from the store with cigarettes, about twenty feet from the house, Preman heard a rustle of leaves. Before he could stretch his head up to look at the source of the noise, a big coconut, like a missile, came aiming for his head. He stood no chance. With a loud thud, his head was crushed. He died instantly.

At the end of Chenda's narration, Vijayan laughed.

"This is no laughing matter, comrade," Chenda said. "Astrology is a serious issue. Our Guru is never wrong. When he says you will win the election, he means it. You should believe him. You will definitely become our MLA."

"Alright. I won't doubt our Guru's predictions," Vijayan said. "Let us paint the slogans on all cement and mud walls. In large letters. Don't leave space for other parties."

ON THE FOURTH day after the RSP district leaders' visit, the same black Ford arrived with a loud roar, made a slow U-turn near the banyan tree, honked twice, and stopped in front of the medical store. Five men—the driver, the front-seat passenger, and three back-seat passengers—got out of the car and looked around as if they were in a strange land. All of them sported beards. A burly man with a thick, scruffy beard—the thickest among the five beards—stepped out, stretched his body backward, straightened, and asked, "Are you Vijayan?"

"Yes," said Vijayan while preparing powdered medicine in a porcelain bowl for a patient.

The man hollered at Vijayan, "Eda, you must stop this joke."

"What joke?"

"Your PPP party."

"It's no joke. I started a new party. People's Power Party," Vijayan retorted. He wanted to assert his new netav status and not be intimidated, not again, in front of customers, in his territory.

"You will regret it," the thick-bearded man hollered again, drawing people's attention. Then, he coarsely spat on the white bodybuilder on the metal sign as if spitting on Vijayan's face. Raising his fist, he yelled, "You bloody rascal, we'll teach you a lesson."

Taken aback by the threat, Vijayan perspired, wiped the sweat on his forehead with the back of his hand, and peevishly said, "Why can't I start a party? I want to improve the living conditions of people here, unlike all these leaders who make promises and forget us after the election."

The man looked at Vijayan with contempt and shouted, "Aha! Does anyone know that you are a fraud? A fake. A real doctor won't work at this stupid medical store. Where did you get your medical degree? Tell me. You are a stupid quack. And you want to be an MLA? What a joke?"

Vijayan trembled and wiped the sweat on his forehead again. His face twitched with anger and humiliation at being called "a stupid quack."

Chenda, who was loading firewood on the handcart at the lumber yard, saw the Ford car in front of the medical store. He ran to the store, noticing that Vijayan had turned pale, and tried to hold his own against the men.

The leader of the group, the thick-bearded man, howled again, "You, stupid quack. We'll teach you a lesson."

Hearing the commotion, Mani also rushed to the store from the marshland. By then, Chenda had moved the kettledrum to the right corner of the store for safety and stood with one leg forward as if ready to tackle the thick-bearded man. Mani furiously curled the tip of his mustache with fingers and stared at the five men from head to toe, apparently sizing up the situation. Tucked under Mani's folded lungi, near the hip, was a big, sharp, shiny scythe, like the ones used by farmers to chop rice corn heads. He made sure the scythe's blade was visible to the uninvited visitors. He also brought a long bamboo stick and gave it to Chenda in their full view.

The threatening posture of Mani with a scythe, his vigorous curling of the tip of his mustache, and Chenda with a bamboo stick shot a strong message to them.

Mani's deep-set, piercing, cold stare, devoid of emotion, unnerved the RSP's henchmen. He unmasked his poker face only when he sold arrack to his regulars. As opposed to

Chenda's muscular build, Mani was slim, and an inch taller. His lean physique had its own benefit. It helped him outrun the chubby Flying Squad members in plain clothes. During their lightning raids. He would easily escape through the narrow zigzag lanes, streets, bushes, and trees. If you saw him gently curling the tip of his mustache, it was simply out of habit.

The posture of Chenda and Mani, both with their lungi folded knee up and ready to pounce, had a sobering effect on the RSP henchmen. What began as a lion's roar was reduced to a cat's meow. The thick-bearded man became less belligerent. "I'm warning you. You'll pay for this. We'll make sure you are defeated and kicked out of this village like a dog with its tail under its butt," he warned Vijayan. He turned to Mani and Chenda and continued, "Put some common sense into this stupid man's head. He doesn't know whom he is dealing with." He turned to Vijayan and waved his finger and warned, "Don't mess with us. You'll regret it."

Vijayan was worried these thugs would throw stones, break the rasayanam bottles, and vandalize the store.

Not to be outdone, Vijayan said, "I don't need your permission to start a party. This is a free country." His lips moved hesitantly, and no one heard these words distinctly.

"We'll trounce you in the election. A medical store clerk starting a party? Ha!" the thick-bearded man said and spat even though he wasn't chewing a paan. Vijayan was miffed that he was being called a clerk.

"I'm the manager, not a clerk," Vijayan corrected the man.

"What's the difference? Manager. Assistant manager. Clerk. Peon. All are the same here. Politics is not a child's play.

Every stupid idiot wants to be a leader," he said and gestured to his companions to get in the car.

As the car roared away from the store, the curious villagers booed them. Elated by their rapid retreat, Chenda shouted spontaneously, "Comrade Doctor Vijayan Zindabad. People's Power Party Zindabad. Down, down RSP." Others repeated, "Comrade Doctor Vijayan Zindabad. People's Power Party Zindabad. Down, down RSP."

And Mani returned to the marshland to resume his arrack sales.

If the RSP henchmen's motives were to intimidate Vijayan, they failed to succeed. It misfired and gave an unexpected boost to Vijayan. It became the talk of Alumaram Village. Soon the word spread to Marakana and other villages, "The Krishnan Good Health Herbal Medical Store's Manager Doctor Vijayan had formed a new political party— People's Power Party. And he stood up to RSP goondas." The community rallied behind him. One knick-knack store owner donated a dozen large sheets of paper to Chenda for making Vijayan's campaign posters. Other store owners donated blue ink tablets and money and volunteered to display PPP's election posters. Homeowners let Chenda superimpose the PPP campaign posters on the "Stick No Bills" warnings on their walls. Vijayan became an instant celebrity, and villagers called him Comrade Doctor Vijayan.

One by one, Appu, Guru, Gopi, and Steven came to the store for their evening discussion of politics. Their topic detoured from the state, national, and the U.S.-USSR Cold War. Instead, their conversation focused on the threat from RSP. Chenda, as usual, from the sidelines, at the right corner of the store, listened to their arguments.

"Chenda and Mani came to my rescue. Those goondas might have assaulted me if these two didn't show up," Vijayan told them. He looked at Chenda with gratitude and said, "As soon as I become an MLA, I will get you an Indian passport and an American visa. I'll send you to America."

Such phony threats were part of the political mind-game, Appu explained. "No one will touch you. Let me tell you something: I make conversations with customers when I cut their hair. They argue that they need a local MLA. They all praise you. You got their votes."

"Thanks," Vijayan said. "I need your support and blessing. From all of you."

Guru had another piece of advice: "We should develop a list of goals. People should know what we stand for. It should be unique. Different from others."

Vijayan repeated what Chenda had painted on walls: "Free electricity. Free pipe water. Tar Roads. Jobs with a pension for all."

"Very good," Guru said. "Now, you must plan street rallies and public speeches here and in other villages.

Vijayan looked at Chenda for an answer.

"It is no problem," Chenda said and gently tapped the kettledrum. "Leave it to me, comrade. We'll have a jatha tomorrow noon."

"A jatha? A rally tomorrow?"

"Yes, comrade."

The PPP's campaign wheels had been set in motion.

8

CHENDA and a few campaign volunteers waited for Vijayan's arrival at the medical store in the morning. One of the volunteers waved a hand-held PPP poster when he saw Vijayan far away on his bicycle. It was a cue for them to chant, "Vijayan Zindabad. People's Power Party Zindabad." They carried crudely made signs that screamed, "Vote for Comrade Vijayan." "V For Victory." "Jobs For All." "Triple-P is India's Future." The full-throated slogan shouting was accompanied by Chenda's animated drum beat.

Vijayan gently bowed his head, clasped his hands like a seasoned politician, and greeted them, "Namaste." He had donned a new handloom juba and a handloom mundu. A large, horizontal sandal paste on his forehead indicated that he had sought the blessing of Goddess Amman Devi on his way to the store. He had offered a special pooja at the temple for his election victory.

On his part, Chenda had cleaned the kettledrum with a wet cloth and applied a coating of coconut oil to make it glisten. He was all gung-ho to play the *chenda* and lead a rally of PPP supporters.

"Look at this, Comrade Vijayan," he said, pointing to the poster "Vote for Vijayan" with a drawing of a blue rocket that he had tied around the kettledrum. Then, he played a few notes to warm up the crowd.

Vijayan, who was ecstatic with the turnout of supporters, asked Chenda quietly, "Who are these people?"

"Our campaign workers, comrade," he explained.

"How did you manage to get so many people so quickly?"

"I promised them free breakfast now and free lunch after the jatha." Before Vijayan could react, he continued, "Otherwise, we won't get people for the rally. No food, no support. No rupee, no vote."

Chenda explained he had already arranged for credits with the Brahminal Hotel and the Military Hotel. They would serve food for the campaign workers and charge the amount to the PPP account. Vijayan didn't have to pay the restaurants until next month. "Isn't it great they gave us credit?"

"Midukkan," Vijayan said, lit a beedi, and took a deep puff. As soon as he finished the beedi, he lit another one. It took a few minutes for the gray smoke to circulate through his lungs and throat and gush like a locomotive train letting out steam.

Over the years, Chenda had observed that Vijayan smoked non-stop whenever he was nervous. So Chenda assured him, "Don't worry about the money, comrade. Things will work out. I'll take a collection."

It was then, Stephen, owner of Lucky Sounds and Lights, came to inquire why people had assembled at the store. When he learned about the rally, he said, "What kind of jatha is without a loudspeaker? No one will hear the slogans without a loudspeaker. Let's use the mic and a loudspeaker from my shop. You also need my diesel generator for power."

"Let's do it," Chenda said. "But, Stephen Chettan, will you give us credit? How much will it cost?"

"Don't worry about it. We'll discuss the payment later. First, our mission is to win the election and make our comrade an MLA," Stephen said and winked at Vijayan as if portending his victory. "We will have super, loud rallies. The loudest ever. But we need a cart to transport the generator and the loudspeaker."

Chenda and Vijayan looked at each other, their eyes exchanging their concerns about the mounting expenses.

"I'll bring the handcart from the lumber yard. We don't have to pay rent," Chenda said.

Vijayan disapproved of the plan and argued it would be impossible for Chenda to pull the handcart and play the kettledrum simultaneously. "You have to play the *chenda* in the rally. Your music is important to draw people's attention. And they love it." For the first time, Chenda felt needed. Belonged. His chest swelled and his eyes became moist. Gently, he caressed the kettledrum.

"Thank you, comrade Vijayan," he said.

"Ask Sivan whether he could ride his bullock cart on credit," Vijayan said, pointing at Sivan who was sitting idle near his bullock cart—the village's taxi—near the banyan tree.

"Good point," Chenda said and approached Sivan, who was happy to haul Stephen's loudspeaker and the diesel generator because no one had hired him for rides. Besides, he had already eaten two appams with egg curry at the Military Hotel at Comrade Doctor Vijayan's Election Credit Account. The word of the free food for campaign volunteers took off faster than the PPP's blue rocket. Sivan had told Basheer, the rickshaw puller—another village hand-pulled taxi—about it. He, too, claimed as a PPP volunteer and ate two appams with egg curry.

Sivan brought his bullock cart to the Lucky Sounds and Lighting, a hundred-foot ride from the northeast of the junction. Stephen placed the diesel generator in the middle of the handcart and fastened it with a coir rope. And he tied the freshly painted green loudspeaker to the vehicle's rear so the bullocks wouldn't be frightened by the sound.

"This is the biggest loudspeaker in my collection," Stephen told Chenda. "You won't find a bigger loudspeaker in any village. Even in the entire state of Kerala."

Both Sivan and Chenda touched the green loudspeaker in admiration, like children with new toys in awe.

Stephen yanked the generator that sputtered a couple of times, cleared its throat, and came to life with a whirr. "Hello, testing. One. Two. Three," Stephen checked the sound system. The mic and the green loudspeaker boomed Stephen's voice.

As soon as Stephen put down the mic, Chenda took it. "Check. Check. One. Two. Three." It was a strange experience for Chenda to hear his voice on the loudspeaker. He smiled and nodded in approval. "Big loudspeaker! Good sound! Let's go."

"Dum…tada…tada…tatatada…dum," the kettledrum sang as Chenda played it, holding drum sticks in both hands. He raised his chin, and his chest swelled with joy. Behind him was the bullock cart with the green loudspeaker that blared Stephen's voice, "Comrade Doctor Vijayan Zindabad. People's Power Party Zindabad. V for Victory. Jobs for All." Other free-food volunteers repeated after him.

Chenda was ebullient as if heading a troupe of musicians at the Travancore Maharaja's Arattu procession from Shankhumugham Beach to Sree Padmanabha Temple at East Fort. In this much anticipated annual event, Maharaja Chithira Thirunal Balarama Varma, who wore a silk mundu with gold thread embroidery and carried a sword in a green velvet sheath, walked the four-mile route. Behind him in the procession were Hindu deities carried on shoulders by devotees, Kerala police cavalry, and a marching band. Despite his royal status, the Maharaja exuded humility and reverence to his subjects, who had converged on either side of the paved street to pay tribute to him. Like the curious onlookers at the Arattu procession, villagers lined up on either side of the gravel streets of Alumaram Village to watch the PPP's first election rally.

"PEOPLE'S POWER Party Zindabad. Up… Up… Triple P," Stephen chanted through his green loudspeaker. The rally participants raised their fists, repeated in full throat whatever Stephen chanted, and waved PPP placards.

Vijayan didn't participate in these rallies. He stayed at the medical store to tend to his patients and sell rasayanam. His patients received an extra pinch of ground ginger powder, extra white sugar-coated pills, an extra ounce of rasayanam, and a reminder, "Don't forget to vote for me. We should win this election. See, there'll be tremendous improvements in the village."

The rally grew longer as more young and unemployed men joined. And the slogan-shouting became louder.

During a lull in the slogan shouting, Chenda whispered to Stephen, "Did you know there were so many men without jobs?"

"No. Not until now," Stephen whispered back. "Most of them are ashamed to admit they are unemployed. I tell you, we won't have any problem recruiting campaign volunteers for a token fee."

The rally wound through several narrow single lanes and cut through the marshland to the street leading to Amman Devi Temple, then to Brahmin's cluster. Halfway through the street, Chenda raised his hand like a traffic constable with a hand-held red stop sign. He stopped playing the kettledrum. The slogan-shouting turned to a whimper, and the rally halted. Stephen's loudspeaker became silent. The reason? Far away, on the other end of the lane, the elephant with Balan perched on its back appeared. The elephant held a stack of coconut tree leaves on its tusks. It walked briskly like a huge rock rolling toward the PPP rally.

"Let's turn back," Chenda told Sivan and Stephen.

"Good!" Sivan said. "The lane is so narrow. There's no space to duck the elephant. If it goes berserk, God, save us! We'll be crushed. Even though the elephant is domesticated, it could turn wild just like that. Animals are not predictable." Sivan snapped his fingers for emphasis.

With the help of a few rally participants, Sivan maneuvered the bullock and the cart in the opposite direction. The rally hastily but quietly retreated and took a detour to the temple via the Brahmin's cluster with rows of narrow homes. The pachyderm ruled the lanes, streets, and M.G. Road. Once the elephant and Balan were out of sight, the cry for PPP votes rose again.

As the rally snaked through rice fields, farmers and laborers stopped tilling to see the procession. A rare sight and entertainment from their back-breaking labor. The booming slogans on the loudspeaker and the *chenda* music echoed through the vast expanse of the rice fields as if they held on to the melody.

Some rally participants, especially teenagers, chanted louder to impress girls. The boys, who watched from the sidelines, punched their fists in the air, imitating the adults, and repeated after them, "People's Power Party Zindabad. Congress Party Murtabad. Pullane, Pullane, RSP Pullane. Down with PSP. Down with the Communist Party." Stray dogs animatedly wagged their tails and barked, either excited or annoyed by the din created by the slogan-shouting paid volunteers.

Every day, for three hours in the afternoon, the rally passed through a different neighborhood.

Before dusk, the volunteers returned to the medical store to drop off the campaign signs. The vegetarians went to the Brahminal Hotel, and non-vegetarians went to the Military Hotel for their reward of free meals, like circus animals looking forward to treats after each performance.

"Ugran jatha," Chenda told Vijayan after a rally. "You should see the enthusiasm in people. We are going to crush our opposition."

"Sabash," Vijayan said. He had another reason to be happy: His candidacy had been a boon for the herbal medicine business. Curious to meet the new leader, people from neighboring villages stopped by the store and bought rasayanam.

The PPP's campaign progress became the focus of the evening discussion of Vijayan, Appu, and Guru. Chenda, as usual, watched them from his right corner of the store. The national and the U.S.-USSR politics had been relegated to the fringes.

"Eda, Chenda," Appu said, "you should include women in the rally. At least one or two women."

Guru chimed in, "There are a lot of women in this area. We need their votes. Good observation, Appu. There should be women in the rally. What do you think, Vijayan?"

Vijayan responded, "I never thought of it." Then, he asked Chenda, "Could you get a couple of women for the rally?"

Chenda looked toward the market at the junction and nodded as if he had found an answer. "I think I could get Cross-toed Ammu and her niece, Kamala, to join. They should be free after selling vegetables in the morning."

"Midukkan," Vijayan said. "You have the solution to every problem?"

CHENDA WENT to the market at the junction and waited for the two women to finish their day's sales. They were sitting on the market's mud floor. Their wares—tomatoes, okra, brinjal, cucumber, bitter gourd, beans, and other vegetables—were spread on banana leaves. Cross-toed Ammu, though in her forties, looked about sixty. The ten-mile trek in the sun and the rain from her mud hut to the market and then to door-to-door sales in the Brahmin's cluster had dried her physique like a raisin. Her weather-beaten wrinkled face, thinning gray hair, scrawny hands, and sagging breasts made her look much older when she sat next to her niece—untanned, voluptuous twenty-something with protruding breasts and long lush black hair. Single and married construction workers whistled and made catcalls at Kamala, making her giggle and Cross-toed Ammu jealous.

Cross-toed Ammu looked at Chenda and asked, "Do you want to buy something?"

"No," Chenda said. "Would you like to make extra money by joining the PPP? Our party?"

"Sure! Tell us what to do."

"You have to participate in our rallies. They start in the afternoon. You could finish your morning sales and then join us. We will pay you."

"How much?"

"Two rupees per jatha, per person."

She looked at her niece for her response.

"Only two rupees?" Kamala asked and looked at Chenda from top to bottom with a sly smile.

"You can also have free meals at the Brahminal Hotel or the Military Hotel," he said, ignoring her smile.

"How long will it take for the jatha?" Kamala asked.

"Maybe three hours. You can do your door-to-door sale after the jatha."

Kamala and Cross-toed Ammu whispered to each other. It was Cross-toed Ammu who spoke up, "We need the money at the end of the jatha every day. No credit."

"OK. No problem," Chenda said. "But this is a secret. I don't want others to know this. About the money arrangement."

They agreed to the deal and were at the forefront of the next day's rally. Thus began the duo's political activism.

"One more thing," Chenda continued. "Could you bring a few other women? Your friends from the market or relatives? But they will be paid only one rupee per day. Plus free meals."

"Good! We'll ask around," Cross-toed Ammu said.

Soon after Chenda left, she admonished Kamala, "What's wrong with you? You looked at him as though you had never seen men before? Smiling at him?"

"He is good-looking. Handsome. Young. Strong. What's wrong with flirting with him?"

"Interested in him? He will make a good husband."

"I know. He is good-looking. But he is black. A low caste. Not interested."

BARELY a month had passed after the campaign kickoff when Vijayan received a torn note from Brahminal Hotel's owner Kuttan: *Rs.105 for meals. Need payment.*

He stared at the note in distress. Again stared as if it was something dreadful. From the store, he searched for Chenda. Unaware of the food bill and Kuttan's demand for money, Chenda came casually to the medical store to get ready for the afternoon rally.

Vijayan gave the note to Chenda and said, "Eda, look at this. This is the bill from the Brahminal Hotel. Did our volunteers eat this much food? Are they eating at both places?"

Chenda raised his eyebrows while reading the note. "This is too much. I didn't expect such an enormous amount. Let me check with the Military Hotel about their bill." He walked hastily there, and owner Kader went through a ruled notebook, added the numbers, and told him, "One hundred-

and-thirty-three rupees as of yesterday. It would be nice if you could settle the bill. I have to pay my workers."

"Ayyo. I didn't know the meals would cost this much. It has been only six days," Chenda said. "Comrade Vijayan will get a heart attack."

Chenda returned to the medical store and told Vijayan about the Military Hotel's bill.

"I'll take money from the store to pay half the amount. We've got to cut down the food bill."

"OK, comrade," Chenda said and suggested that he would prepare a list of volunteers—one for vegetarians and the other for non-vegetarians. They should check in with the owners of the hotels whether they were on the list. It would also stop double-dipping. "Now they won't be able to eat at both hotels."

"Good! We also should restrict the amount of food they can eat," Vijayan said.

Chenda agreed. "Yes. No more than two dosas or idlis, one vada and chai at the Brahminal Hotel, and no more than two appams and egg curry at the Military Hotel. No take-outs. And no guests unless we give permission."

"Excellent! The only exceptions should be you and me," Vijayan said. "We could eat at both hotels on the election account."

WITH CHENDA at the helm, the campaign gradually expanded to adjoining villages. The chanting "Vote for Comrade Doctor Vijayan" and "People's Power Party Zindabad" blared from the green loudspeaker. Chenda and Vijayan decided to organize the party's first Sunday rally. Men who didn't have to work and teenagers who didn't have schools joined the rally, making it longer than its weekday campaign.

"Eda Chenda, this is the largest turnout we have seen so far," Vijayan said with exhilaration. "I should have opened our store. We would have sold a lot of rasayanam today."

Other stores at the junction also were happy. The paan shops sold three days' worth of betel leaves, betel nuts, and snus that addicts wedged under their lips, beedis, and Panama cigarettes. Mani had more customers than he had expected near the marshland, and he had to bring an extra jar of arrack and a bottle of spicy mango pickle.

"Now we should organize a public meeting, not just a jatha," Chenda said. "You should make a big speech."

"I've never given a speech. Perhaps I should ask Appu and Guru to write a speech for me. With lots and lots of big words. Big, big words to impress our villagers."

"Great idea."

"Comrade, you should announce our manifesto. It should be longer than one sentence. Include more items. You can make up something."

Later that evening, Vijayan, Chenda, Appu, and Guru put their heads together to craft the PPP's manifesto. After a prolonged session, including headshaking, nodding, and hand gestures, they came up with a set of goals. Vijayan took a blank paper from his desk and scribbled down the manifesto: "The People Power Party promises to bring city pipe water and electricity to every home. The PPP will create jobs for all, irrespective of the person's gender, caste, and religion. The PPP will build a modern hospital and a high school for boys and girls. As the president, secretary, and the first and the only MLA candidate of the People's Power Party, I dedicate my life to improving Alumaram, Marakana, and other neighboring villages. Now, the power is concentrated at the Secretariat in Trivandrum and in New Delhi. The PPP will give the power back to the people."

Vijayan read it aloud, and others clapped. Pleased, Vijayan gave a glass of rasayanam to them.

"It should be a super event," Vijayan said. "The community should know what our party stands for."

They also made a list of guests for Vijayan's public meeting at the junction. Prominent among them was Arul, owner of the Oil Mill Factory—the wealthiest man in the village.

"We should make him feel important," Vijayan said.

Chenda became quiet. After a pause, he was about to say something when Vijayan interjected, "Mr. Arul will donate large sums to our campaign. We need his support."

"I understand," Chenda said. As if changing the subject, he added, "I can ask Hassan to donate a marigold garland to put on you at the end of the speech. Stephen will take care of the sound system and music. I will play the *chenda*."

With a temporary agenda drawn, the evening gathering of the regulars at the medical store dispersed.

The next two rallies included frequent announcements about Sunday's public meeting at the junction.

THE JUNCTION, especially near the banyan tree, buzzed with a rush of activities on late Sunday afternoon, attracting a scattering of people like the early arrivals for services at the Sacred Heart of Jesus Church. Chenda and Appu brought a table and a chair from the medical store and placed them in the middle of the area. More people arrived and formed a circle around the table.

Stephen brought a ladder, leaned it against the banyan tree, climbed on it, and tied the green loudspeaker on a branch. He was assisted by a friend whom he introduced as dancer Prabhu.

"Dancer Prabhu?" Chenda asked.

"Yes. He is a friend from another village. He is going to perform at this event. For free!"

"What? A dance? Nobody told me about it. Does the comrade know this?"

"Of course. I got our comrade's permission. Prabhu is a great dancer. He had done auditions for a movie role."

"Comrade didn't tell me about this."

"He might have forgotten."

"I guess so. I'll include him in the program," Chenda said and focused on priming the kettledrum for his concert.

Stephen and Prabhu decorated the banyan tree with two fluorescent bulbs—one facing the table and the other facing M.G. Road. They hung a string of red, blue, green, and white bulbs through the branches. Bats, awakened from their sleep, ferociously fluttered around the tree and found spots to lie upside down on other branches. The electric decorations and the loudspeaker were connected to a long black wire that sucked energy like a leech from the power line. Free electricity. Stolen from the Kerala State Electricity Board.

Stephen kept the mic on the table and checked the sound system. "Check One. Two. Three," he tested the mic. The green loudspeaker didn't sputter or clear its throat this time, and it sounded perfectly healthy. Chenda listened from different corners of the junction and waved his hands as if giving a thumbs-up sign to Stephen.

"Play a few notes in front of the mic," Stephen told Chenda. "Let me check the sound from M.G. Road."

Chenda tapped the kettledrum, which was already wrapped with a blue "Vote for Vijayan" sign. Pleased with the sound, Stephen waved at him to continue the music.

"Dum…tada…tada…tatatada…dum," Chenda began to play. The drum sticks appeared to multiply from two to four, then to six, to eight and to twelve as if the birds were dancing on the leather face of the kettledrum. When Chenda finished the music, the crowd broke into a long applause.

"Sabash," Appu and Guru shouted.

Chenda smiled and bowed his head.

Stephen took the mic and announced, "Our candidate, Comrade Vijayan, will be here soon. Before that, we have a surprise program for you. A special performance by an up-and-coming film star, dancer Prabhu.

He placed a 60-rpm HMV black vinyl disc on a gray gramophone record player and turned on the switch. Then, he moved the handle with a shiny, sharp needle on the spinning vinyl disc. "Mm… mm… oh, oh, yeah, yeah!" Elvis crooned through the green loudspeaker on the banyan tree. Startled by the strange loud noise, the bats that hung upside down on the tree like coal rocks fluttered, circled the banyan tree, whined a cacophony, and flew away for the night.

Elvis continued to croon in his inimitable baritone voice, *"A well I bless my soul… I'm all shook up… mm… mm… oh, oh, yeah, yeah!"*

The aspiring actor, who sported a red and white plaid shirt and a white mundu, put on a show. The mundu was folded up to his knee and tucked into his waist to avoid tripping over it. He swung his arms, twisted, and spun around to the beat. Once in a while, he would put his finger under his chin and shake his head as if asking trivia questions. It was a fusion of Indian classical Bharata Natyam moves and Elvis Presley's *"All Shook Up"* beat. East and West, the twain shall meet through dance and music.

Dancer Prabhu shook his head, shoulder, and his famished hip. As the song and dance ended, people clapped loudly. And Stephen thanked the dancer, adding, "He is an up-and-coming movie star. Isn't he a superb dancer? He is the Elvis Presley of Kerala. Give him another round of applause." Dancer Prabhu bowed and gestured namaste. Chenda didn't clap or tap the kettledrum.

"Nalla dance," Guru said. "Super! Is that an American dance? Do it once more." Heeding the request for a repeat performance, Stephen played *"All Shook Up"* again, and dancer Prabhu twisted and pirouetted. A couple of girls imitated his moves and giggled.

At the end, dancer Prabhu said to impress Guru and the audience, "This is Elvis Presley's song. He is an American. World-famous!"

By then, Vijayan had closed the store and walked toward the meeting venue. He wore a long-sleeved juba and a mundu. They were clean and neatly pressed. No one knew the clothes were borrowed, thanks to the local dhobi.

The Elvis Presley of Kerala took a break from prancing around. Chenda shouted in full throat, "Comrade Doctor Vijayan Zindabad." The crowd repeated after him. "V for victory."

"People's Power Party Zindabad."

"Down, down, PSP."

"Down, down, Congress Party."

"Down, down, Communist Party.

"Down, down, RSP."

"Up, up, PPP."

Vijayan took the mic, cleared his throat, and said, "Namaste. Namaste, my brothers and sisters. Today, Alumaram Village is creating history. I thank each and every one of you from the bottom of my heart for coming at short notice. I'm running for election because this constituency needs a strong leader. A leader who will really take care of you; work for you; work with you."

Chanda was the first to clap. Taking the cue from him, the crowd clapped. Loudly. Energized by the applause, Vijayan raised his voice, "I can relate to your struggle to feed your family. I'm also poor like you. The cost of rice is going up. The cost of vegetables is high. We cannot afford to buy kerosene. There is no wage increase and no job opportunities. The politicians at the Secretariat, the Statehouse, don't care about our Alumaram and Marakana villagers." This statement generated louder applause, and Chenda tapped his kettledrum as an accompaniment.

Vijayan referred to himself in the third person. "Comrade Vijayan will never forget his humble roots. He is not like other greedy, power-hungry politicians at the Secretariat. Comrade Vijayan will bring free city pipe water and electricity to this constituency. Comrade Vijayan will create hundreds of government jobs with a pension and build a hospital and a high school. Comrade Vijayan will fight for equal opportunity for women and fight discrimination." He peppered his speech with phrases such as "people's power," "bourgeois revolution," "uplifting the downtrodden," "fight against corruption," and "stop red-tape." He repeated them three times, pumped his fist in the air, and ended his speech with, "Comrade Vijayan will honor his words. PPP Zindabad."

The crowd clapped. Young boys, clueless of what Vijayan had said, also clapped.

Appu and Guru stood up in awe.

"Where did he learn to speak like a professional politician?" Appu asked Guru.

"I didn't know he was capable of public speaking, let alone giving such a powerful speech. He was not nervous at all. He might have had a glass of rasayanam," Guru replied, and chuckled. "I think he had watched political speeches at the East Fort grounds." Politicians have a knack for stirring up the audience's emotions. First, they would speak slowly in a low voice to win over the audience's sympathy. Then they would talk fast and furious, raising their voice into an emotion-charged high pitch to stir anger against their opponents. Anger is the best tool to sway public opinion in your favor. Vijayan employed the same strategy.

As soon as the speech ended in a crescendo, Hassan put a marigold garland around Vijayan's neck. The crowd applauded, and Chenda shouted, "V for Victory," "People's Power Party Zindabad," and "Triple-P Zindabad." The crowd repeated his every chant and dispersed, fully charged.

Stephen quickly removed the loudspeaker from the tree and unplugged the power hookup from the lamppost before anyone could complain about the illegal siphoning of electricity.

Hassan and dancer Prabhu carried the chair and the table back to the store. They hung around to congratulate Vijayan on his speech and offer advice and suggestions.

Chenda was jubilant and tapped the kettledrum as if patting Vijayan's back for his rousing performance.

"Eda, Chenda, what do you think about my speech? My first public speech?" Vijayan asked.

"Ugran! You are amazing, comrade. If you give such speeches, we will easily win the election," Chenda said, applauding the evolution in Vijayan.

He took the mic as a nervous manager of Krishnan Good Health Herbal Medical Store and emerged as a seasoned political leader. The transformation was swift and solid.

9

AT NOON after the day of Vijayan's debute public address, Proprietor Krishnan's blue Chevrolet Impala, announcing its arrival by honking incessantly, pulled up in front of the medical store. A few boys and old men milled around to admire the car and see the goings-on at the medical store. Other store owners peeped at the medical store. Chenda quickly grabbed the election posters and hid them at Appu's barber shop. Vijayan cleaned the desk with a cloth and moved the blue paint can and the coconut husk brush to the backroom, partitioned by the shelf containing rows of black bottles of rasayanam. Only he knew which bottle contained rasayanam and which had water.

"Do you think our comrade is in trouble?" Chenda, who was standing in front of the barbershop, asked Appu.

"Why? Didn't he tell Proprietor Krishnan about his campaign?" asked Appu, gently massaging his swollen leg.

"I don't think so. How did the news reach Kottayam so soon?"

"Arul might have tipped him off. He is the only one with a telephone in the village."

"I'm going to the store. Comrade may want me to fetch chai and vada for Proprietor," Chenda said and left the barber shop.

Inside the Impala were Proprietor Krishnan and the General Manager. They had come from the store's headquarters in Kottayam. Vijayan stood nervously in front of the shelf, blocking the view of the rasayanam bottles filled with water, and said, "Namaste, Proprietor. What a surprise! Come in. Please come in."

As he entered the store, Proprietor Krishnan said, "I didn't know you had big political ambitions. I know that you'll do big things in life."

Vijayan unfolded his mundu, bowed, stood up in reverence, and greeted the owner like an obedient servant, "Namaste, saar," and pushed the big chair in the store toward him. Proprietor Krishnan sat in the chair, looked at the shelf, and massaged his chin. He ordered the driver to buy three cups of chai—for himself, Vijayan, and the General Manager—from the Brahminal Hotel. Proprietor Krishnan glanced at the stores near the junction and asked Vijayan, "How are the sales?"

Proprietor Krishnan looked away, avoiding eye contact whenever he spoke to his employees and others he considered inferior to him. He would tilt his head toward the person as if looking at the person with his ears.

Vijayan scratched his head, ostensibly apologizing and replied, "The business is a little slow, saar. Other stores here have the same complaint. The sales will pick up soon, saar."

"How is your election campaign?"

Vijayan hesitated, wondering whether it was a trap. He could accuse Vijayan of ignoring the store's sales and fire him. Hiring and firing was Proprietor Krishnan's hobby.

"Just started the campaign, saar. It was a sudden decision," he said. "The villagers forced me to start a party, saar. I thought I had to oblige them because they had been good customers. Our sales will go up."

Proprietor Krishnan ignored Vijayan's sales pitch, tilted his ears toward him, and asked, "Will you win?"

"I'll win, saar. The community is behind us."

"Good! Do I have to hear such good news from others?"

"I'm really sorry, saar. I'll never hide anything from you. I couldn't leave the store. I thought of coming to Kottayam tomorrow to tell you in person and seek your blessing. Sorry, saar."

Proprietor Krishnan massaged his chin and smiled. "Umm! It is OK. You've been a trustworthy manager."

"Thank you, saar."

"How old are you?"

"Twenty-eight, saar."

"You're getting old, you know. It's time for you to get married and settle down."

"Maybe after the election, saar."

Proprietor Krishnan looked at Vijayan, making eye contact for the first time as though measuring his height and weight, and turned to the driver, who had brought chai. Vijayan's nervousness evaporated because Proprietor Krishnan didn't ask for the sales report or check the petty cash.

"Drink... drink, chai before it gets cold," Proprietor Krishnan instructed Vijayan and the General Manager, who was sitting on a chair across from him. Chenda, who stood at the right corner outside the store, noticed the Proprietor was massaging his chin while looking at the junction as if plotting his next move. The Proprietor looked at the General Manager, raised two fingers, and mouthed two. The General

Manager walked to the store's stuffy back room and motioned Vijayan to follow him. He took a black pouch tucked under his armpit, fished out two hundred rupees, and gave them to Vijayan. "This money is for your election. Don't mix this with the store's account. Keep them separate. Spend this carefully. If you are good to our Proprietor, he will be good to you. He will help you more. Do you understand? We know you are a loyal and trustworthy servant," the General Manager said.

"Thank you, saar. I'll be a loyal, trustworthy servant to the Proprietor. I promise."

Both of them came out of the office. Vijayan was all smiles, which pleased Chenda because comrade Vijayan didn't lose his job.

"Let me know the campaign's progress," Proprietor Krishnan said. "Don't ignore the store. That's our bread and butter. Umm! We should get you an assistant soon. Let me know if you know any honest and hardworking person like you. He must be reliable. From a good family."

"Thank you, saar. I'll search for a good worker," Vijayan said, his face still sparkling with happiness.

"There's one more thing," Proprietor Krishnan's baritone voice turned into a whisper. "Arul. You know him, don't you? Be good to him. He will be generous to your party. He has a dozen workers in his oil mill. He thinks those idiots plan to start a union. Make sure it doesn't happen."

"OK, saar."

Proprietor Krishnan's baritone voice returned, and he massaged his chin. "Good! If you want anything, contact the General Manager. I saw your campaign slogans on the walls all over the village. Did you paint them all by yourself?"

"No, saar. The party volunteers painted them."

"Impressive," Proprietor Krishnan said, then motioned the driver to start the car. Without saying goodbye, Proprietor Krishnan got into the car, followed by the General Manager. The Impala announced its departure with incessant honking the way it arrived.

SOON AFTER the Impala drove off, Vijayan gestured Chenda to come and told him about the Proprietor Krishnan's contribution. "We could pay off the debt to Kader, Kuttan, Stephen, and Sivan."

"That's good, comrade. I think the Proprietor is bribing you."

"What do you mean?" Vijayan asked and lit a beedi.

"He'll definitely ask you favors once you become an MLA. You told me he was stingy. A kanjoos! A money-pincher. He will tell you to vote for prohibition, so he could sell a lot of rasayanam. He has ulterior motives."

"Good point," Vijayan said. "I think it is OK to return the favor. Should I ask for more money from him? Say, five hundred rupees?"

"Not now. Wait for a month. He is filthy rich. Richer than Arul. Look at his Impala. How much does it cost?"

"Maybe one lakh rupees."

"I think it's more. When I go to America, I'll buy an Impala bigger than the Proprietor's car."

THAT AFTERNOON, Chenda led the rally in the adjoining Marakana Village with the usual crew in tow: Stephen on the mic, Sivan and his bullock cart with the generator and the long green loudspeaker, Cross-toed Ammu and Kamala and their friends with "Vote for Vijayan" signs. The women's presence attracted a few young men to the campaign. A few stragglers, who were unemployed, tagged along for the free meal. Vijayan stayed at the store to sell rasayanam and other herbal medicines. He took part only in Sunday rallies, giving speeches so that he didn't come across as if he, too, was unemployed. Chenda's plan was to make Vijayan available only for major campaign events and let the volunteers pound the pavement.

Chenda also scouted for venues in populated areas in other villages to promote the campaign. A small patch of land, with garbage strewn all over, in Marakana Village got his attention. It didn't matter whether it was private, government-owned, or unclaimed property. All Chenda needed was to shoo away the stray cows and dogs that made it their home and remove the garbage. The area's proximity to Vijayan's house made the spot appealing for the following Sunday's public rally. Appu and Guru made the trip to Marakana Village to show their support. Chenda, as usual, primed the kettledrum, Stephen brought his long green loudspeaker, and dancer Prabhu warmed up to shake up to Elvis' music.

"Today, you will see a special performance. A bonus for coming," dancer Prabhu announced to the crowd like a circus manager boasting about an impending daring act. "You won't forget this. I promise this will be an unforgettable event," Prabhu said. He took out a shiny sharp object from a brown bag he had brought, like a magician pulling a rabbit from his hat, and raised it for the crowd to see. "I'm going to swallow this sword. This is a very sharp sword. If you're not careful, it will slit your throat and puncture your heart. You'll die instantly. To see my daredevil act, you'll have to wait until the end of Comrade Doctor Vijayan's speech."

Chenda, seeing the object, told the dancer, "This is a long kitchen knife, not a sword."

"Shh! Keep quiet," the dancer Prabhu whispered.

"People can see it. They know it is not a sword," Chenda pointed out.

"If you keep telling them it is a sword, people believe it. Got it?" Dancer Prabhu, his face seething with anger, told Chenda. "Mind your own fucking business. Go, play your stupid kettledrum." He turned toward the crowd and asked, "Anyone wants to try this? Swallow this sharp sword?"

No one raised his hand.

"I know you can't do this risky act except me," dancer Prabhu said. He saw Vijayan coming to the venue and bellowed, "Now, please welcome our next MLA...Comrade Doctor Vijayan!" He shouted on the loudspeaker, accompanied by the *chenda* music that rose to a crescendo.

Vijayan repeated his speech interspersed with the same promise of more power to people, free city pipe water, free electricity, a high school, a hospital, equal opportunity for women, jobs with a pension and no discrimination. Another successful speech. Loud applause. And a fresh garland of marigold from Hassan. People nodded, and one by one, returned home.

"We are waiting for your special act. We want to see you swallow the sword," one boy told dancer Prabhu.

"Look, the crowd has already dispersed. They didn't wait. I need a large crowd. I'm not going to swallow this sword just for you. Come to our next meeting," he said.

THERE WERE a few people who waited to congratulate Vijayan. Among them were his sister, mother, and father.

"That was an ugran speech," his sister said and teased him. "Look at you…A big netav!"

His father, beaming with pride, said, "Excellent prose. Where did you learn to speak like this?"

"Achan, I practiced during my bicycle rides to the store and back home."

"If you give such speeches, you will become India's Prime Minister," Vijayan's father said. "I thought you were joking when you said you wanted to be an MLA. Midukkan!"

His mother caressed his face and said, "I'm proud of you. Many people came to the meeting. Big crowd. I've been praying to Amman Devi that you win the election."

"Thanks, amma."

"Come home soon after talking to your friends. I made fish curry and kappa for you," his mother said. She gestured toward Chenda and told Vijayan, "Bring him along. He plays the *chenda* really well. He is handsome and would be a good match for your sister. Do you know him well? What does he do for a living?"

"Shh, amma. Talk quietly. He is a parayan. I don't want our Omana to marry him. And he is a little loose," Vijayan whispered and made a mini circle with a finger near his head. "He carries the *chenda* all the time, day and night. And he talks about going to America. A parayan going to America? Could you believe it?"

Vijayan's mother responded, "He can't be crazy because he is an excellent musician. He could be an eccentric, like some brilliant artists. It's OK with me."

"Yes, amma. He is gifted. But he is obsessed with going to America. That's all he talks about. Something is really wrong with him. Don't worry, amma. Once I win the election, I'll find a light-skinned rich husband for Omana. I promise."

"Alright. You know what's good for your sister. She is your responsibility," Vijayan's mother said and wistfully looked at Chenda, who was helping Stephen load the green loudspeaker and the generator in Sivan's bullock cart about two hundred feet away.

"WE HAD a great campaign yesterday," a smiling Vijayan told Chenda, who stopped by on his way to deliver and chop firewood in the morning. "You did a great job."

Encouraged by Vijayan's praise, Chenda said, "Comrade, the Proprietor asked you to search for an assistant manager. You could hire me. I already told you I would do all work: Load empty bottles and unload boxes from the lorry, sweep the floor, do the morning and evening poojas, fetch your food."

Vijayan lit a beedi, took a deep puff, and spewed the gray smoke. He did this a few times to stall for a nicotine-fueled excuse.

"You should focus on going to America. You don't need the dead-end job at the store. Besides, I need you for my campaign. You are my right-hand man. That's more valuable to me than as the store's assistant manager. Eda, I want you to be in charge of the election funds. I cannot trust anyone else."

"Treasurer! PPP Treasurer!" Chenda repeated and tapped the kettledrum. It made loud, happy music. "OK, comrade. I'll do it if you want me to be your collection agent. Thanks!"

"This is my strategy," Vijayan explained. Chenda had to contact all businesses in the village and solicit a fixed weekly donation, in addition to the blue ink tablets and the papers they had given. "Eda, you also should approach Arul. Proprietor Krishnan told me Arul would contribute to our party. We will get a large amount from him."

Chenda recoiled at the mention of Arul's name as if he had come across a real cobra. He shook his head and declared, "You should contact him, comrade. Not me. I won't ask him."

"Why not?"

"He is not a good man," Chenda said. His excitement about being the PPP Treasurer quickly wilted. After hesitating, he continued softly, "Once, he wanted me to meet him at night behind the haystack in his compound."

"Did he really say that?"

Chenda swallowed the saliva as if swallowing his pride and whispered the details: He had been dodging Arul's invitation to meet him at night. Arul offered him a job in his coconut oil mill and wanted to discuss the job description at night behind the haystack. When Chenda declined the job, Arul tried to give him Onam gifts. Arul sent a servant twice to remind him to collect them. When Chenda went to meet Arul in the afternoon, his servant told him that Arul was busy and he would be free at night.

"I don't know why he wanted to give me Onam gifts. I don't work for him. Comrade, he is not a good man," Chenda reiterated.

Vijayan lit another beedi and took a few quick puffs that were mixed with confusion and anger. "Isn't he married? He has two children, right?"

"One girl and one boy."

"You know, that pervert is trying to take advantage of you. He wants to do his wife as well as you. Rascal!"

"Comrade, people won't believe me because he is rich. His home has electricity, a telephone, and a tiled roof."

"Then what happened? Did you meet him?"

"No. I didn't meet him. I don't need his stupid Onam gifts."

"Good! But I'm so sorry you didn't get any gift for Onam."

"I did receive a gift. Patti-Amma gave me a white shirt."

"Alright, I'll deal with Arul. You go ahead and solicit donations from stores. We need the money."

10

CHENDA, the kettledrum clinging to his shoulder, was on his way to the lumber yard to pick up the handcart and firewood for delivery. He was surprised to see Appu and a couple of farmers with bullocks standing in front of the Brahminal Hotel, listening to the news on the dust-covered Murphy radio at the eatery. Kuttan stood at the hotel's door, both ears screwed up to the broadcast from All India Radio. At Kuttan's instruction, one of the hotel servers offered free chai to Chenda, Appu, and the farmers as though providing sustenance to those grieving at a funeral. Fear and confusion were written on their face as if they had been hit by a cyclone. The All India Radio's news bulletin repeated: "Kennedy was assassinated. U.S. President John F. Kennedy was shot and killed by a gunman in Dallas, Texas. We are waiting for more information."

"Oh! My God…oh my God, this can't be true," Chenda screamed as the news bulletin was broadcast again by a sad baritone voice on the backdrop of soft sarangi music, plucking the strings of emotions one by one. Startled by Chenda's loud cry, the farmers' bullocks lurched and let out loud brays. The farmers reined in the animals by holding on to their harnesses while Appu consoled Chenda.

"Calm down. Please calm down. We don't know the full detail," Appu said and patted Chenda's shoulder. Chenda squatted on the road and put his head on the kettledrum like a young boy resting his head on his mother's lap. His body quivered as he wept bitterly, "Who will do such a thing to Kennedy? The great President of America."

Appu said, "Bad people are everywhere. America is no different."

"Why would someone do that? To Kennedy?"

"We don't know. Let's wait for more news."

"Do you think our Prime Minister Jawaharlal Nehru is safe?"

"Yes, he is safe. No one will touch him. We don't have guns as is in America," Appu said.

Chenda tightly held the kettledrum, looked at the Murphy radio, and waited for All India Radio to update its dispatch. Appu went back home to check on his wife's and two-month-old son's safety and quickly returned. Appu, Guru, tailor Gopi, Stephen, and Mashe came and stood somberly, their ears glued to the Murphy radio. The last to join them was Vijayan.

Another news bulletin: "The American authorities have arrested a suspect. Vice President Lyndon B. Johnson will be sworn in as President of the United States of America."

"Good! They caught him. Hang the motherfucker," Chenda shouted at no one in particular.

Chenda didn't deliver and chop firewood. He returned the handcart to the lumber yard that owned it. The Murphy radio repeated the same news to the background of the heart-wrenching sarangi melody.

"Comrade, we should hold back our campaign today," Chenda said. Vijayan nodded his head. Cross-toed Ammu and Kamala didn't object and gave up their daily compensation of two rupees. "Someone, a big leader in America, died," she explained to Kamala and others. "Killed. I think he was the President. Shot. Like what happened to our Gandhi. Crazy people are everywhere!"

Vijayan, Appu, Gopi, and Hassan shuttered their stores and went home to be with their families. The market at the junction closed early. Hassan didn't sell flowers. Chenda's kettledrum didn't sing in the evening at the junction. Out of habit, he tapped a note that sounded like wailing. Teenage boys didn't play cricket on M.G. Road. Stray cows, buffalos, and dogs roamed aimlessly. The bats in the banyan tree stayed upside down. The banyan tree didn't rustle its branches and leaves.

Before dusk, the All India Radio broadcast another news bulletin: All flags in India's central and state government buildings had been lowered to half-mast. The country would observe a week of mourning.

THE MORNING newspapers screamed in large, bold letters: "JFK assassinated." But they had little more to say because it was about ten o'clock at night in India when the shooting took place in Dallas. The newsroom teleprinters spitted out the same breaking news that had already been broadcast by the Murphy radio.

Chenda, Vijayan, Appu, and Guru read the news repeatedly in all three Malayalam newspapers. They had the same news story transmitted by the Associated Press, UPI, AFP, and Reuters. Even the headlines were the same. So were the file photos of a debonair John F. Kennedy, his wife Jackie, and his children.

"I think the Soviet Union is behind it," Guru said and made a calculation with his fingers. "Kennedy should have stayed home...not an auspicious time for him to travel."

Vijayan interjected, "He has a lot of enemies. There are a lot of jealous people in the world."

Appu speculated it could be the mafia. "Can you imagine assassinating the world leader? Shocking! No one is safe."

Chenda listened to their loud conversation and wept silently.

"Don't let this discourage your American dream," Appu comforted.

THE ONLY business unaffected was Mani's arrack sales. People hit the bottle when they are happy or when they are sad. To celebrate or to grieve.

"Can I have a drink, please?" Chenda asked Mani, who curled the tip of his mustache and looked at Chenda's taut face as if wondering why he asked for liquor. After curling his mustache a few times, Mani gave Chenda a glass of arrack. He had never requested arrack and never refused when Mani offered him. Mani never demanded money from Chenda, who emptied the glass in two consecutive gulps, scooped the spicy mango pickle with his finger, and ate it. Both conversed in silence, tightly held by the cord of empathy.

While pouring arrack, Mani said, "I heard a mad man killed the American President."

"The President's name was Kennedy," Chenda said as his lips quivered. "He was like the world's President."

Mani patted him on his shoulder. "Be careful when you go to America." Chenda nodded and thanked him for the drinks. As soon as he emptied the glass, Mani replenished it. "You're tired. This one is for the road. Go, get some sleep."

Chenda drank it and felt the burning sensation created by the pungent potion as it flowed through his throat, liver, and stomach and numbed his heart and mind. He tapped the kettledrum with his tired hands. There was no rhythm. No music. No life. Somewhere far away, a sleepless dog barked, followed by the rustle of the leaves caused by a slithering yellow rat snake. Chenda shooed the reptile away.

"*Ulagae Maayam, Vaazhve Maayam,*" he sang as he set out to Patti-Amma's back porch.

"The world is an Illusion, Life is an Illusion."

11

TWO WEEKS had passed. The Murphy radio at the Brahminal Hotel resumed playing Malayalam and Hindi movie songs. The market at the junction buzzed again. Chenda began to deliver and chop firewood in the morning and lead the PPP rallies in the afternoon.

By late afternoon, Vijayan had an unusual visitor: A postman on a bicycle. He handed an envelope to Vijayan. It was addressed to the Manager, Krishnan Good Health Herbal Medical Store, Alumaram Village, Kerala State—God's Own Country, India.

"We don't get letters. I don't know who sent this," Vijayan said and was buoyed by the "manager" salutation on the envelope. He looked at both sides of the envelope. "There is no sender's name and address?"

"I don't know who sent it," the postman said. "You are the manager. You can open the envelope and find out."

"You came all the way from Marakana Village to bring this letter?"

"Yes."

"Good. When I become an MLA, I'll push the central government to start a branch here."

The postman nodded his head, rang the bicycle's bell out of habit, and pedaled back to the post office in Marakana Village.

Vijayan checked both sides of the envelope again before opening it. Inside was a ruled paper with large writing. His eyebrows puckered. He reread it, "Vijayan is a Parayan Lover. The PPP is the Parayan People's Party. No Future for Upper Castes. We will boycott the medical store."

His lips moved when he read the letter for the third time, word-by-word. There was no name. And no signature. The handwriting was neat and legible. Vijayan lit a beedi and realized he was trembling with trepidation. Beads of sweat were forming on his forehead. He looked around and on M.G. Road, hoping to spot the letter's author. Other store owners were busy attending to customers, and there was no unusual activity or strangers at the junction. Chenda was preparing for a rally with a few volunteers; Appu was lathering a man's face for shaving; Hassan was busy slicing mutton; Cross-toed Ammu and Kamala were busy selling vegetables; Guru was not to be seen; and the brown Murphy Radio at the Brahminal Hotel was blaring the popular "*Annathinnum*" song from the 1962 blockbuster movie *Laila Majnu*.

Holding the envelope, Vijayan plunked on the wooden chair behind the desk to hide his trembling legs. His hand still shaking, he took deep puffs from his beedi. Then, he went behind the shelf, poured a glass of rasayanam, gulped it down, and lit another beedi. He scrutinized other store owners and passing men, wondering whether each person was the anonymous author. Then, he looked at the religious pictures on the wall and, on impulse, performed a quick pooja.
SWISH. SWISH. SWISH.

Vijayan raised his head and looked for the source of the swishing sound. It was Cane-Swami who swished his cane. He carried the four-foot cane with both tips fastened with elephant hairs, purported to bring strength and good luck. The cane swished whenever he whipped it in the air to drive away devils that he had claimed only he could see. *Swish. Swish. Swish.* Often he stroked his flowing gray beard or the long wavy, oily gray hair that reached over his shoulder. On his forehead were three broad lines of sandal paste he had drawn with fingers. Donning a saffron juba and a saffron mundu over his five-foot four-inch-tall stocky frame, Cane-Swami stood out in any crowd. He enjoyed the special attention drawn by his appearance, especially the saffron apparel and the swishing.

"Come in. Swami, come in," Vijayan said, his eyebrows still furrowed over the anonymous letter. "Need any medicine?"

"No…no medicine for me," Cane-Swami said and entered the medical store, *swished* with his cane over a chair as if sprinkling holy water, sat on it, and looked at Vijayan. "I heard you gave a great speech the other day, here at the junction, and another rousing speech at the other village. Good job!"

"Thanks, Swami."

Cane-Swami looked around. "Where's the boy? Chenda?"

"He went to deliver firewood."

"Good! I'm glad you are alone. Here's something I want to tell you," Cane-Swami whispered.

Vijayan tossed the beedi on the floor, snuffed it with his foot, and pushed the *beedi* stub out of the store. "Go ahead, Cane-Swami."

"You are a good man. I want you to win the election. But there's something you should do. Get rid of him. That parayan."

"What?"

"Somehow, get rid of the boy. You don't need the *chenda* player. He is a Harijan. You don't want an untouchable to campaign for you."

"Cane-Swami, what are you saying? Did you write the letter?"

"What letter?"

"What I'm going to show is highly confidential. I received this anonymous letter today. You are the only other person to know this. OK?"

"Yes," Cane-Swami said and stroked his flowing gray beard.

Vijayan removed the letter from the envelope, gave it to Cane-Swami, and closely watched him read.

"I didn't write this," he said. "But I'm not surprised by its contents. Whoever wrote this didn't want to offend you, I guess. Many villagers are turned off by the parayan's presence. They tell me these things. They like you, not him."

"But Cane-Swami, Chenda was the one who motivated me to run for office. He is the backbone of the party. The PPP was his brainchild."

"I don't know what to tell you, Vijayan. I hope people don't boycott your store. You'll lose the election and your job if it happens," Cane-Swami said, followed by a quick prayer. "Hare, Rama. Hare Krishna. Good, God! Save this country."

Befuddled, Vijayan studied Cane-Swami, wondering whether he shared the words of wisdom, or the words of destruction, or the words of politics. Vijayan lit a beedi, took a deep puff, and waited for the tobacco to form his thoughts. A few seconds later, he blurted out, "I want to become an MLA. What can I do to win the election? I cannot simply kick him out of the campaign or tell him not to come to the store. The villagers like him. And they love his music."

"Don't worry about him. He is like a curry leaf. You use it for flavor, then toss it out," Cane-Swami said and combed his long oily gray beard with his fingers. "When you eat your meal, you toss the curry leaf in the garbage. Don't you?"

"Yes. No one eats it."

"It's the same case with him," Cane-Swami explained, combing his beard with his fingers. "Send him to the Harijan hamlets. Let him campaign far away from our village. Far away from public view. The villagers wouldn't doubt you. Gradually you could force him out of the campaign. How about that?"

Vijayan was quiet. After a pause, he asked, "Can I get you chai from the Brahminal Hotel?"

"I don't drink tea or coffee. Only milk. Don't worry," Cane-Swami replied and looked at the pictures on the wall. "Why do you have the pictures of Jesus and the Kaba? You're a Hindu. You should worship only Hindu Gods."

"I've been praying to all of them for a long time. Appu, Gopi, Hassan, and Stephen do the same."

"Don't worry about them. You need the Hindu votes, not they," Cane-Swami said. Before leaving, he added, "If you need help, let me know. I'll ask some of my disciples to campaign for you. You know where I live. Don't you?"

"Yes, Swami. Near the Amman Devi temple."

"Alright," he said and left the medical store with a swagger like a king's chief counsel who had crafted a winning war strategy.

Swish. Swish. Swish.

AFTER THE RALLY, Chenda arrived enthusiastically with the kettledrum at the medical store. The Vote for Vijayan sign was still strapped around it.

"*Eda,*" Vijayan said, "we have to extend our campaign outside the village. We should reach out to the poor. I mean, the poor people in the hamlets near the forest. We need their votes, too. Tomorrow, take the rally there and put our signs in front of the huts there."

Surprised, Chenda said, "Comrade, there are not many votes in those places. People there are moving out of their hamlets. They are finding jobs in the city. I think we should concentrate more on heavily populated areas."

Vijayan insisted, "There are many residents in those hamlets, and we need their every vote. I have a solution. Let us create a small rally of a handful of people just for the hamlets. You lead it. Dancer Prabhu and Stephen will take care of the campaign here. What do you think?"

Chenda didn't respond.

As if to pacify him, Vijayan said, "Let's try it out. Eda Chenda, remember. You are a valuable part of my election. I won't win without you. You got me into politics. You started this party. PPP. You are the only one who can help me get the votes from the hamlets. We should get to them before other parties do."

"OK," Chenda said. The following day, Chenda invited the vegetable vendors to join his mini-rally to the hamlets. They declined.

"We must walk ten miles one way and another ten miles back," Cross-toed Ammu complained. "You have got to give a lot more than two rupees for each of us. It's a long trek."

Other volunteers echoed similar excuses. So, Chenda set out alone to the hamlets through the northeast of the junction. He passed the Alumaram River bridge and a hill. The slope on the other side would lead you to a swath of rice fields surrounded by a forest of tall coconut trees interspersed with banana, jackfruit, papaya, and an assortment of other trees. A few coconut trees in the middle had grown crooked, circumventing other trees to bathe in the sun and breathe fresh air. A narrow, rough dirt track, formed over the years of traversing on the same route by farmers and their tilling ox, led to the rice fields. They were carved into hundreds of different sizes and shapes, like the patches in a quilt. An elevated mud path—perhaps a foot high and wide—let tiller-carrying farmers pass through with their ox. Some fields needed tilling, some had buds of rice crops, and some were ready for harvesting. On the right side of the rice fields were the hamlets, whose residents worked at these rice fields. In heavy monsoons, these rain-soaked paths would become mushy and slippery. A misstep would land you in the wet rice field. Like a tightrope walker, you had to maneuver a mile through these little squares and rectangular rice fields to reach the first hamlet. A man-made stream functioned as a buffer between these fields and the hamlets.

HAULING THE kettledrum on his shoulder, Chenda deftly navigated through a narrow bridge, which was made by knotting long tree trunks and reached the first hamlet. It was composed of six mud huts with thatched roofs.

Chenda tapped the kettledrum in front of a house. The music, a rare treat for the hamlet, brought out elderly people and children. He gave them PPP signs with a blue picture of a rocket and urged them to display them in their front yards. "Remember to vote for the People's Power Party. It's our party," he exhorted them. The residents were amused to see a dark man campaigning for a political party.

"Come, come…sit," said an old woman. He looked at her wrinkled, weather-beaten, leathery face. Her hands and legs were frail as dried tree branches. Like hay, her hair had become pale after years of bearing the brunt of life in the hamlet. She had a slight hunch—the reward for bending down to plant, weed, and harvest rice during her youth.

"OK, ammachi. I have a little bit of time. I have to visit other hamlets," Chenda said and sat on the mud verandah.

"I'll make black chai for you," she said and went inside the hut before Chenda could tell he was not hungry.

It didn't take long for her to bring chai in a small, thick glass.

"Don't be shy. Drink," the woman said. "I'm sure there's room for a glass of chai in your stomach. We don't get visitors. We are the forgotten ones. You stopped by because you must be a parayan. One of us. Aren't you?"

He didn't respond and sipped the chai. "Hmm…very good."

The woman's grandchildren and their friends from neighboring huts milled around him and touched the kettledrum.

"You want to play?" Chenda asked. A boy vigorously nodded as if screaming, "*Yes, yes!*"

Chenda made them stand in a circle and let them tap the kettledrum. The first to try was a girl. She tapped the kettledrum with the drum stick. "Dum." Her eyes widened, and her jaw dropped. "Dum…dum." She let out a giggle laced with the thrill of making music. Each "dum" was her own melody. Her own rhythm. Her own creation, like the first stroke of a brush on an empty canvas. And the kettledrum hummed a medley of the children's music, enriched with pure joy.

He gestured with his hand to pass on the drum stick to a boy who impatiently waited for his turn. The boy tapped a few more times than the girl and swayed his hips like a professional *chenda* player. "When I grow bigger, I want to be a musician like you," the boy said.

Chenda laughed at the unexpected admiration and told the boy, "You should aim high. Go to school. Get your SSLC certificate and get a government job. You'll have job security and a pension."

The children looked puzzled at each other.

"There's no school here," the boy said. "We have to walk miles and miles to go to the elementary school. The rich children will make fun of us because we wear the same clothes every day. So, we don't go to school."

Chenda's eyes became moist, and he wiped his eyes with the back of his hand.

The boy continued, "Did you go to school? Do you work in a big government office?"

"No. I didn't get a chance to go to school. That's why I want you all to go to school. I play the music and chop firewood. But I have big plans," Chenda explained.

Hearing the conversation, the woman interjected. "You children ask too many questions. Treat him with respect. No more silly questions."

Chenda finished the chai and put the empty glass on the verandah's mud ledge.

"More chai?" she asked.

"No. I'm already full."

"What's your good name?"

"Chenda."

"Chenda? That's your real name?"

"That's what the villagers call me."

"Which village?"

"Alumaram."

"No…no. What I meant was, where were you born? Which hamlet? I know the families of all hamlets here."

"I don't remember, ammachi."

"You don't remember where you were born?"

"Yes. Honestly, I don't remember. People won't believe me when I say it."

"What's your father's name? Or your mother's? I can find them."

Chenda caressed the kettledrum to avoid the confused stares of the children and said, "Ammachi, you won't believe it. I don't remember them, either."

"You are an orphan," she murmured. Seeing Chenda's face that had turned sallow, she continued, "You are always welcome here."

"OK, ammachi," he said and looked around. The mud huts sat about twenty yards from each other. They were surrounded by an assortment of banana, coconut, jackfruit, papaya, and mango trees. There were bushes and switch grass—a perfect hideout for scorpions, snakes, and other critters. If you were not careful, you would touch poison ivy in the bushes and end up with a wild rash all over your body. In the middle of the hamlet was a well with a stone wall that supplied water to these huts. Each hut had a cow or a sheep and a few chickens. Crows cawed, mynahs chirped, and a stray dog asserted its territory by peeing on trees. Chenda took a deep breath, which was filled with tranquility and contentment.

The woman looked at Chenda and said, "We'll find you a wife, a pretty young wife. And a hut. You are so young and have strong muscles. You need a family. Without a family, you are like a loose kite. Drifting aimlessly. You need a home."

Chenda listened to her calmly. "I have other plans, ammachi. Right now, I've to ensure our comrade's victory. Please vote for Vijayan. Tell your relatives and friends, everyone, to support him. Put these PPP signs in your front yard or tie them on trees," he said.

He proceeded to the next hamlet. Alone. There was no blare of the green loudspeaker. No Sivan's bullock cart. No procession of the hired supporters. And no chanting of "Vote for Comrade Doctor Vijayan."

Idly, Chenda tapped the kettledrum out of boredom that sounded like a slowly dying heartbeat. A few seconds later, you could hear the kettledrum's sound, a single "dum," which ricocheted in the hills like an afterthought. From a long distance from the hill, you could see a tiny lonely image—a dot in the vast panoramic landscape of rice fields below, carrying an oblong object on its shoulder and hitting it lazily.

THAT EVENING, when Chenda returned from the hamlet, Vijayan asked, "Eda, how did it go?"

"It is OK, comrade. I distributed a few PPP posters. You should build an elementary school there."

"Sure. Tell them to vote for me. I'll build a first-class school for them. With a tiled roof and black boards," he said and poured a glass of rasayanam from a half-finished bottle and offered it to Chenda. "Now on, you should concentrate on securing votes from those hamlets. Find out their needs. Tell them I'll fulfill their needs once I become an MLA."

Between drinking the rasayanam, Chenda explained that an elderly woman at the hamlet would drum up support for the PPP. Vijayan listened with interest and replenished Chenda's glass. "Excellent! Eda, we've got to make some adjustments in our strategy."

"What's that?"

"You are a great campaigner, a successful one," Vijayan said. "You've put together a good team to work here in the village. I want you to be in charge of the campaign in the hamlets."

"Who will handle the rallies here…in Alumaram, Marakana, and other villages?"

"The dancer will handle it. You need to focus more on the hamlets and other rural areas. What do you think of this plan?"

Chenda took a gulp of rasayanam and asked, "Who will collect the money? We need a big election fund."

"I will make the dancer in charge of the village funds, and you will be in charge of the hamlet funds."

"Comrade, the people in the hamlets are broke. They cannot afford to donate even a paisa."

Vijayan lit a beedi and nodded his head as if agreeing with Chenda. "We will accept whatever they give. Let us talk more about it tomorrow. You must be tired. Get some rest."

INSTEAD OF going straight to Patti-Amma's back porch, Chenda went to the marshland to meet Mani.

"I'm glad you came," Mani said, pouring arrack into a thick glass with yellow rings of the liquor residues and giving it to Chenda. "Have a drink and help me with these jars."

Chenda took a gulp, put the kettledrum on the grass, and got ready to help Mani transfer arrack from a big jar into small jars. Once filled, Mani closed the small jars with corks, wrapped them with old newspapers, and fastened them with coir. He stepped into the knee-deep marshland, and Chenda passed on the small jars to him, one by one, as if they were bottles of white liquid gold. Mani carefully thrust them into the swamp, hiding from public view. Then, he littered bits of snakeskins to scare away the Flying Squad members from raiding his livelihood. For Mani and Chenda, the long bits of snakeskins were the clues to the hidden spots in the wide swath of water, grass, reeds, and lotus. Chenda knew Mani collected snakeskins from the marshland. For his part, Chenda also picked up dry brown-and-yellow snake skins whenever he saw them under the rocks. The villagers avoided the marshland because it was a breeding ground for mosquitos, frogs, and yellow rat snakes.

After hiding the jars except one, both sat on a nearby grass patch. Mani refilled Chenda's glass, poured one for himself, and said, "I didn't see you in the jatha here. Is everything OK?"

"Now I'm focusing on the hamlets near the forest. Comrade wants me to campaign there," Chenda said and sipped the arrack.

"Doesn't he know that you're more valuable here?" Mani said.

"I think he is trying to get rid of me. He is sending me off to faraway hamlets that are not even in our constituency. He also doesn't want me to play the *chenda* at public meetings anymore. He wants me to take rest. Can you believe it?"

"Hmm. That's interesting," Mani said and offered him the spicy mango pickle to go with arrack. "Listen, do whatever he asks you to do. You need his help to get your passport and visa. After that, ignore him."

Chenda nodded.

"Tell me, why do you want to go to America?" Mani asked and gently curled his mustache. "To escape from discrimination?"

Chenda pondered over the question and looked at the marshland for an answer.

But Mani continued, "Wherever you go, there's discrimination. You cannot escape from it."

He shrugged his shoulder and said, "America is a great country, Mani Chettan. There are no upper castes or lower castes. There are no poor people. All are equal. And they are so rich that they drink beer instead of water."

Whenever Chenda spoke of America, his face would light up. He would become energetic and create vivid images of that country. He would show the pictures of the Carnegie Hall and the Empire State Building and say, "Mani Chettan, look…look at this huge hall. The stage is so big it can hold ten elephants. There is no other such massive music hall in the whole world. Only famous artists are allowed to perform there. One day, Mani Chettan, I'll play the *chenda* there. White madammayums and sayippums will be astonished by the music. You'll be proud of me."

Mani asked whether Americans would enjoy the *chenda* music.

"Of course! Who doesn't love music? It's the universal language of love."

"Then you'll be a famous musician. A big-shot sayippu. And rich. Richer than Mr. Arul. Will you take me there?"

"Sure, why not?"

"Eda, I was joking. I'm happy here," Mani said. "You go to America. You are an artist. Artists dream big. Will you bring me a big Murphy transistor when you visit us?"

"Yes, I will," Chenda said, emptied the glass, and tapped the kettledrum.

"Dum. Dum…dum."

12

THE ALUMARAM Village junction's landscape dramatically changed as election day neared. The first sign was the appearance of other parties' campaign posters, plastered over "Vote for Vijayan" slogans and the PPP's blue rocket symbols on the walls.

Malayalam movie advertisements would muzzle their way over the party posters, adding to the clutter. The next day, you would see new election signs on top of the movie posters. It was a war between election and movie posters—between false promises and make-believe worlds.

Other parties' banners and flags popped up like festoons at every nook and corner. The banyan tree became the favorite real estate for political signs. Every branch had either a flag or a banner fastened on it. From far away, the tree's top looked like an old woman's bun-shaped hairdo with different colors and sizes of flags and banners. Agitated by the invasion of foreign objects, the bats squawked and fluttered.

The first rally of the Congress Party was the wake-up call for Vijayan. Three dozen men, chanting "Congress Party Zindabad," cruised through M. G. Road and side streets. They were loud enough to bring housewives out of their kitchen.

Within two days, the Communist Party's and RSP's slogan-shouting supporters showed up like a stream of enemy platoons invading the village in broad daylight.

Vijayan peered out of the store, a beedi dangling from his lips. He took a few puffs and tried to make smoke rings when Appu stopped by to read the newspapers. "Are you worried about the election?"

"A little. Other parties have landed in full force. We've got to ratchet up our campaign."

Appu massaged his right hand and pointed out, "Our PPP jathas are not loud and lively as they were before. The PPP is now like a flat balloon."

"We are trying our best to keep the momentum," Vijayan said. "People are fascinated by other parties because they just entered the fray. Once the novelty is over, they will come back to us. We are local."

"You are losing the magic. Where's Chenda?" Appu asked.

"He went to the hamlets. We are trying to get the Harijan votes."

"Guru and I have been wondering what had happened to him. I think you should bring him back. He is the life of our PPP. Send someone else to those areas," Appu said.

THE FOLLOWING afternoon, the PPP rally was dull as if the volunteers were on valium. "Vote for Vijayan" and "PPP Zindabad" slogans had become tedious whimpers. One man would shout a PPP slogan, and two or three out of a dozen volunteers would repeat it, that too, half-heartedly as if saying "whatever." Women and children didn't come out of their homes to cheer them. It was like a rerun of black-and-white movies when color movies were in vogue. There was another surprise: The rally was short of two familiar faces—Cross-toed Ammu and her niece. Perturbed by their absence, Vijayan asked dancer Prabhu why didn't they show up.

"Oh! Those vegetable ladies? Saar, they have been asking for Chenda."

"Why?"

"I don't know. They said they had joined the RSP."

"RSP? Did they defect us?"

"Yes. Because that party offered them four rupees per day."

But Vijayan argued, "We've been paying for their food on top of two rupees."

"They demand more money; six rupees," dancer Prabhu said.

"Greedy women! We gave them more than what they earned by selling vegetables. Tell them we will give five rupees plus food. We need them on our team. They are valuable. You know, they also sell vegetables door-to-door after the morning market. They are like our ambassadors," Vijayan said and instructed him to give a one-rupee raise to all PPP volunteers. "We don't want other parties to steal our people."

"OK, Vijayan, saar," dancer Prabhu said. He hesitated before asking, "Could you hire me as your assistant?"

The first thing Vijayan wanted to know was his religion and caste.

"Hindu. Pillai."

"Good," Vijayan said. "I'll recommend you for the assistant manager's position here at the store. This is top-secret. I don't want Chenda, barber Appu, or Guru to know this. For the time being, your main job is to work aggressively on my campaign. Get me elected. Understood?"

"Yes, saar."

"Your monthly salary will be sixty rupees, and you won't get overtime for the extra work for my campaign."

"OK, saar. I need a job. I haven't received any movie roles except as an extra in a local drama at the Onam festival. I'm really indebted to you for the job, saar."

Vijayan explained to dancer Prabhu that he would officially start the new position after confirming with Proprietor Krishnan, which would take a week. Until then, he had to work for free at the store and perennially campaign for free.

"Your major responsibility is to cut the cost of my campaign and develop creative ways to raise money. We need cash," Vijayan said. "First, let us streamline the party workers' food bill."

Vijayan and dancer Prabhu made two revised lists of volunteers eligible for free food—one for the Brahminal Hotel and the other for the Military Hotel. Exempt from the one-restaurant rule were Vijayan and dancer Prabhu. Chenda was not on either list.

The new assistant manager had to collect two rupees per week from each store owner. He also had to ask for one hundred rupees from Arul.

"Should I tell Chenda not to contact these people?" dancer Prabhu asked.

"I'll talk to him. He needs to focus on Harijan hamlets. He can eat at a chai shop somewhere there. You are in charge of the campaign in Alumaram and Marakana villages. You are the Chief Treasurer, and Chenda will be your assistant."

Dancer Prabhu was so happy that he shook his shoulder and pelvis.

Without realizing the changes, Chenda ate at the Military Hotel after an arduous campaign through rice fields. When it came to paying the bill, owner Kader said he was not on the PPP's free-meal list.

"There should be a mistake," Chenda said.

"No mistake. Comrade Vijayan said the dancer is the new treasurer and gave me the list," Kuttan said, and showed him a sheet of paper with a row of names. Chenda studied the list and shook his head in disbelief.

"Don't worry about this meal. It's on me," Kader said. "You should play the *chenda* in front of my shop often. Alright?"

"Alright." Flustered, Chenda approached Vijayan, who had already rehearsed an explanation.

"I thought it would be convenient for you to eat in a tea shop in the hamlets," Vijayan said. "You may open an account with a chai shop there. You can pay from the collection there and give the rest of the money to dancer Prabhu. This is a temporary arrangement. OK?"

Chenda was reticent. Noticing his silence, Vijayan offered Chenda a glass of rasayanam. He didn't drink it and stared at the "PPP Zindabad" and the blue rocket poster wrapped around the kettledrum.

"Comrade Doctor Vijayan," Chenda said, "there are not many voters in those hamlets."

Ignoring his explanation, Vijayan instructed him to campaign aggressively. "You are a smart man. Go to every hut. You'll find more people."

Without responding to Vijayan, Chenda went straight to the barbershop.

"It looks like he is trying to get rid of me," Chenda told Appu. "I know when people shun me."

Appu heaved a sigh and said, "People are complex. And selfish. Put up with his nonsense until you get your documents. Sit on the chair; you need a haircut."

13

WHILE RETURNING from the hamlets, Chenda saw a group of RSP workers at the village junction. They were erecting a make-shift wooden stage for a political rally at the same venue where Vijayan was transformed from a manager of the medical store to a politician. A team of musicians from Marakana Village played the *chenda*. Fastened atop the banyan tree was Stephen's long green loudspeaker.

The RSP candidate wore a white handloom mundu and a juba, and had a white handloom towel with a red and white border on his shoulder. He took the mic, and in a booming voice, he promised the villagers that he would "fight for better wages for the poor and farmers. We will build schools and provide higher education to the poor in the villages and the rural areas. Mark my words; people don't have to toil in the sun." He repeated the last part of his sentences. Soon, his speech took a different turn. "I challenge my opponents to show one good thing they did for this village." Then he shouted loudly, "I heard some store clerk had formed a new party and promised you all sorts of goodies. Don't fall for it. He is a liar. I know it because I know he is a fake doctor. A con man. A quack."

Chenda looked around and saw Appu and Guru staring at each other, stunned by the name-calling. Chenda inched toward them and asked, "This is outrageous. He stole our election agenda. He is insulting our comrade. Should I yell at the speaker?"

"Ignore it," Appu said. "These are election rhetoric. Don't take them seriously."

"It hurts," Chenda said. "I feel as though these people had broken into our home and ransacked it."

Guru interjected, "This is a major part of the election game. The real fun begins when other parties start their meetings and call each other names." His prediction came true. Two days later, the Congress Party held its public rally, and on the third day, the Community Party took the stage.

The name-calling and character assassinations became a regular feature of the rallies and public addresses. The nastier the name-calling, the greater the applause from the crowd. They called each other "imbeciles," "suck-ups," "morons," "hypocrites," and "corrupt." The gloves were off.

Chenda overheard other party leaders lambasting the People's Power Party he had helped found.

The candidates never addressed their opponents by their names. Instead, they used pronouns. "He gives wrong medicines. You know why? Because he is a quack. He is merely a clerk. He doesn't have any legislative experience," said one opponent in his campaign speech. "Have you ever heard of this PPP before? Eh? This high school party won't last long. This is a one-man party without any base," another candidate said.

Vijayan wasn't ready to let go of these criticisms. In his next day's public speech at the junction, he came back swinging. He blamed his rival parties for the spiraling cost of rice, pepper, sugar, salt, chili, coconut, and other staple items.

"Who ruled this country, this state, our beloved God's Own Country, for so many years?" he asked the crowd. "What did they do? They destroyed the village. They and their friends became rich. Super rich! Look at the high unemployment rate, dowry deaths, and a lack of educational opportunities for the poor. India is suffering because of these parties' red tape, corruption, and nepotism. Mark my words. I'll end them when I become an MLA and go to the Secretariat." Inspired by Vijayan's speech, Appu, Guru, and Chenda clapped.

"Great speech," Chenda complimented Vijayan.

"You heard it, eh?"

"Yes, comrade. I came early from the hamlets to attend your meeting. I was standing there, near the marshland."

"It is OK this time. Don't ignore the hamlets. Go to the hamlets as soon as you finish your morning firewood delivery and chopping. No need to stop by my store in the morning," Vijayan said and walked away from Chenda toward Appu and Guru.

But Chenda followed Vijayan, so he didn't have to raise his voice. "See, our crowd is getting smaller. I think I should be campaigning in villages, not in the hamlets. I heard Cross-toed Ammu, Kamala, and Sivan work for the RSP. I can bring them back to our party."

Vijayan turned back and said, "Eda, don't worry. We will manage here. You focus on the hamlets. Make sure they vote for me." Vijayan didn't wait for Chenda's response, walked further from him, and pretended to be busy talking to Appu and Guru.

Chenda waited near the banyan tree for Vijayan to leave. Then, he asked Appu, "What's going on? Why is comrade avoiding me?"

"I don't know, Chenda. He has been behaving strangely lately," Appu said and rubbed his right hand to ease the pain from carpal tunnel syndrome. "If he wants to run the campaign himself, let him do it. Less headache for you. Concentrate on your music."

"Definitely, some strange thing is going on," Chenda muttered and went to the marshland to assist Mani whose illicit liquor business flourished with the arrival of RSP, PSP, Congress and Communist Party election volunteers. The cooks at Brahminal Hotel and the Military Hotel worked overtime to cater to them. Kuttan and Kader were ebullient as their cash boxes filled with rupees. So were the stores that sold paans, beedis, cigarettes, bananas, and snus.

AN AVALANCHE of opposition parties' banners, posters, and signs shook Vijayan's confidence like a marathon runner pushed back from the lead. He stared at them, lit a beedi, and told dancer Prabhu that he would be gone for a while. He also instructed him not to dispense medicines until he returned and set out on his bicycle to meet Cane-Swami. He knew that Cane-Swami lived near the Amman Devi temple, but didn't know the exact house. He asked one of the boys who was playing soccer near the temple.

"There," the boy said, pointing to a house one street off the temple. "The widow's house." Its porch had iron bars, and the door was locked from the inside.

Vijayan pulled over his bicycle in front of the house, rang the bicycle's bell, and called "Swami. Swami."

A woman peered out the window and asked, "What do you want?"

"Is Cane-Swami in?"

"Wait. Wait," the woman replied and went inside. Her voice was timid, and Vijayan could see part of her head, not the face, through the window's iron bars.

A few minutes later, Cane-Swami came out swinging the cane. *Swish. Swish. Swish.*

"Oh, our comrade. Is everything OK?"

"Not really. Can I come in? I want to discuss something important."

"Not here," Cane-Swami said. "Let us meet at the temple's atrium. No one will bother us there. Wait for me there."

CANE-SWAMI sat leaning against a pillar, his legs stretched out, at the temple atrium. The cane was meticulously kept on his lap. It glimmered with an oily polish. Vijayan stood near Cane-Swami like an obedient disciple.

"Tell me, what bothers you?"

"I think my campaign is faltering. Our jatha is becoming shorter and shorter," Vijayan said. "The number of people at our meetings is becoming fewer and fewer. We can't afford to lose people's support. We should do something to shake up the campaign.

"Hmm," Cane-Swami said. He looked around. The temple was empty except for two women worshippers who entered the sanctum sanctorum for a pooja. They carried a betel leaf, a coconut, two bananas, and a piece of the saffron root as an offering to the goddess.

"Well. This is my strategy," Cane-Swami said. "It is confidential. Top secret. You have to promise something exclusively for Hindus in your campaign. Promise them you'll take care of them. You'll protect them from a Muslim and

Christian takeover of the country. Muslims and Christians won't be happy. You will lose their support, but you will get Hindu votes. That is all we need to win the election. We should somehow bring all Hindus on your side."

"Won't it create communal tension?"

"So what? Let me tell you something. Muslims love Pakistan, not Hindustan. Christians are loyal to the pope. Rome. Not to India. They don't care about us."

"Swami, it is not true. Most Muslims and Christians are loyal to India. I don't want to set one group against the other. Is there any other solution?"

Swish. Swish. Swish.

Swami swished his cane and said, "This is the best solution. If you don't want to do it, it is OK. But some other party will do it and corner the Hindu votes. They will win the election, not you."

"Oh, Swami. It's not right. It is deceitful."

"Politics is deceitful. You want to win the election, don't you? Be shrewd. See what the British did to India for two hundred years: Divide and conquer."

"Hmm," Vijayan heaved as if agreeing with Swami and lit a beedi.

"Then do what I told you. Let us keep this between us."

Vijayan nodded.

"Don't worry," Swami continued. "I'll send a few men. We'll make your rallies longer and stronger than others."

"Thank you, Swami. Namaste, Swami," Vijayan said and walked around the temple's sanctum sanctorum three times in reverence, prayed to the goddess, and went to the medical store. Cane-Swami whipped his cane as if he had won a trophy. *Swish. Swish. Swish.*

ONCE AT the medical store, Vijayan smoked more beedis and pondered over Cane-Swami's advice. By the time he finished a ten-pack beedi, his face had become serene and peaceful as if he had enlightenment induced by the raw tobacco. From the maze of the tobacco smoke, like emerging from the morning mist, he found the perfect solution to bolster his campaign: Divide and conquer.

Soon, the Brahmin enclaves, once the haven of the Congress Party, were peppered with Vote for Vijayan posters and the blue PPP rocket signs. PPP banners and posters popped up near the temple, playgrounds, and on many walls in Brahmin's cluster. New faces appeared at the PPP rallies and meetings.

VIJAYAN FOUND the perfect opportunity to launch his plot to resurrect his floundering campaign when the glass showcase that displayed special delicacies in the Military Hotel was shattered with a loud noise. It was late afternoon.

"Some rowdies smashed my glass case," shouted Kader, owner of the Military Hotel. Carrying a butcher knife from the kitchen, he rushed outside the hotel and yelled, "Who did it? Where are the motherfuckers?"

A server ran to the side street, searching for the perpetrators. Glass shards were scattered on the floor, benches, and long dining tables. A large portion of mutton curry, appam, idiyappam, and vadas had fallen from the glass showcase and splattered on the floor. Petrified, patrons stopped eating and ran out, though no one was injured. The atmosphere was ripe for an explosive reaction triggered by rage, hatred, and an impulse to hit back.

Kader yelled again, "How many men were there? Two? Three? Did anyone see them? Let's teach them a lesson and never let them forget it. Bloody rascals!"

A crowd had formed at the Military Hotel, checking out the shattered showcase, glass shards, and the splattered food on the floor. Some were anxious. And some were curious. "Oh, my God! Do you know who did this?" one man asked Kader.

"I'm going to find and chop their hands off," Kader yelled, and brandished the knife.

Vijayan stopped mixing medicine in a porcelain bowl for a patient and looked at the Military Hotel. He was piqued by the ruckus and people in front of the eatery. Being a self-made leader, Vijayan went to the Military Hotel to check it out. When he learned what had happened, he whispered to Kader that his business had been the target of Hindu extremists.

"Kader, sorry this happened to your hotel. I should have warned you they have been planning to attack you and the other Muslims for a while. It was a matter of time. They are jealous of your success. If you keep quiet, they will attack you again. They will drive you and your people out of this place," he said.

These words made sense to Kader, especially from a Hindu MLA candidate. *"Vijayan must be sincere,"* Kader thought. *"Otherwise, why should he put down his own people?"* Kader shook in astonishment that Hindus would attack him.

"Somebody has to pay for this," Kader said. "We won't let them get away easily."

"I'll talk to you later. Be careful. I'll do whatever I can to help you," Vijayan said, returned to the medical store, and resumed mixing medicines.

FROM THE foot of the banyan tree, Chenda, who had returned from the hamlets early and relaxing, watched the events unfold. Soon after Vijayan left the Military Hotel, Chenda approached Kader and described what had happened: A few boys were playing cricket on M.G. Road, and the batter hit the ball. It was not a heavy cricket ball, but an old tennis ball. It flew straight through the glass showcase. "Believe me, Kader Chettan. I saw the whole thing with my two eyes. It was an accident."

Kader stared at Chenda suspiciously and yelled, "Really? I don't see any boys there. Do you?"

"They ran away with their stumps and bats. I think they got scared."

"Oh really?" Kader yelled again. "If so, where's the tennis ball? Did you see it in the hotel?"

"It must have bounced off."

"You stay out of this," Kader reprimanded. "Those bloody Hindus have been trying to drive us out of India. They killed my grandfather and uncle during the Partition. Did you know that? Bloody rascals!"

Chenda pleaded again, "Kader Chettan, it was an errant tennis ball. I'm not making this up. I swear. If you don't believe me, ask those boys. I know where they live."

"Why don't you shut your dirty mouth and go to the banyan tree and play the *chenda*?" Kader asserted. "Don't blame those innocent boys. They play there," he said, pointing to the middle of M.G. Road about two hundred feet from the eatery. "No one can hit the ball this far—all the way from there to here. I know who is behind this. Even Comrade Vijayan knows it. Jealous, stupid Hindus."

Soon, Kader's friends and a few members of the Juma Masjid came to his aid. They carefully removed the glass shards and wiped the spattered food on the floor. Two men covered the big hole in the glass showcase with newspapers.

"Next, they will attack our homes," a waiter said. "We should stick together and protect our families and homes."

Chenda rushed to the medical store and repeated what he saw to Vijayan.

"Why do you want to poke your nose in everyone's business," Vijayan said and smirked. "You are good at making this up."

"No, Comrade Doctor Vijayan! I'm not making this up."

"Here comes the peacemaker," Vijayan mocked. "Let Kader handle it. It was his business that was attacked. You stay out of this. Go, continue campaigning at the hamlets."

Having been shut out by Vijayan and not knowing what to do, Chenda went to Appu's barber shop, hoping he would persuade Kader to calm down. In between cutting an elderly man's gray hair, Appu listened to Chenda as if listening to desultory conversations with his customers, who long for a patient listener.

Chenda recreated the scene he witnessed to Appu in one breath and declared, "Kader is angry."

"Oh! That was all the ruckus about. I didn't get a chance to look out," Appu said.

Chenda raised his voice, "Kader is holding a knife. He could hurt someone. I'm scared."

The later part of Chenda's pleading grabbed Appu's attention as if someone knocked on his head. "I'll talk to Kader after finishing this haircut," Appu said. "Wait for me."

One of Kader's servers was still cleaning the glass shards and the food on the floor with a broom.

"What happened?" Appu asked Kader.

"Some bloody motherfuckers broke my glass showcase," Kader said, spewing the words of venom. "They are trying to destroy my livelihood."

"I don't think so, Kader. Who would do that?" Appu said.

"I'll find out who did this. I was minding my own business. I didn't harm anyone. Didn't bother anyone. Why me?"

"Please calm down, Kader. No one is going to harm you. Chenda says he saw the boys playing cricket with a tennis ball, and it flew into your glass showcase. Please believe him."

"Nonsense! What does he know? He is a parayan," Kader shot back. "Look. Look at the damage. Could a tennis ball break such a solid showcase? Where's the tennis ball? Where is it? No one can find it."

Meanwhile, Kuttan came to enquire. He observed the damage to Kader's restaurant, took a few steps toward him, and commented, "Who will do this to you?"

Kader was curt, "You tell me."

"I don't have any clue," Kuttan said. "If you need any help, please let me know. I can supply you dosa and appam batter. Chutney and sambar for your customers. For free."

"Don't worry, Kuttan. I can manage. Luckily, my kitchen is not damaged. Thanks, anyway," Kader said.

"I wanted to stop by when I heard something happened to your hotel. Alright then," Kuttan said and returned to his eatery.

Chenda and Appu lingered around to comfort Kader.

"It was an accident," Appu reiterated. "We should tell those boys to play cricket somewhere else."

"It's not a ball, Appu," Kader said. "I know who is behind this. I'll hunt down those hooligans and teach them a lesson."

"Kader, you are talking about a broken glass case. You can repair it. Or buy a new one," Appu said. "Let us not make things worse."

"It is easy for you to give advice, Appu. I feel humiliated. Rejected. We Muslims are treated like foreigners. Second-class citizens. Why should we be the ones to be tolerant? Thanks for coming," Kader said and walked briskly inside the kitchen.

In silence, Chenda and Appu left the Military Hotel.

CHENDA GOT up during the morning twilight and decided to visit Kader, hoping he might have slept off the anger. *With a clear head, he would believe that tennis-ball incident,* Chenda thought. The street was deserted except for two stray cows rummaging through a pile of garbage for breakfast. The sun was hesitantly waking up, touching the horizon, crows were cawing, and the bats were returning to roost at the banyan tree after foraging for dinner.

On his way to the Military Hotel to meet Kader, Chenda took a detour via the Brahminal Hotel. He was puzzled to see a small gathering of Kuttan's cooks and servers who were flustered. Kuttan was animatedly talking to his customers: the farmers. They came for their morning chai and dosa on credit and paid the bill on the way back home in the evening after earning their wages.

Chenda looked at the eatery and screamed in shock, "Oh, my God! What happened, Kuttan Chettan?"

Kuttan, his face sallow and his hair disheveled, didn't respond. Instead, the servant said, "The Muslims, the motherfucker Kader's men, destroyed our hotel. We saw this when we came to open the hotel this morning."

Chenda peered inside and flinched.

The Brahminal Hotel was smashed to smithereens. Its interior was reduced to shambles. The stoves were broken into several chunks with a pick ax. The brass chai kettle had been hammered into a mass of twisted metal. The tables were turned upside down. Chairs were flung out of the restaurant, breaking their legs. Several mud pots used for preparing curries, chutney, and dosa batter were pummeled into bits and pieces. The showcase was shattered and glass pieces were strewn all over the floor.

The Brahminal Hotel looked as if it had been hit by a hurricane.

"Ayyo, this is terrible!" Chenda screamed again. He could hear his heart pound like a loud wrong beat on the kettledrum.

Kuttan, the cook, and his assistant tip-toed into the eatery to assess the damage for the third time. They navigated carefully not to step on glass pieces. Chenda followed Kuttan closely, partly to catch him if he passed out. Chenda pulled up a chair and straightened it. But the chair wobbled and fell. Seeing it, Kuttan, who was stoic until then, let out a loud cry as if someone had died. "Who did this to me? My livelihood has been destroyed. What did I do wrong?" Kuttan lamented and wiped his tears with bare hands.

Meanwhile, the server ran to Kuttan's house and alerted his wife. She, along with her son, hurried to the hotel.

"What happened?" she asked after seeing her husband's taut face, looked inside the eatery, and cried. He haplessly stretched his hands toward the kitchen and said, "I never thought such a thing would happen to us. I never thought people would harm us. We've been kind to everyone. Very kind. Oh, Amman Devi," Kuttan lamented. His body shook as he pressed his hands on his head. Tears flowed down both their faces.

She caressed his shoulders, gently wiped his tears with the tip of her sari, and wiped her tears, too. "I'm glad you are safe. God will punish those people. We never harmed anyone," she said and looked inside the hotel again. "Did you call the police?"

"Will do later," Kuttan replied. "By God's grace, we all are safe."

Their teenage son surveyed the destruction and cried, "We should kill whoever did this. Every one of them."

"Don't say such bad things. Never," Kuttan admonished his son and told him and his wife to go home.

THE WORD of the attack on Brahminal Hotel spread quickly in the village early morning, spread by milkmen who dragged their cows from house to house and milked them in front of their customers.

Before opening his barber shop, Appu went straight to the Brahminal Hotel. Guru also came briskly, the black umbrella tucked in his armpit. They looked at the damage and sympathized with Kuttan.

"This is shocking," Appu said. "Unthinkable!"

Guru said he would ask Kader whether his men attacked the Brahminal Hotel. If so, he would try to de-escalate the tension.

"Such violence has never happened in my life in the village. Never," Guru said. "We should have a meeting with Kader and Kuttan. What do you think, Appu?"

Appu nodded his head.

"Good idea," Chenda interjected.

They were distracted by the sound of the swishing. *Swish. Swish. Swish.* They turned around and looked at each other with raised eyebrows when Cane-Swami showed up like the fabled wolf lured by the smell of blood from head-butting goats. *Swish. Swish. Swish.* He was accompanied by a dozen men who carried long bamboo sticks, knives, and bicycle chains.

"This is not good," Appu whispered to Guru and Chenda. "He is going to make things worse."

"Shh," Chenda whispered back. "He is bad news. God, help us."

Cane-Swami spoke with Kuttan and whipped his cane. *Swish. Swish. Swish.*

He didn't look at Appu, Guru, Chenda, or anyone else.

"We cannot keep quiet," Cane-Swami told Kuttan. "Hinduism is a tolerant religion. These Muslims are taking advantage of us. We should get rid of them. They deliberately destroyed your business. Look! Look at the Military Hotel. They are still there, with sickles and bamboo sticks. Ready to attack you, I mean us. Again."

Appu took a peek at the Military Hotel from M.G. Road. Cane-Swami was right. Kader and his workers had assembled a few men in case Kuttan and his supporters attacked Kader's eatery. A pall of hatred began to hover over Alumaram Village.

THE SUN hesitantly rose as if dreading to see how the day would turn out. The brown dusty Murphy Radio at the Brahminal Hotel didn't broadcast the All India Radio news.

The farmers who drank their morning chai and ate idlis and appams on credit made small talk and went on empty stomachs to till the farms.

Cross-toed Ammu and Kamala returned to their huts as soon as they saw men with bamboo sticks, knives, and bicycle chains in front of both eateries. Fish and fruit vendors followed suit. Hassan didn't sell mutton and beef and hid the make-shift butcher's table behind his house. Then, hastily he dragged his flower cart and hid next to the butcher's table. Young men who usually hung around the junction stayed in their homes. So did young women. The boys didn't come to the junction to show off their bicycle riding skills. No cricket game, either. And Chenda's kettledrum was silent. Again!

The Kerala State Road Transportation Corporation's green bus arrived on time to pick up morning commuters to the city. Sensing an uneasy calm in the air, the driver asked Chenda what had happened. Chenda, sleepless and tensed, said a simple misunderstanding had created racial tension. The Brahminal Hotel was destroyed by vandals.

"Must be the bloody Muslims," the driver said and moved the bus from the designated stop near the banyan tree to a safer place, about two hundred feet south on M.G. Road. The bus drove off as soon as the passengers, mostly government and bank clerks and peons, regular faces to the driver and the conductor, boarded.

A wave of panic swept across the area when one of Cane-Swami's disciples hit the floor with a bamboo stick and screamed, "Watch out, you...fucking Muslims! We are coming after you."

The challenge was met with an equally loud response from the waiter at the Military Hotel at an earshot. "We are not scared of you. You feckless cowards."

The profanity-filled verbal spats of each group flew back and forth diagonally across the street. They became frequent. So was the sound of the bamboo sticks slamming on the floor or a wall. Frightened, the bats that hung like square rocks on the banyan tree flew helter-skelter and let out battle cries.

The two factions waited impatiently: The Hindu faction at the Brahminal Hotel was led by Cane-Swami, and the Muslim faction at the Military Hotel was led by Kader. Like soldiers ready with bayonets aimed at the enemy, they impatiently waited for a command to charge. They had folded up their lungi and mundu from the knee up and tucked around their waist, exposing their hairy, thin legs. This made it convenient for them to kick and run toward or away from each other.

The air was pregnant with apprehension and anger when something fell on the Brahminal Hotel's roof. It was bat droppings from the banyan tree. But that noise was enough for Cane-Swami to yell, "Stones. They are throwing stones at us." It was the clarion call needed for his men. Armed with bamboo sticks and knives, they charged toward the Military Hotel. In a counter-offensive, the Muslims ran toward the Brahminal Hotel wielding their weapons. What ensued were blood-curling screams and the whacks of bamboo sticks striking human flesh. The sound of the bamboo sticks hitting the head is uniquely different from hitting the chest or the back. The former cracks, and the latter thwacks. A hail of stones pelted by Hindus and Muslims rained on many roofs, irrespective of the residents' religion. Stones cracked tiled roofs and tore holes in thatched roofs.

The sound of stones landing on roofs and M.G. Road resembled the bellicose fireworks finale. Women locked their doors and closed windows, and their children clung to their mothers and sobbed. Trembling with fear, some women slipped through their back doors to their neighbor's home for safety and moral support.

Gopi, Stephen, and Prabhu quickly closed their stores and ran away. Appu was slowed down by the dragging of his swollen right leg. He sat inside the half-shuttered shop, shaking and whimpering. Two Muslim men noticed him hiding behind the barber's high chairs. They crept under the half-closed door and dragged Appu out of the store. He fell flat on M.G. Road with a thud. One man aimed a long bamboo stick at him and Appu held his hands above his head as a shield.

Hassan, who took cover under the bushes, came out running. He brandished his butcher's knife and yelled, "Leave him alone." He whipped the sharp knife and was poised to slit the man's throat. "He is with me. Leave him alone. We don't want any trouble here." The man recognized Hassan, having seen him in the mosque, and brought the bamboo stick down. The butcher knife had something to do with his change of mind. The man stared at Appu, poked his right leg with the bamboo stick, backed off, and looked for another target. Appu let out a cry, hurt by the poking on his swelled leg and the inability to run quickly as others did.

There was no let-up in the bedlam unleashed by both groups. Before someone could stab, the purported victims would back off and return, hitting the road with long bamboo sticks. When one group got the upper hand, the other would retreat. After a few minutes, they would return menacingly, and the other group would pull back. It was a see-saw game of attacks, retreats, and counter-attacks. The groups, fueled by the frustration of their inability to inflict fatal wounds on each other, turned their wrath in another direction. The mom-and-pop stores became their target. Muslims vandalized Hindu shops, and Hindus retaliated. They hit the stores' wooden and metal doors with bamboo sticks, creating shattering noise.

Terrified, Chenda took cover behind the banyan tree, which was a grave mistake. The tree couldn't hide him and the kettledrum. A server from the Military Hotel, accompanied by a stranger, charged at him. The server had a sharp kitchen knife, and the other man, a stranger, carried a long bamboo stick.

"Are you Muslim or a Hindu?" the man with the bamboo stick asked. Chenda didn't reply. Too numb to utter any word. The server told his companion, "He is a parayan. You'd get leprosy if you touched him. Let him go."

"What is this stupid untouchable doing here?" the man asked and kicked the kettledrum. In the impact, it slipped from Chenda's shoulder and fell on the ground. The man forcefully kicked it as if it was a football. The kettledrum was airborne, twisted and landed with a thud, bounced, and rolled over the dirt.

Chenda ran after the kettledrum and grabbed it with one hand. He managed to save the percussion instrument from landing on a garbage-filled ditch. He missed a heartbeat when he realized the tension cord had snapped. It was not the only damage inflicted upon the kettledrum. There were cuts and scrapes all over its brown shell. Chenda hugged it and patted as if comforting a battered soul mate.

"Tell your Hindu friends not to mess with us," the man said. "This is a friendly warning for them. Next time, it'll be worse." The server and his accomplice left on a different route, avoiding the gang of Hindu extremists.

The Muslim mob then moved to the western section of M.G. Road and was cornered by the Hindu gang. The outcome was inevitable. The air reverberated with rapid full-throated yelling, screaming, and shouting. The spine-chilling battle cry could be heard as far away as the next village.

With loud blows, bamboo sticks landed on people's backs, shoulders, and heads. Whack! Whack! Whack! Equally loud were cracks of punching each other in the jaw, stomach, and wherever they could reach. Those carrying sickles and knives stabbed their opponents as if piercing watermelons. Blood gushed from people's heads, torsos, shoulders, arms, and faces.

Kader watched the scene from his eatery. Realizing that Muslims were outnumbered by Hindus, he ran through the back alley to call for reinforcement. And he stepped on a rubbery object and almost tripped. Exasperated, he kicked it. The dirt-covered tennis ball bounced a couple of times, rolled on, and landed in a sewage ditch. He saw the ball and flinched but didn't stop because of the advancing footsteps of the Hindu mob.

It didn't take long for Cane-Swami and his men to pummel Kader's kitchen and utensils beyond recognition and take off before Kader's men arrived. Puffing and panting, Cane-Swami and his men returned to Brahminal Hotel.

"I think we've taught them a lesson," he told Kuttan and mouthed one of his followers to yell, "police...police." This warning was an excuse to throw in the towel after scoring points.

The threat of police coming held back the Muslim gang. While retreating, both groups taunted each other. "We'll be back. We'll teach you motherfuckers a lesson," someone from one group yelled.

Promptly, the other group responded, "You bastards. You'll pay for this."

"We'll never forget what your fathers' fathers did to us."

"You'll regret messing with us."

The wounded were helped by their friends. They covered the gashes with wet towels to stop bleeding and carried them to their homes. Men who suffered deep lacerations were taken on bicycles to private clinics in other villages.

14

POLICE DID arrive perfunctorily as if going to work on Monday morning. It took almost an hour for a dozen constables in two Jeeps led by two Sub-Inspectors, to come to the village. Chenda, who was repairing the kettledrum's tension cord, saw the constables jump out of the Jeeps and spread out. One Sub-Inspector and three constables went to the Military Hotel to inquire. The other Sub-Inspector and three constables went to Brahminal Hotel. The rest of the constables patrolled M.G.Road littered with rocks, glass shards, debris, and blood.

"What happened? Is there any eye witness?" the Sub-Inspector asked Kuttan, who was standing in front of his eatery.

Kuttan, the cook, and a server stood around the Sub-Inspector in reverence and showed the damage caused by Muslim thugs at night. A constable took statements from Kuttan and his servants, their addresses, age, and date of birth.

"Any eye witness?" the Sub-Inspector asked.

"No, saar. No one actually saw the perpetrators. This happened at night. We were sleeping."

"So, there's no proof that Muslims attacked you."

Kuttan didn't reply.

Chenda stopped fixing the kettledrum, went to the Sub-Inspector, and told him, "It all started with a tennis ball. It flew through the Military Hotel's glass showcase yesterday. I'm telling the truth, Sub-Inspector saar. A tennis ball from the cricket game hit the glass showcase. I swear! Hindus didn't attack the Military Hotel first," Chenda said.

"Who are you?" the Sub-Inspector asked.

"Chenda."

The Sub-Inspector smirked and asked Kuttan, "Who is this boy? What's he doing here?"

"He is a handcart puller," Kuttan said. "He delivers firewood and plays good *chenda* music."

The Sub-Inspector didn't buy that explanation. He stared at Chenda and said, "Eda, go home and stay out of trouble. The IG will arrest you if he sees you. Run before he comes."

Chenda returned to the banyan tree and got busy repairing the kettledrum.

Shortly after that, the Inspector General of Police, IG for short, came in an olive-green car with a state flag on its hood. Both Sub-Inspectors reported their findings to the IG. Not included in them was Chenda's version.

The IG, accompanied by Sub-Inspectors, spoke with Kader and Kuttan separately to investigate the cause of the riots and who started them. Each pointed out the finger at the other.

"The Hindus attacked us first," Kader claimed. "They completely broke my glass showcase yesterday. This morning, they were after us again. They assaulted us with lathis, cycle chains, and whatnot. We had to defend ourselves."

Kuttan gave his side of the story. "Those Muslims destroyed my hotel in the middle of the night. This morning they threw stones at the crowd in front of my hotel. So we went after the Muslims to stop them. They had bamboo lathis and knives."

The constable religiously wrote down their statements, despite their inconsistencies.

"Did you see who started first?"

"No one in particular."

"We cannot make arrests unless there's a witness," the IG said. He ordered a half dozen constables to patrol the village. One constable was stationed at each eatery until the situation returned to normalcy. A Jeep with constables drove around the village to make their presence known.

Soon a horde of reporters and photographers arrived in taxis with white license plates and black letters. They were tipped off by the Public Relations officer in IG's Office. The reporters spoke with the IG. Photographers snapped pictures of the IG flanked by two Sub-Inspectors walking on M.G.Road. Then, reporters proceeded to interview Kader and Kuttan.

"We were minding our own businesses, and unexpectedly, the Hindus provoked us. They're trying to sabotage my business," Kader said. "They broke our glass showcase first and came after us with knives, bamboo sticks, sickles, etc."

One of the reporters asked, "Have such religious attacks happened before?"

"Never. But we don't know what's going on in people's minds," Kader said. A photographer asked him to stand next to the broken glass showcase. He declined to be photographed and asked his cook to stand beside it. The cook posed in front of the glass showcase, holding a broken ladle. He smiled. But the photographer told him to look sad or angry.

The reporters and the photographers moved on to interview Kuttan.

"I started this hotel as a street chai shop many, many years ago," Kuttan said. "Look at this now. Muslim goondas ruined my livelihood. It's all gone."

The reporters jotted down Kuttan's words, and the photographers wanted to shoot his photo near the damaged kitchen. Kuttan, too, refused to be photographed and asked a server to stand in for him. The server, looking grim, stood near the damaged kitchen, pointing his hand at the broken big brass chai kettle. The lensmen were pleased.

Chenda followed the horde of reporters at both eateries, tapped a reporter, and said, "I know what happened."

"Tell us about it," asked a reporter, who wore thick eyeglasses and a well-trimmed beard. Not wanting to be scooped, other reporters edged toward him to catch every word that would fall from his mouth. And Chenda recreated the tennis ball story. They looked at him quizzically, questioning the veracity of his version, "Do you want us to believe the religious riot broke out because of an errant tennis ball?"

"Yes."

"People are not stupid," the bearded reporter said, eyed the photographer, indicating that Chenda was crazy, and walked away as if let down by an anticlimax in an action movie.

TIMING IS everything. Vijayan arrived on his bicycle and was pleased to see the journalists. He introduced himself as the candidate of the People's Power Party. Taking the opportunity for the press coverage, he excoriated other parties for instigating the communal riots. The reporters, eager to add a political dimension, avidly jotted down every word uttered by Vijayan.

"Remember, I'm the only candidate to show up here. Where are the other political leaders? Did you see any?" Vijayan asked the journalists. "I'm really concerned about the well-being and safety of our people." In the interview, he exhorted the villagers to be patient and strive for peace and harmony. "This is God's Own Country," he said. "We should respect each other's faith. It's a shame that career politicians with ulterior motives fuel religious fanaticism."

"I'm also the manager, hmm…the General Manager, of this store," Vijayan told the reporters. "Do you need more quotes? "

He excitedly posed for photos in front of the medical store. Then, he introduced himself to the IG and the Sub-Inspectors and posed for photos with them.

Chenda, who stood in his usual spot under the banyan tree, watched Vijayan's politicking and shook his head in disgust.

With enough quotes and images of broken kitchens to fill the front pages, the reporters and photographers took off as quickly as they had landed in Alumaram Village.

The IG and the Sub-Inspectors followed suit. A few constables with khaki match stick turbans stayed behind, shooing away curious onlookers.

Late afternoon, Appu's barber shop buzzed with the snipping of scissors. Stephen's green loudspeaker belted out Malayalam movie songs. The medical store dispensed rasayanam. And farmers gulped down Mani's arrack near the marshland and ate spicy mango pickles from the jar with their hands.

"Thank you, Hassan. Thank you for saving my life," Appu said, holding Hassan's hand and narrating the harrowing scene to Guru.

"It's no big deal," Hassan said coyly, showing his awkwardness in accepting compliments. "I know you will do the same for me."

Appu nodded and smiled.

Guru chimed in, "Great job, Hassan. This is what we need. A good example of Muslim-Hindu friendship. Unity. It should be on the front pages."

15

IT WAS A restless night for Chenda. *I wish I had a glass of arrack to put me to sleep*, he thought. He sat with his head leaned on the kettledrum, his legs stretched, on Patti-Amma's back porch, and looked at the sky for divine intervention to bring peace to the village. Any message: a tablet with tips from Heaven, enlightenment, or at least a heavy monsoon downpour to cool the Hindu-Muslim tempers. The sky didn't open with directives. The Gods on the medical store's wall looked the other way. The soothing morning wake-up calls of chirping mynahs, the crowing roosters, and the cawing crows sounded like ominous bugle calls.

He got up, drew water from the well, brushed his teeth with black tooth powder made out of burned rice husks, splashed water on his sleepless face, applied Cuticura Talcum powder under both armpits and behind his neck for relief from humidity, and on his face to make it a little lighter. The result was a powdery face like a dusting of ground wheat on coal. The powder would fade away when Chenda wiped the sweat on his face with the towel. With the kettledrum on his shoulder, he set off to the lumber yard to deliver firewood to homes.

THE MORNING newspapers ran front-page news stories with a photo of Vijayan with the IG, the damaged kitchen, and the shattered showcases. In bold letters, the reports highlighted Vijayan's call for communal harmony. He became an instant celebrity and a peacemaker.

"You are in the newspaper, Comrade Doctor Vijayan," Guru said excitedly. "You are a famous man. I told you...I told you...whatever your touch will turn into gold. Your time is very auspicious."

Appu applauded Vijayan's efforts to bring peace to the village. "You're going to win this election, comrade," he said. "The newspapers have made you popular."

After delivering and chopping firewood, Chenda stopped by the medical store and noticed the clippings of the front-page stories displayed prominently under the pictures of God Ganeshan, Jesus, and Kaba on the wall.

"Good article," Chenda said. "This is good for our campaign. I hope Cross-toed Ammu and Kamala would leave the RSP and will come back to us."

"I hope so," Vijayan said and forced a smile as if he was not thrilled to see Chenda at the store. He looked on both sides of the street lest the anonymous letter writer notices them together. Hastily, he said, "We have to do a lot of work. Get going. I'm counting on you for the votes from those hamlets."

Vijayan was curt. Less conversational. And he stopped offering him rasayanam. The change in his demeanor was conspicuous.

"I've got to meet a few important people. I'll talk to you later," Vijayan said. Without waiting for Chenda's response, he lit a beedi and went to Brahminal Hotel.

THE CONSTABLE guarding Brahminal Hotel recognized Vijayan from the newspaper articles and saluted him. Kuttan, seeing Vijayan, came from the kitchen and said, "Namaste, Mr. Vijayan."

Until then, Vijayan didn't know the impact of positive news coverage. The proof: "Vijayan" had become "Mr. Vijayan" for the owner of Brahminal Hotel.

Vijayan smiled and said, "Thank God you're not hurt. We can always rebuild the hotel, Kuttan, but not lives."

"Thank you, Mr. Vijayan. Thank you for trying to bring back peace to this community. We need leaders like you," Kuttan said. "I'm shocked by Kader's behavior and fury. We've known each other for so many years. We used to borrow rice, dal, etcetera from each other. During last year's Eid, I made fifty appams for him because he ran out of batter. But I never thought Kader would do this to me."

"You know, the riots were incited by Kader and his men. Somehow, we've got to stop them. These Muslims have no loyalty to India. They are back-stabbers. We, Hindus, have to stick together. You see, the goondas were brought in from outside. I know this for a fact. They want to attack the peace-loving, tolerant Hindus. They want to drive us out of our homes and take over this village. Our village! I won't put up with this. Congress Party, PSP, Communist Party, and the RSP won't help us. They are afraid to take on Muslims. Believe me, they won't come to our rescue. The People's Power Party will. I will. Do you know why? It was founded here, in this village."

"What should I do, Mr. Vijayan?"

"Tell your workers, relatives, customers, and friends to support the PPP. Our party! We need more muscle power. That's the only way to save our village from those Muslims."

Kuttan nodded in reluctant agreement and apologized for not being able to offer him chai or coffee. "My hotel is in shambles. I won't be able to open it for a few days. My workers' livelihood depends on this business. The farmers eat here on credit. They will starve. They don't have any other place to go for food."

He patted Kuttan on his shoulder and said, "I'll get you a good compensation for your loss as soon as I become an MLA." He reminded Kuttan that his election victory was vital for Kuttan to receive the government's financial aid.

After pacifying Kuttan, he returned to the medical store, smoked a beedi, and went to the Military Hotel to express his sympathy and support for Kader. Rage and disillusionment were written all over Kader's face. He acknowledged Vijayan's arrival by saying, "I saw your picture in the newspaper."

Vijayan coyly said, "The reporters recognized who I am and wanted a few quotes from me. The Press! You know how they are! I'm so sorry that your hotel has been damaged. Thanks to Allah that you and your family are safe."

Kader didn't find his words comforting, and he went on a tirade. "It's your people…your people who did this to me. First, they broke my glass showcase and then destroyed my kitchen. I worked hard, day and night, to build this business. I wanted to hand it over to my children for their future. Look at it now. They destroyed everything. That motherfucker Kuttan brought people from other villages to kill my people and me. They plan to drive us out. We're not going anywhere. We didn't go to Pakistan during the Partition. You know why?

Because India is our home. This is where I was born. My father and grandfather were born here. We are here to stay. For good," he said and pointed his finger at the floor for emphasis. "My workers and I depend on this business. There's no reason to attack us. Who started this? Tell me... tell me, Comrade Vijayan. Who broke my glass showcase first?"

Patiently, Vijayan listened to Kader's outbursts and interjected, "I understand what you're going through. Hindus, by and large, are peaceful and tolerant people. I know it. I'm one of them. But this is the work of the extremists," Vijayan said, looking at Kader's damaged eatery. "I know this riot is engineered by our opposition. They are plotting to ruin my election. Believe me when I say this is their handiwork. We never had such problems before. Has such a thing ever happened before? Now on, there will be more police protection for you Muslims."

Kader didn't reply, but his eyes displayed rage.

"I know you suffered a lot of loss," Vijayan said, showing sympathy. "The first thing I would do as an MLA is to help you; compensate for the damages. It's a promise to you and other Muslims. You, minorities need someone like me in the legislative assembly to protect your family and business. This is our country: yours and mine."

Be cautious. He is a Hindu, Kader's brain warned while his heart argued, *Trust him; he is a member of the village, and he means good.* There was no winner in the tug-of-war between the brain and the soul. So, the brain and the soul came to a compromise. And Kader's face softened.

"Don't worry, Comrade Vijayan," Kader said. "I'll ask the Muslim League to field a candidate from this constituency. The Muslim League will protect us."

Vijayan was caught off-guard by Kader's alternative and blurted out, "You don't need a Muslim League candidate. You don't need another party to come in. That will create more friction and confusion. I'll take care of you and your people." After a pause, Vijayan continued, "Do what you think is best for your community. I'm always available to help you. Come to the store if you need anything."

Dancer Prabhu was creating PPP posters when Vijayan returned from the Military Hotel.

Smiling, he told dancer Prabhu, "We have good news. The Muslim League is fielding a candidate."

Dancer Prabhu raised his head as if asking for clarification. Vijayan explained, "This will immensely benefit our campaign. Look! The League will siphon Muslim votes away from others. Somehow, if we corner Hindu votes, we could win the election."

OVER THE next few days, the number of constables who patrolled the village became fewer and fewer as the village limped back to normalcy. The aadhan chants from Juma Masjid and pooja bells from the Amman Devi temple filled the morning air. In the evening, the boys played cricket with a new tennis ball on M.G. Road. Women gossiped from their verandahs, and men smoked beedis and spat paan juice on the street.

The Brahminal's Hotel and the Military Hotel resumed serving dosas, idlis, and appams. The curry aroma permeated the junction. The Murphy Radio at the Brahminal Hotel boomed Malayalam music and news from All India Radio.

Chenda's kettledrum hummed again at the foot of the banyan tree.

16

TWO DAYS before the election, Chenda was on his way to deliver and chop firewood when Vijayan called him from the medical store. "Eda, Chenda! Come for a minute."

Chenda dragged the handcart, loaded with a half-ton of firewood, a sharp-edged ax, and the kettledrum meticulously fastened with a coir rope, to the store.

"What's up, comrade?"

"Don't forget that the election is the day after tomorrow," Vijayan said. A strong smell of rasayanam mixed and the odor of beedi oozed from Vijayan's mouth. Overpowered by the scent, Chenda coughed.

"I know Comrade Doctor Vijayan," Chenda said. "How can I forget it?"

"Good! Do you think we will win?"

"Of course, we're going to win. This election is ours, and our PPP signs are all over the hamlets. There are not many Congress, PSP, RSP, and Communist Party posters. The same scenario at the Amman Devi temple and its neighborhood. We are everywhere."

"Yes. Cane-Swami and his men are doing a great job. They are working hard," Vijayan said and looked at Chenda pensively. "I really hope that we win. If not, I'm in big trouble. I borrowed two thousand rupees from Proprietor Krishnan and a thousand from Arul. A lot of things are at stake, you know."

Vijayan, then, offered a glass of rasayanam.

Chenda was surprised by Vijayan's friendly overture, like a divorcee trying to woo his ex-wife to get his dowry back.

"No thanks, comrade," Chenda said. "Too early for me. I have to deliver and chop this firewood. Then, I have to campaign at the hamlets. I don't want to go to these places smelling of alcohol."

Vijayan took a deep puff from the beedi and let the nicotine swirl inside his lungs before exhaling it. He took a sip from a glass and asked Chenda, "Are you nervous? Are you worried?"

"No. I'm not," Chenda said. "You, too, shouldn't be worried. Remember what Guru told you. This is a very auspicious time for you."

"Eda, Chenda, we have to do something big, something special, to get people on our side on the election day. Any suggestion?"

Chenda urged Vijayan to hire Sivan's bullock cart and Basheer's rickshaw to transport voters from their homes to the polling booth and back. "Once they are in the bullock cart or the rickshaw, they will vote for us." He also had another game plan: Lure Cross-toed Ammu and her niece from the RSP back to PPP. They should be asked to serve free lemonade to voters before entering the polling booth. "Their presence will motivate women to vote for us," Chenda continued. "The lemonade is not a bribe. It's a free drink to quell thirst in this humid weather. When they serve lemonade, they should tell people to vote for us. We should keep a large Vote for Vijayan sign near the lemonade jar."

"Excellent!" Vijayan said. "You know, I haven't forgotten about your American trip. Your Indian passport and American Visa. I promise, I'll send you to America."

"Thanks, comrade. Here's the thing: A tennis ball broke Kader's glass display case. It was an accident. Why didn't you believe me?"

"Let us not worry about it. It's time to move on," Vijayan said, shrugging his shoulders. He didn't make eye contact with Chenda. "The village is peaceful. That's what matters now. Go and finish delivering firewood and your visit to the hamlets. OK?"

ELECTION DAY. Chenda had never seen Alumaram Village so busy—busier than the Thiruvathira Onam celebrations when the residents donned new clothes and exchanged goodies. Music blared from the green loudspeaker, and villagers gathered to see the play of Mahabali, the King of Kings, at the junction on the last day of the Onam festival.

At the break of dawn on Election Day, Chenda loudly tapped the kettledrum at hamlets to remind them to vote for the PPP. He had brought Sivan and his bullock cart so old people didn't have to walk all the way to and from the polling stations at the Alumaram Elementary School. The bullock cart was stationed on the slope near the rice fields. The hamlet residents had to walk through mud paths from their huts to the cart. While helping people get inside the bullock cart, Chenda would ask, "You will vote for Comrade Doctor Vijayan, right?"

"Yes."

"Don't let me down."

"I won't."

As soon as Sivan returned with his cart packed with people from the polling station, Chenda would be ready with another batch of voters. By afternoon, most of the hamlets' residents had voted. So, Chenda went to the polling station to campaign for Vijayan. Chenda recognized the PPP was being outdone by its rivals. They had brought horse-drawn jatkas. The villagers were fascinated by these jatkas, especially their aluminum roofs, windows, and wooden steps. The horses wore leather bridles decorated with long feathers. Those who had never traveled or couldn't afford to hire a horse-drawn jatka took advantage of the free rides.

Having helped the hamlets' residents vote, it was Chenda's turn. Excited to vote for the PPP, Chenda dusted off his mundu, removed the towel wrapped around his head, put it on his shoulder, and entered the polling station. Inside were one Presiding Polling Officer and two Polling Officers. All of them were outsiders. On their desks were thick, long books with people's names and addresses and stacks of long ballots with the candidates' names and their parties' symbols. There were political party agents to ensure no voter fraud was committed by their opponents. But they milled around betting on who would win the election.

Chenda went to the Polling Officer sitting near the entrance and told him he wanted to vote for Comrade Vijayan.

"What's your name?" the Polling Officer, tired and aggravated, asked.

"Chenda."

"Your full name?"

"That's my full name. That's what people call me."

The man laughed and asked for his address.

"I don't know. I live in Patti-Amma's house in Brahmin's cluster. Everyone in the village knows me."

"It doesn't mean anything to us," the Polling Officer said. "You cannot vote unless you tell me your address or show the voting slip delivered to your house. We need verification."

Chenda looked at other Polling Officers to see whether they could help him. "My name should be somewhere in the book."

"That's not a real name," the Polling Officer said, directing him to the Presiding Officer. Chenda had the same discussion with the Presiding Officer, who laughed. The party agents who listened to the conversation also mocked him. "Police will arrest you for trying to cast an illegal ballot. Run before they come. You are committing fraud," the Presiding Polling Officer said.

Chenda stood outside watching others come and go after casting their ballots.

SWISH. SWISH. SWISH.

Chenda turned around and saw Cane-Swami arriving with a horde of supporters. Among them were young men who looked like high school students and had yet to grow facial hair.

"This is what you should do," Cane-Swami told one young man. "Walk confidently to the polling booth and go to the agent wearing a blue shirt. He is our man. Don't talk to others and have no eye contact with anyone else. Give this voting slip to our agent and tell him that I sent you, and your name is Kumaran. The card has the same name. He will take you to the Polling Officer. The officer will give you a ballot box and put a black ink dot on your finger. All you must do is check-mark the PPP's column with the blue rocket symbol and quietly leave."

After a few minutes, the young man came out of the polling station, flashing a big smile.

"Everything went well. No problem, Swami. The agent in the blue shirt was very helpful. I voted for PPP," he said and showed the black dhobi ink on the tip of his finger as if it was a trophy.

"Sabash! Here are two rupees," Cane-Swami said. "Now, wipe the ink mark on your hair. If it doesn't disappear, go to that man on the corner, and he will clean it with a chemical. Put on a different shirt and come back after about thirty minutes. I'll give you another voting slip."

CHENDA AND Cane-Swami were nemeses. He earned Cane-Swami's wrath because he had revealed to Appu, Guru, Vijayan, and Mashe that the "fake sage was taking advantage of the widow in whose house he lived. Cane-Swami had convinced her that he was the reincarnation of her late husband and made her do all sorts of bad things. He had brainwashed her. While chopping firewood for a neighbor, I have seen him touching her."

Cane-Swami never missed an opportunity to argue for Chenda's expulsion from the village. "He is a parayan. If you touched him, you would get all sorts of diseases," Cane-Swami would say. "The untouchables practice voodoo magic, drink animal blood, and eat raw flesh. We should banish him from the village."

But in the election, where every vote counts, enmity takes the backstage. Cane-Swami looked at Chenda with a taut face standing outside the polling station. He called Chenda and asked, "Did you vote for our comrade?"

"No. The Polling Officer wouldn't give me a ballot because I don't have a proper name or an address."

"Don't worry. Do you still want to vote for the PPP?"

"Of course!"

"This is what you should do," Cane-Swami explained. "Wait for about thirty minutes, put on another shirt, and go to the PPP agent in a blue shirt. Tell him I, Swami, sent you. And your name is Pradeep and give him this voting slip. He'll take care of you."

"Won't he ask for an address?"

"No, he won't."

Chenda looked at the voting slip. It had an address and the name Pradeep.

"Another thing," Cane-Swami continued, "you won't get money for this."

"OK. I understand."

Chenda ran to Patti-Amma's porch, left the kettledrum there, wore the white shirt she gave him for Onam, and rushed back to the polling station. Almost thirty minutes had passed, and it was time to try again to vote for Comrade Vijayan.

The confidence he mustered evaporated as soon as he entered the polling station. He was besieged with the fear of being caught for impersonating. Sweat formed on his forehead, neck, and chest. His legs shook. He took a deep breath and walked straight to the agent in the blue shirt.

"My name is Pradeep. Swami sent me," he mumbled and gave him the voting slip. The agent took him to a Polling Officer who twitched his eyebrows as if he recognized that Chenda was denied a ballot earlier. Ashamed, Chenda felt a strong urge to run out of the room. But the Polling Officer pretended as if he had not seen Chenda before.

"You are Pradeep. Right?" he asked loudly so other Polling Officers and agents could hear him.

"Athe. Yes, saar," Chenda said, the words slipped out of his tongue.

The Polling Officer gave him a ballot, check-marked a column in the long vertical book, and told Chenda to stretch his hand, which trembled. Nonchalantly, as if he had seen several trembling hands, the Polling Officer dipped a thin stick in a bottle of black dhobi ink and put a dot on Chenda's finger.

After drawing a check-mark on PPP's column with a blue rocket on the ballot, Chenda walked briskly out. His shirt was soaked with perspiration. He breathed a sigh of relief. He didn't look at Cane-Swami, who was busy passing voting slips to men and rewarding them with rupees.

Chenda went to Patti-Amma's porch, took off his shirt, drew a bucket of water from the well, washed up, took the kettledrum, and went to his usual spot under the banyan tree.

THE COUNTING of the ballots started the following morning. Vijayan paced in the medical store and smoked beedis. Appu, Guru, Stephen, and Hassan anxiously sat inside the store. Chenda stood at the right corner of the store and tweaked the kettledrum's tension cord. Also gathered outside the medical store were a few PPP's paid volunteers.

Late evening, dancer Prabhu telephoned the results from the Chief Electoral Office to Arul, the only one with a telephone in the village. As Arul came to the store to break the news, his cheek-to-cheek smile said it all. Vijayan beamed with joy and said namaste. Soon Alumaram Village was startled by the exploding firecrackers at the medical store and full-throated chants: "New MLA Comrade Doctor Vijayan Zindabad. PPP Zindabad." And Chenda's kettledrum sang the song of victory.

In this six-party race, the People's Power Party squeezed a narrow win with eighty-six votes.

"Now that you're an MLA, don't forget us," Appu said.

"How can I, my dear Appu? You people are my strong supporters," Vijayan said.

Guru chimed in, "My prediction came true. I told you that you would win. Whatever you touch will turn into gold."

"Thank you, astrologer Guru. I always believed in you. You gave me hope," Vijayan said and offered them free rasayanam.

Hassan made a long, thick garland of rose petals, which he put on Vijayan's neck. The sound of laughter, applause, and firecrackers filled the air again. Stephen played music on his green loudspeaker at full blast. The bats on the banyan tree fluttered back and forth.

THE NEXT afternoon Proprietor Krishnan's Impala's honking could be heard from far away. Even if there was no traffic, motorists honked as if the horn was the driver's toy. The honking, this time, sounded a mix of habit and celebration. Vijayan came out of the medical store to welcome his boss. With hands clasped above his head in reverence, Vijayan greeted Proprietor Krishnan with a warm namaste. The General Manager who accompanied Proprietor Krishnan grinned. Vijayan motioned to his supporters to make way for the VIPs so they could sit inside the store.

"Great job! Congratulations," Proprietor Krishnan said. For the first time, Proprietor Krishnan looked at Vijayan with his eyes, not with his ears—A sure sign of Vijayan's elevation from a servant to a higher status.

He bowed and said, "I was able to win the election because of your blessing, Proprietor. Without it, I would have lost it." Then he sent dancer Prabhu to buy coffee from Brahminal Hotel and stood with folded arms like a servant eagerly waiting to take orders. The General Manager slipped a thick envelope into Vijayan's hands. "This will cover some election expenses."

Vijayan thanked Proprietor Krishnan for his generosity.

"Hmm. You are an MLA now. You have to think about your future," Proprietor Krishnan said. "You should think about your marriage and settling down. Have a family. You shouldn't waste your youth."

"Yes, saar," he replied. "First, I've got to find a suitable alliance for my sister. She is my top priority."

Proprietor Krishnan patted Vijayan on his shoulder and said, "You are a responsible man. I admire it. You also will make a good husband. When do you take the oath of office?"

The MLA-elect said he would be sworn in within a month, and he would train dancer Prabhu in dispensing and managing the store.

"Is he a good worker? Honest?"

"Yes, Proprietor. You can trust him."

Dancer Prabhu came with coffee, and Proprietor Krishnan and the General Manager took a few sips from their cups.

"The GM will talk to you later about the shop and other things," Proprietor Krishnan said, massaged his chin, and left with the General Manager. The driver drove off, honking and whipping up clouds of dust.

HARDLY THE dust from the Proprietor Krishnan's Impala had settled, it was yanked up again by the black Ford that had brought RSP's District President and District Secretary. With a whirr, the Ford made a U-turn and stopped in front of the medical store. The District President, the District Secretary, and the driver stepped out of the car.

Vijayan's forehead wrinkled as he looked at them with suspicion. The joy and euphoria he had during the Proprietor's visit had turned into scorn. He quickly looked out for the backup of Chenda and Mani if the District President attacked him. Chenda and Mani were nowhere to be seen.

"Namaste," the District President said and smiled. There was no angry face. No threats. And no yelling. Now, Vijayan was confused like the mouse caught in the paws of a big cat, wondering whether it would gobble up or harass or simply play with the hapless creature.

"Congratulations. You won," the District President said and smiled again.

Vijayan nervously smiled back and thanked him. "It was a tough election. Sorry, your candidate lost."

"Don't worry about him. We knew he wouldn't win, but we had to field a candidate," the District President said. "I'm happy others didn't win this seat."

Vijayan gestured, inviting them to come inside the store. Promptly, the District President and the District Secretary entered the store and sat on the wooden chairs. And the driver stood near the Ford.

"Would you like to drink a glass of rasayanam?" Vijayan asked hesitantly. Still fresh in his mind were their threats against his running for office and the rejection of his peace offering.

"Sure! Why not?" the District President said and looked at his companions, who nodded in affirmation.

Vijayan poured the black potion into three glasses and gave them. The District President took a gulp. "This tastes really good. Super!" he said.

The District Secretary, holding the glass, said, "Let's forget what we said during the election. That's how politics works. You know that, don't you?"

"Yes," Vijayan said.

"The boy, who painted your slogans, did a great job. Good handwriting."

"You mean, Chenda? The coolie? He delivers firewood. He didn't write those slogans. I had to write them on paper so he could copy them onto the walls. That's it," Vijayan said and waited for the District President to reveal the purpose of his visit.

"You've got a great future in politics," the District Secretary said. "We'll make you a great leader. All you need to do is join our team."

Vijayan paused and said, "I cannot defect from my own party."

"You don't have to leave PPP. Your agenda and our agenda are the same: The well-being of the people. What we need you to do is join our coalition. You could be part of our government. Our man will be the Chief Minister, and you can get your things done."

"Let me think about it."

"Listen, comrade," the District Secretary explained as if a high school teacher clarifying a point to a student. "If we don't form a coalition government, others will do. They are corrupt to the core. They'll bankrupt the country. You know that, don't you?"

Noticing Vijayan's hesitation, the District President jumped in, "We are the first to approach you. Not the Congress or the Communist Party." Then he dangled a bait. "We will give you a portfolio, say, Forest. The government has a big budget for forest expansion and maintenance. Don't wait too long to give us an answer. We might give the portfolio to someone else."

Then the District President looked at the District Secretary as though hinting at him to fill in the blanks.

The District Secretary took a pinch of brown powder from an aluminum foil in his shirt pocket, snorted it in both nostrils, took the handkerchief wedged between his shoulder and shirt collar, and wiped the nostrils with it. "Once you get a portfolio, you can do whatever you want there," he reiterated. He rubbed his fingers as if counting cash, winked at Vijayan, and continued, "You can make as much as you want. You can pay off your loans, build a home, and save plenty of money for your sister's dowry and wedding."

"What am I supposed to do?"

"Simple," the District Secretary added, "join our coalition. We'll tell you what legislation to support and what to oppose."

Meanwhile, the District President took a sip of the rasayanam. "Good stuff. Pour more for us, not for the driver. We don't want him to drive the car into a ditch," he said, looked at the driver, and laughed.

Vijayan emptied the bottle into the District President's and the District Secretary's glasses.

"By the way," the District President said. "We're having a big celebration at our party headquarters tomorrow evening. There'll be foreign whisky and vodka. Chicken biriyani. Fried chicken. Fish curry. Fried Fish. A lot of food. We'll send our Ambassador to pick you up and drop you back at your house."

"You will send an Ambassador car for me?" Vijayan asked like a boy excited over a free ride on Sivan's bullock cart.

"Yes. But you should promise that you will join our coalition. Can we trust you?"

Vijayan agreed. That magic word was the key to the door for the mouse's transformation into a fat cat.

"You're a wise man," the District President said. "We'll see you tomorrow. Now, go, celebrate your election victory."

IT WAS the time for the MLA-elect to make a victory speech at the junction. People from other villagers—young and old—came to meet and greet him. Stephen brought a mic and his green loudspeaker and hooked it to the lamp post. Dancer Prabhu's hip swung and hands flailed to Elvis' *"I'm all shook up."* There was no announcement of his sword-swallowing daredevil act. Vijayan got ready to make an impromptu speech, which was interrupted by the chanting of "People's Power Party Zindabad," "Up…up…up…Triple-P," "Comrade Doctor MLA Vijayan Zindabad."

Applause broke out again when Vijayan took the mic. He thanked the residents of Alumaram, Marakana, and other villages for "having faith in me." He thanked "the hundreds

of volunteers for your time and donations for my campaign."
He renewed his vow to bring peace and unity to the
community. He repeated his campaign promise of job
creation, free city pipe water, a hospital, a high school, and an
end to discrimination. "We should not lose our focus," and
thanked God for "giving me an opportunity to serve the great
people of Kerala, God's Own Country, especially the
Alumaram and Marakana villages." At the very crescendo of
his speech, he made sure to pause so that his party workers
could clap and chant, "Comrade Doctor MLA Zindabad."

He also thanked Proprietor Krishnan, Arul, Cane-Swami,
Appu, Guru, Hassan, Stephen, and others. Left out on his
thank-you list was Chenda.

The taste of Vijayan's election victory was felt inside the
Brahminal Hotel and the Military Hotel. The cooks and the
servers worked overtime to keep up with the demand for food
from Vijayan's supporters.

Both hotels had displayed their best dishes in glass
showcases that were repaired and installed near the doors,
facing the street to lure customers. Hanging in the corner of
each glass showcase was a sheet of paper smeared with oil to
trap flies and bugs drawn by the pungent aroma of curry. By
evening, these oily papers were peppered with black dots, like
an intricate art created by flies, mosquitos, and other bugs.

To serve Vijayan's supporters, the eateries prepared more
kaara vada, appam, and idiyappam. The special fares in the
Military Hotel included fried chicken, egg masala, fish curry,
and parottas that were neatly placed on banana leaves. The
extra items in the Brahminal Hotel were puttu, masala dosa,
and papadam.

"Edi, eat as much as possible," Cross-toed Ammu told Kamala and ordered an extra helping of mutton curry and parotta, each for her and her niece. "You won't get free food any more. The election is over."

The brisk business helped both establishments recover a large portion of the financial loss they suffered in the communal riots.

Mani had brought additional bottles of arrack. He served it openly without fearing a raid.

The mom-and-pop stores ran out of beedis, cigarettes, and paans.

VIJAYAN OFFERED a special thank-you pooja at the Amman Devi temple before coming to the medical store to continue his victory celebration the next day. He had applied a thick coating of sandal paste on his forehead and a dash of ash that the temple priest gave during the pooja.

"Eda dancer, what is today's program?" he asked Prabhu.

"We will have a rally all over the village. You will be leading it. I've arranged with the Marakana Music Group to play the *chenda* music. Stephen will bring his green loudspeaker, and Sivan will bring his bullock cart. We will make a dozen stops where you have to give short speeches. There will be volunteers to put a garland on you at every stop."

"Excellent," Vijayan said. "How about Chenda?"

"We don't need him anymore. I didn't tell him our plans."

"Good. Very good!"

Vijayan, wearing a marigold and rose garland donated by Hassan around his neck, led the procession that wound through the main and side streets and the Amman Devi temple. Cane-Swami came out of the widow's house. Vijayan said "namaste" and shook both his hands. "Thank you for your help," Vijayan whispered, "Please let me know if you need anything."

The victory lap continued. Marakana Music Group played the *chenda*, and PPP's volunteers clapped and chanted "People's Power Party Zindabad," "Comrade Doctor MLA Vijayan Zindabad."

In his speech at several stops, Vijayan repeated his promise to create jobs, and build a hospital and a high school, extend the city's water pipeline, and expand the electricity supply.

Halfway through the victory parade around Alumaram Village near the marshland, Vijayan heard a familiar kettledrum beat. He turned around and saw Chenda playing the music. Alone at the end of the procession, like a one-man band.

He played the music in tandem with the Marakana Music Group in front of the procession. It was as if he was an extension of the group. He played so well that his kettledrum ruled the scene as if silencing the opponent in a shouting match. The music group's leader looked at Chenda and eyed the group members to take a break to throw Chenda off the track. Undaunted, Chenda continued to play the instrument like an obsessed musician. His music stood out loud and clear and dominated the air. When the group realized they were being outdone, they resumed the drumbeat slowly. Appu and Guru looked at each other and chuckled.

"Look," Appu told Guru, "Chenda is leading the music. Listen to the repertoire."

"Yes! He is clever," Guru replied. "The group is following his repertoire. See, he played three beats, and the group followed up with three beats. He did seven beats, and the group did the same: seven beats."

"How true!" Appu said. "He is going for two beats, a pause, and three beats."

Keeping up with Chenda, the group repeated—two beats, pause, and three beats. Both Appu and Guru chuckled again.

"Aha," Appu said. "Look, our Chenda. He is messing with their rhythm and is taking over the music. Smart! Midukkan!"

When the music group's leader realized what had been happening, he stared at Chenda for taking over the music, that too, by a parayan. But Chenda didn't stop and continued to play alone. His eyes closed, his body swayed to the beat, and his hands and the drum sticks pulsated like a hundred kettledrums' beats synchronized into one rhythm. The music reverberated in the area. Vijayan and the procession stopped to watch him. And listen to him. His two drum sticks transformed into four drum sticks, then to six, to eight and to twelve, and a flock of birds fluttered and danced on the kettledrum. At the end of Chenda's enthralling performance, the crowd clapped. The hired group members looked at each other in humiliation. Still, the group members didn't invite him to play with them. Vijayan pretended as if he didn't notice the whole episode.

Then, Chenda walked away from the victory procession and returned to his usual place in the junction under the banyan tree.

17

GURU, HIS BLACK umbrella tucked under his armpit, stopped when he saw Chenda squatting, sullen, under the banyan tree, hugging the kettledrum.

"Eda Chenda, you were great. You gave the group a music lesson."

Chenda didn't respond.

Perplexed by Chenda's unusual behavior, Guru asked, "What's wrong?"

"Nothing."

"Nothing? You didn't answer to my compliments; you looked away. Why didn't you join the PPP's victory celebrations after the rally?"

"Not invited."

"Not invited? How come? You started the party."

"So?" Chenda asked. "Our Comrade Vijayan has changed. He is friendly only when he needs a favor from me. Otherwise, he doesn't want me near the medical store." After a pause, Chenda continued, "The Polling Officer didn't let me vote because I couldn't prove I live here. I don't have an ID with my name and address. Then, Cane-Swami helped me vote for our Comrade Vijayan." Chenda showed the black dot on his finger as a badge of honor. "But I had to use someone else's name."

Guru studied Chenda's puffy, pensive face and said, "I understand. Don't worry too much about it. These elections are rigged anyway. Comrade Vijayan promised you a passport and a visa. So you did what you needed to do."

Chenda slowly shook his head and said, "How will I get a passport without a proper name and an address?"

Guru pondered and said, "OK. Let us go to my home."

"Why?"

"You'll see. You are not an orphan."

Carrying the kettledrum on his shoulder, Chenda walked behind Guru on a narrow dirt street created by thousands of footsteps to Guru's house. The silence was their communication. As they neared Guru's house, the only tile-roofed one on the street, their silence was interrupted by the barking of Guru's dog. It was excited to see its master from far away.

Once they reached Guru's house, Guru patted the dog. Wagging its tail, the dog ran around Chenda and licked his legs. Guru drew water in an aluminum bucket from a well, located south of the front porch and washed his feet. Seeing him, Chenda did the same. Guru entered the verandah, dusted a wooden chair on the verandah, sat, and called his wife, who was in the kitchen. And Chenda sat on the verandah's ledge. Guru's wife, Leela, came out of the kitchen. Seeing Chenda, she said, "Good to see you. You're a gifted musician."

Chenda said, "Thank you," and Guru smiled as if endorsing his wife's observation and urged her to make two cups of chai. Leela, wearing a white mundu, a red blouse, and a long towel diagonally across her upper body, nodded and went to the kitchen.

Guru placed the umbrella in a standing position near the door. Then, he took a sheet of white paper from the brown gunny shopping bag he had carried. He meticulously drew a large square and twelve smaller squares around it with a blue fountain pen.

"I'll make your horoscope. What's your date of birth?" he asked and quickly corrected, "Sorry, you already told me you didn't know it. Then, how do you tell people that you are twenty-four?"

"Patti-Amma told me that I looked twenty-four."

"That's a nice way to decide your age," Guru said. By then, his wife had brought chai in steel tumblers and banana chips on an aluminum plate. She placed them on a stool, stood near the door, and listened to their conversation.

"Is Patti-Amma related to you?"

"No," he replied emphatically. "I wish she was. But she lets me sleep on her back porch. That's all. She's a kind woman."

Guru became quiet, and his wife went inside the house, so Chenda wouldn't see her tears.

To distract himself from becoming emotional, rather than to quench his thirst, Guru drank chai and gestured to Chenda to eat the round, yellow chips.

"Do you remember your religion? Caste? Anything about your childhood?"

Chenda sipped the chai, belched, and shook his head in the negative. "All I remember is that I used to sleep in front of the lumber yard and later inside the shop. And one day, Patti-Amma asked me to sleep on her back porch."

Guru paused and said, "If there is any problem with Patti-Amma or other Brahmins, you can stay here. We've got an extra room," Guru said. "Leela!" He called his wife, who came out to the verandah. "He can sleep in the extra room. Can't he?"

"Sure! We don't have any objection. Come any time."

Chenda smiled, showing his gratitude to Leela—thin as Patti-Amma, but younger with thicker, darker hair.

Guru urged Leela to bring betel leaves from the house. She obliged and brought a brass plate with betel leaves stacked on each other, betel nuts cut into bits, and lime paste in a small aluminum cup to make paan.

He urged Chenda to pick a betel leaf from the plate. Chenda randomly picked one from the middle of the stack and gave him. The leaf had black dots and was partially eaten on the edges by moths. And Guru recoiled as if he saw a ghost on the betel leaf.

"What's wrong?" Chenda asked.

"Throw it away. Right now." Guru was terse. He heaved, took a deep breath, slowly exhaled as if calming down, and said softly, "Pick another betel leaf." This time, Chenda picked one from the bottom of the stack. It was a sturdy green leaf, neither tender nor ripe like a teenager. Guru was pleased with the new betel leaf.

He tore the first betel leaf and the sheet of paper into bits, crumpled them into a ball, and tossed it out of the verandah. He took another sheet of paper and drew the squares again. A fresh start. He opened a handbook with various charts and zodiac signs, which had been frayed by years of matching and rejecting marriage proposals. He went through a few pages and drew symbols on each square that revealed the secrets of one's future. He made a few calculations with his fingers and wrote down a few numbers. "This is your date of birth. And this," he said, holding a chart, "is your horoscope."

Chenda looked at the piece of paper and tried to figure out his future, the fate of his American dream, hidden in the large square in the middle and fortified by a dozen small squares around it.

"Guru saar," Chenda asked, "how do you know the time of my birth?"

"I selected the best day available twenty-four years ago. It doesn't matter whether you were born in the morning, noon, or night. On that day, any hour was auspicious for birth."

Chenda laughed, mixed with joy and skepticism as if he had won a jackpot. "How accurate is it? You just made it up."

"Eda Chenda, I'm telling you, it is one-hundred percent accurate. I prayed to Amman Devi before I prepared your horoscope. These squares are zodiac houses. If you need a copy of your horoscope, let me know."

Chenda replied he didn't need a copy of the horoscope, and Guru could keep the original.

"OK. Ask me whenever you need it. Now, we've to come up with a proper, good name for you," he said and asked his wife, who was standing near the door. "Edi Leela, what do you think about the name Narayanan for him?"

Leela looked at her husband, stunned. And her face became ashen. "Are you sure you want to give him that name?"

"Yes," Guru asserted and looked at her sympathetically as she wiped her moist eyes with the tip of her long towel. "Yes," Guru repeated. "We know that name has a special significance. Doesn't it fit Chenda's personality?"

Leela nodded her head in approval. Guru looked at Chenda and said, "The name Narayanan is perfect for you based on your horoscope I made. Do you like the name? If not, we could come up with another name."

"No…no! Narayanan sounds good to me. It is the lord's name."

Guru's face lit with pride as if he had just adopted a son. And Chenda's heart swelled; his eyes twinkled as if he was lost and found. Still beaming with joy, he turned toward Guru's wife. She looked at him, from top to bottom, as if he was a newcomer to the village, and quickly retreated to the kitchen. There, she wiped the tears again.

Confused by Leela's tears, Chenda asked Guru, "Is everything OK?"

"Yes. My wife gets emotional easily. She is happy that you liked the name Narayanan."

A few minutes later, she brought more chai and banana chips. A celebration for Chenda's christening.

Guru had another surprise for Chenda. "Give my address, this address, if anyone asks you. Now you can vote. Apply for an Indian passport and an American visa with this address. When you go to America, write me a letter. In English. Use big, big words."

Chenda smiled. "Sure, Guru saar. You know I'll write to you and the entire village."

Soon after Chenda left, Leela sat on the verandah and helped Guru make a paan. While applying the lime paste on a betel leaf, she broached the subject of Mashe's eldest daughter Sita, who was single.

"You have her horoscope on the shelf, don't you? Let's compare her horoscope with Chenda's. If they match, ask

Mashe whether he would be interested in pursuing an alliance between Sita and our Narayanan."

Like an obedient husband, Guru took Sita's horoscope, compared it with Chenda's newly crafted horoscope, and heaved a sigh of relief.

"Are they compatible?" Leela asked.

"Yes. They match well. Sita's horoscope shows a major development. I think she'll get married. But there's a blip in Chenda's horoscope. A special pooja to Amman Devi will fix it. But I don't know whether Mashe, his wife, and Sita will agree."

"No harm in asking them," Leela said. "Tell them that Chenda has a new name and an address."

GURU AND Leela were alerted by their dog's barking about the arrival of a visitor. It was Mashe.

"We were just thinking about you," Guru told Mashe.

"How so?" Mashe asked.

"I'll explain later. First, tell me, what brings you here?"

Mashe had brought a new horoscope from a prospective groom for Sita as he had done in the past two years. Guru would study those horoscopes with Sita's for their compatibility. A previous horoscope was a good match. But the groom's parents demanded a dowry of ten thousand rupees, ten ounces of twenty-eight-karat gold jewelry, a new bicycle, plus the wedding expenses.

He had told the groom's father that he couldn't afford such an exorbitant dowry, and the proposal fell through.

The new horoscope he had brought today was not fully compatible with Sita's horoscope, Guru said. However, if the groom's parents didn't insist on a large dowry, Mashe could agree to the proposal. "Let them pursue the alliance. We could negotiate for a lower dowry. If it works out, we need to offer a special pooja to Amman Devi. The Goddess will take care of the compatibility issue. It is very minor."

"What will I do if the boy's parents demanded a huge dowry," Mashe said. He wiped his Gandhian-style round-framed eyeglasses with the tip of his mundu, a habit started as a strategy to stall for time while fielding questions from students. His gray hair was neatly combed and partitioned in the middle. Every morning he shaved his thin face with a 7 o'clock blade, an unusual ritual in a village where most men sported a beard or a mustache. "I have to save money for the other two daughters' weddings."

It was the perfect opportunity Guru was waiting for to propose Chenda as a possible husband for Sita. He looked at Mashe sympathetically and said, "I've got a suggestion." Then, he took the pouch from the brown gunny bag, took a betel leaf from it, meticulously applied the lime paste on it, placed two bits of betel nuts and a pinch of processed tobacco, rolled the betel leaf, and offered it to Mashe, "Paan?"

Mashe took the paan, chewed, and spat the initial tart juice as Guru made another for himself.

"Tell me, Guru, what do you have in mind? People don't make paan this slow. You are hesitating to tell me."

Guru chewed his paan and said, "Mashe, don't get me wrong. Have you ever thought about our Chenda? I think he will make a good husband for Sita. He is strong. Bright. And talented."

Mashe's face turned pale with indignation that he would suggest a low-caste man for his daughter. That resentment was reflected in how he spat the paan juice forcefully, landing at the spot near the verandah already red with the residues of Guru's paan spit.

He wiped the round-framed eyeglasses with the tip of his mundu and was about to say something when Guru interrupted, "I gave Chenda a new name. A great name: Narayanan. Named after our Lord Narayanan—Maha Vishnu. I also made Chenda's horoscope."

Leela, Guru's wife, who listened to the conversation from inside the room, came to the verandah and interjected, "He is good-looking, too. He will be a good provider. You should tell your wife. Would you like me to talk to her? Women listen to other women than to their husbands."

Her words had a calming effect on Mashe, and his face muscle relaxed.

"I'm glad you gave him the God's name, Narayanan. But he still is a parayan. A crow is always a crow. It cannot transform into a peacock. The villagers will ridicule me. They will say I'm incapable of finding a husband from my own upper caste for my daughter."

Leela was in no mood to let it go. "We don't know for sure whether he is a parayan. Yes, he is dark. But we cannot jump to a conclusion," she argued.

No one spoke for a while, like a lull in the rain. Leela went to the kitchen, brought a plate of banana chips and a cup of chai, and gave them to Mashe. He ate them, making crunching noise, and pondered Guru's and Leela's suggestions.

"Even if you changed his name, people would call him Chenda, not Narayanan," Mashe asserted. "First of all, Sita and my wife have to agree. Then, Chenda has to agree. Now that Vijayan has become an MLA, Chenda hopes that he will get an Indian passport and an American visa."

"Don't worry about it," Guru said. "He will change his mind about America once he gets married. Marriage changes people's lives. Everything changes."

"How can you predict it in Chenda's case? He is crazy about going to America."

"Well, according to the horoscope I created, he is not going anywhere. He is going to stay put here. He doesn't know it."

"You mean," Mashe paused, "you didn't tell him that?"

"I didn't. It is a sin to kill people's dreams."

"Then, what did you tell him?"

"I simply told him I am making him a horoscope, and his name is Narayanan."

"Poor boy," Mashe commented.

"We must be realistic. Trust me, once he is married to Sita and settled in life, he will slowly forget about Carnegie Hall. Here is another secret: I checked his compatibility with Sita. Sorry, Mashe. I should have sought your permission before doing it. They match one hundred and ten percent. Ugran! Perfect!"

Torn between the possible humiliation of Sita's marriage to Chenda, and Guru's pragmatic solution, Mashe crunched the banana chips.

Guru had another suggestion. Instead of paying a dowry to Chenda, Mashe could set up a grocery store for him. And it would be less expensive and an investment. "He doesn't have to chop firewood anymore. He is a good boy. No scandal. He never disobeyed us. And everyone loves his music."

"What about his parents?" Mashe asked.

"No one knows. It doesn't matter because we are his guardians now," Guru asserted, pointing his finger at himself and his wife. "Once you agree, we can take the next step. Here's another thing," Guru continued in between chewing the paan, "While going through Sita's horoscope, I noticed something major would soon occur in her life. It must be her wedding."

"Are you sure?"

"What else it could be?"

"OK. Let me talk to my wife and the girls about this. I don't want anyone else to know this now. Not even Chenda," Mashe said.

ON THE WAY to his home from Guru's house, Mashe bought four strings of jasmine flowers—one for his wife and the rest for his three daughters for them to adorn their long, lush black hair.

At night, while lying next to his wife on the wooden cot, Mashe cautiously broached Guru's proposal. "Our astrologer Guru predicted there would be a major event in Sita's life. I think she would get married in this wedding season."

Mashe's wife smelled the jasmine flowers, tucked them between her braided hair, and commented, "God bless him. Did anyone contact him with a proposal for Sita? I hope it is from a good Nair family."

"He didn't receive any proposal," Mashe said. "Don't get upset about what I'm going to say. It is Guru's and his wife Leela's idea. Just a suggestion. That doesn't mean we have to agree to it."

"Who is it?"

"Chenda. They think Chenda would make a good husband for our Sita."

"What? What did you say?"

He ignored his wife's question. Like a student who didn't know the answer to a question and tried to wing it, he replied, "Guru has given him a new name: Narayanan."

His wife sat up and stared at him. "Are you serious? Ask Guru and his wife whether they will give their daughter, if they had one, to a parayan. Ask them. I bet they wouldn't."

"Shh…be quiet. The girls in the next room can hear this." He could see anger twitching in his wife's face. She was ready to strangle him. The fear of waking up their daughters and the neighbors held her back. She didn't want to make a scene at night. And she was terse: "We can do much better. We don't have to stoop low and let her marry a parayan. Our relatives won't invite us for Onam. They won't talk to us. No one will marry the other two daughters. Listen, as long as I live, Sita will not marry a parayan."

They halted the conversation when they heard the noise of one of her daughters getting up in the next room. When the rustle in the next room stopped, Mashe's wife whispered, "I think the girls heard us."

"I hope not. We'll know tomorrow morning."

"You know," Mashe's wife continued. Having spewed her anger, she had calmed. "I'm worried about what the villagers will say about us. They will avoid us. How will I face them on the street? Will the priest let me inside the Amman Devi temple?"

In a hushed, firm voice, Mashe said, "To hell with others. We cannot live in fear of what the villagers and relatives will think of us. They won't lift a finger to help us. Edi, try to understand me. We all know Chenda. His new name is Narayanan. He is a good boy. Our astrologer Guru, Appu, Gopi, Hassan, Stephen, and MLA Vijayan will support us. They will come to the wedding. Sita will be happy. We could give Chenda money to start a grocery store. He wouldn't have to cart firewood. If you say 'yes,' Sita will agree. The horoscope I showed Guru is not at all compatible. Look what happened with the other alliance? The groom's parents demanded a huge dowry. Rascals! They also complained that Sita is not fair-complexioned as Gauri and Paru. The boy wouldn't mind marrying anyone of them for a lesser dowry."

His wife was piqued by his comment as if she was responsible for Sita's dark complexion. "It's not my fault that Sita is dark. I didn't make her darker than the other girls," she said.

"I know it's not your fault," Mashe said. But the accusatory tone in his voice was subtle. "I asked you to mix gold powder in your milk when you were pregnant with Sita. I asked you several times to scrape gold from our wedding rings, mix the gold powder with milk and drink it. You never listen to me."

"Our children's skin color won't change even if I ate a kilo of gold," she said in protest. "You are not white. You are not a sayippu."

He wanted to yell at his wife that she didn't even try to consume gold powder. All he could say was, "Didn't your mother tell you to mix gold powder with milk?"

"I don't remember."

Mashe realized that further discussion on Sita's skin hue would escalate into a full-blown argument in the middle of the night. He stopped arguing. Instead, he massaged his wife's shoulder and hugged her. The fragrance of fresh jasmine flowers she had tucked into her hair tickled his legs, and he hugged   and   kissed   her.   She   didn't   resist.

ALUMARAM Village woke up to a gruesome discovery. The residents were stunned to see Sita's body hanging from a jackfruit tree like an abandoned sari-clad plastic doll in Mashe's back yard. Her long hair obscured the head and neck that hung limply from a coir noose. The body swayed slowly in the breeze as if in no hurry to come down to earth. Mashe beat his chest in anger and grief, and his wife rolled on the floor and wailed, "Ayyo. Dhyvamey! My God! What have you done to my Sita?"

Paru, his youngest daughter, ran, holding a rope to another tree to hang herself. The neighbors ran after her, screaming "stop... stop" and tackled her and snatched the rope from her hand. Paru fell on the ground with a heavy thud, hitting her head on the dirt. The neighbor's wife grabbed and lifted her, consoling her, "Please calm down. Please. Sita is with God. In a better place." Paru stared at her, emitting contempt and desperation, and sat on the ground, resting her head on her knees and her hands on her head.

The other sister, Gauri, passed out after seeing the body. The neighbor's wife sprinkled water on Gauri's face. When she regained consciousness, the neighbor's wife gave her a glass of water to drink. Gauri sat dazed, with a vapid look on her face.

Sita's body slightly swayed in the breeze. Chenda came running with Appu and stood stunned. Chenda stared at her serene face. *You might think she was smiling. Was she smiling at the foibles of the living? The dead have no sad faces. Nor angry faces. Just tranquil like the Gandhi statue at the junction,* he thought.

Mashe, in between sobbing and beating his chest, begged Appu, "Let's bring her down. Please. I can't see her hanging like this. Please!"

"We shouldn't touch the body," Appu said. "Let us wait for the police. They would charge us with tampering with the evidence." As an afterthought, he said, "If they don't show up within an hour, we will bring her down. I'm so sorry, Mashe. I never thought such a thing would happen to us."

Sita's suicide was the main topic of hushed talks at the medical store, the Military Hotel, the Brahminal Hotel, the market, and the junction.

CROSS-TOED AMMU, on hearing Sita's death, stopped her vegetable sales and rushed with Kamala to Mashe's house. "Paavam! Poor Mashe," she said and went to Mashe's back yard to help the grieving family. They tried to force Mashe, his wife, and their two surviving daughters to eat idlis, sambar, and chai brought by a neighbor.

"You should have some nourishment. Please... please eat this idli and drink chai," Cross-toed Ammu pleaded. Mashe, his wife, and their two daughters didn't even look at the food.

By ten o'clock, two constables came on bicycles. They looked at Sita's body from different angles: the position of the knot on the choir, the neck, and the swaying body.

"We should bring her down quickly before her neck severs," the senior constable, middle-aged with a paunch, told his partner. By then, another neighbor had brought a ladder. The other constable, young and robust, climbed on it and cut the noose with his pocket knife. The senior constable, Chenda, and Appu held the body and gently brought it down. Chenda held her by the shoulder, bearing much weight, and wondered whether people weighed heavier when dead. They laid Sita on freshly cut banana leaves that were covered with a clean white cloth given by Mashe's next-door neighbor. By then, Hassan, Stephen, and Gopi had arrived. Already, a crowd of onlookers, sad and bewildered, had formed. Hassan sprinkled marigold and rose petals on Sita, and stood somberly.

The junior constable tucked the noose, still around her neck, under the white cloth.

"We cannot remove it. Sorry, this is for evidence," he told Mashe and stood like a security guard near the body. Mashe sat on the dirt next to it. In between sobbing, he answered the questions from the senior constable, who wrote them down with an ink pen.

"I don't know," Mashe replied when the senior constable asked why she committed suicide. He said 'no' to the next question if he suspected foul play. "She was not pregnant, either."

The next-door neighbor, the first to notice the body, told the senior constable that he was awakened by his dog's barking in the morning. When he looked in the direction of the dog's barking, he saw something long hanging from Mashe's jackfruit tree.

"At first, I thought it was a broken tree limb," the neighbor recalled. "I went to my back porch for a better view. Then, I was shocked to find it was a woman. I can't still believe it. It is like a nightmare. A horrible dream. Such a thing has never happened in the village. In this village."

Guru, who came running, stood stunned. He sat crouched in the back yard with his face cupped in his hands and the black umbrella tucked in his armpit. He let out a loud cry, "Oh, Devi! Amman Devi! This is terrible." Tears streamed down his cheeks. It took tremendous effort for him to look at Mashe, his wife, and their other two daughters. Guru looked at Mashe and then at the body. Guru's wife Leela, who had followed him, covered her mouth with mundu, to muffle her sobs, and stood near Mashe's wife.

In hush-tone, the constables discussed the next step.

"The pretam will be taken to the coroner's office for a post-mortem," the senior constable with a paunch said. "We've got to find a way to transport her."

Chenda whispered to them he would take care of it, ran to the lumber yard, and brought his handcart. Meanwhile, Hassan rushed to his house and returned with a basket of rose petals and a garland.

The neighbor brought a straw mat and spread it on the cart. Another neighbor cut leaves from the banana trees in his back yard and placed them on the straw mat for cushioning effect. The constables, Chenda, and Appu gently raised the body from the ground and placed it on the cart. The junior constable removed the noose from Sita's neck and tucked it under her head. Hassan sprinkled rose petals and gave the garland to Cross-toed Ammu, who slipped it around Sita's neck.

The constables didn't object to the rose petals and the garland. It was a scene of a strange paradox—a rose garland and a coir noose on the same person. A celebration of life and death in one body.

Appu went to the barbershop and came with a white mundu.

In a trembling voice, he asked Mashe, his wife, and their two daughters to take a final look and say goodbye before he covered Sita from head to toe.

A stream of wailing rose. Mashe cupped Sita's face and kissed her forehead. His wife stroked her face. Paru and Gauri grabbed their elder sister's hands and would not let them go. The neighbor's wife tenderly removed their hands from Sita, and it was time to take her to the coroner's office.

Appu covered the body with the white mundu. The neighbor placed more banana leaves and covered the body with another straw mat. The senior constable fastened the body with a coir rope around the cart to prevent it from rolling out. Hassan sprinkled rose petals again. On a cue from the senior constable, Chenda gently pulled the cart, as if it was precious cargo, from Mashe's back yard onto the front of the house and waited. Mashe's wife, Gauri, and Paru came to the verandah to say goodbye to Sita. Their eyes were red with dried tears. A wave of wailing rose along with loud chants: "Rama…Rama…Rama…Devi…Devi…Devi."

Mashe looked at his wife and the two surviving daughters. His eyes apologized to them for failing to come up with a hefty dowry. His face was stooped on his shoulder, like a warrior leaving after a humiliating defeat.

Sivan had brought his bullock cart. "Mashe, I'm sorry about your daughter. In happy times and sad times, your daughter would become our daughter in God's Own Country," Sivan said. "Come. Please sit in my cart. Don't worry about the transportation charge."

Mashe was helped by Appu and Stephen to get into the bullock cart. Before entering, Mashe looked at his wife and two daughters again and beat his head with both hands. Appu grabbed his hands so that he would stop beating his head again. He implored, "Mashe, don't do that. Don't hit yourself. This is God's will. There's nothing we can do about it. It's providence." Mashe's ears were closed for such philosophical advice.

Chenda looked helplessly at Mashe and thought, *No words of sympathy and condolences would lessen his grief. There are no books or newspaper advice columns on handling grief.*

Guru came to the bullock cart and didn't know whether to enter it. After a pause, he apologized to Mashe, "I'm sorry. I shouldn't have opened my mouth. Sita would have been alive if I had kept quiet."

Mashe didn't respond. Instead, he gestured Guru to get in the bullock cart. Appu and Stephen sat on one side, and Guru, Mashe, and his neighbor sat across from them in the bullock cart.

"It's all my fault. My fault," Guru lamented. "I didn't know the major event predicted in her horoscope would be this. I'm blindsided. I'm so sorry, Mashe. I'm really sorry."

Mashe's eyes were stoic, without any expression like the dead Sita's. He didn't respond to Guru's self-reproach.

Chenda, accompanied by Hassan on foot, pulled the handcart. Hassan wanted to lend a hand to Chenda if he got tired during this emotionally-charged long haul on the gravel road.

The constables, on their bicycles, led the slow funeral procession in front of the handcart carrying Sita's body, followed by Sivan's bullock cart. No one spoke. The silence was broken by Mashe's occasional sobbing and the clanking of the bullocks' collar bells. Chenda wore the long-sleeved white shirt Patti-Amma gave and a mundu that he folded knee upwards for easy mobility. Usually, he wore a lungi, a checkered towel wrapped around his head, and no shirt. Today he dressed up. The dead warrants respect. He had left the kettledrum at Patti-Amma's back porch. This was no time for music.

As Chenda pulled the cart, his shoulder muscles bulged. They were as big as the muscles of the white bodybuilder on the metal signs at the medical store. He was barefoot. Mashe watched Chenda pull the cart with ease, sighed, and commented to Guru, "I agree. He would have been a good provider for Sita. Or, for that matter, to any girl. It's a shame he is black. A parayan."

Mashe intently looked at Sita's body carried on a cart by Chenda.

Chenda looked over his shoulder to check how Mashe was holding up. At one such moment, Mashe noticed tears flowing over Chenda's face. Hassan, though he had no experience in the rigors of handcart pulling, told Chenda, "I can take over. You need a break."

Chenda motioned with one hand that he didn't need help, wiped his face with the other hand, and pulled the cart slightly faster.

Villagers stopped on either side of the road to see the rare procession. A few curious onlookers gestured to Chenda as if asking, "What's in the handcart." Chenda ignored them and pulled the handcart steadily. Unlike Vijayan's election rallies, this convoy didn't have Stephen's green loudspeaker. No *chenda* music group. No chanting of slogans.

Alumaram villagers struggled to explain the cause of Sita's suicide to their children, who bombarded them with questions:

"How did Sita die?"

"Why?"

"Is it because she was poor?"

"Is it because she was dark?"

"Will she reincarnate as a rich woman with a big house, a car, a telephone, and servants?"

"Will she be light-skinned?"

18

CHENDA WAS woken up from his deep slumber by the torrid sun and an acrid smell at the corner of Patti-Amma's back porch. With a red towel, which he had rolled into a pillow, he wiped the sweat from his face, shoulder, and armpits from the unforgiving humidity. He fanned his nostrils with the towel as if whooshing away the pungent smell that permeated the back porch. He looked for the source of the putrid smell and realized it was not a rotten rat, but a splat of yellow vomit.

"Oh, my God!" he mumbled. "I don't remember coming through the porch's backdoor and throwing up. I drank too much arrack." He hastily covered the vomit with dirt when he heard the whooshing of Patti-Amma's sari.

"Drink this. You'll feel better," Patti-Amma said and extended a tumbler of hot black chai.

"Thanks, Patti-Amma," he said, without looking at her to hide his bleary eyes and the embarrassment of throwing up at night.

Chenda took the tumbler from her, still looking at the floor, and sipped the chai. "I have a severe headache. I feel better now. Much better."

"You were drunk last night," Patti-Amma said. "You yelled and cried. Remember?"

"Sorry, Patti-Amma. I won't do it again."

"That's what you told me the last time. It's your life. Hmm...I heard you transported the girl's body. For free. Nice. Good boy."

Chenda's lips quivered, and he wiped his face with the towel again. This time to wipe the tears. "Yes, I took Sita to the coroner's office. The coroner is Mashe's former student. He did Mashe a huge favor. He didn't cut open the body. The coroner removed the noose from her neck and wrote it was an accident in his autopsy report. We took the body to the crematorium. Mashe passed out soon after he lit the funeral pyre. We had to catch him from hitting the ground. Sad! Pretty sad!"

Chenda drank the chai and let out a long burp, which made Patti-Amma smile. For her, the burp was a sign that Chenda's stomach was content. Chenda washed the tumbler with water in the aluminum bucket at the well and gave the cleaned tumbler to her.

"I hope you took a bath after visiting the crematorium."

"Yes, Patti-Amma. All of us took a dip, with our clothes on, in the river."

"Good! You should wash away the grief and the past. Well...you called her name loudly last night. Several times. You loved that girl, didn't you? When people drink, they tell the truth."

He didn't reply and gazed at the heap of dirt that covered his vomit.

"Would you have married Sita if she had agreed to it?" Patti-Amma asked.

"Yes. She was a nice girl. She had a nice smile. She once told me she liked my music. No woman told me that. I don't think she would marry me. Who wants to marry a parayan?

You know many people here won't invite me inside their homes. When I was little, people did not let me play cricket with their children. I pretended as if I didn't notice it," he said and caressed the kettledrum. "They gave me water in a coconut shell, not in a tumbler."

Patti-Amma wiped her face with the tip of her white sari and said, "You knew what people were thinking about you?"

"Of course!"

"Are you really from a low caste?"

"I don't know, Patti-Amma."

"Why don't you tell them you are not a parayan?"

"Look at me, Patti-Amma. I'm black. Who would believe me if I told them I'm not a parayan? I'm black like charcoal."

Patti-Amma ran her hand over her gray hair as if looking for an answer.

"Hmm…Paavam. Pour soul," Patti-Amma said. "Don't dwell on the past. It will pull you down."

"It is not easy," Chenda said. "I've got a question for you. Who started the caste system?"

"Eda, it is a long story," she said. "Hundreds and hundreds of years ago, maharishis wrote the Vedas. Have you heard about the Vedas?" Patti-Amma answered her own question. "It is a collection of words of wisdom in poems. Written in Sanskrit. In Rig Veda, people are divided into four categories based on their profession. People who can read and write are called Brahmins. Those who are warriors are called Kshatriyas. The business people and the merchants, like the grocery store owners at the junction, are known as Vaishnavas. And those who did the manual, back-breaking labor work in the field are known as Shudras. They are the lowest in the Hindu caste hierarchy."

"You mean the rishis are responsible for the caste system?"

"No. I don't think they created this caste system. People did. I'm sure the rishis wouldn't have created such categories if they had known it would tear people apart. My Mister knows about the Vedas a lot more than I do. Unfortunately, he is down with vaatam. And he can't talk," she said, looking into the bedroom where her husband lay on a straw mattress in a wooden cot.

Chenda said, "So, I've been called a low-caste man because I'm a coolie. Delivering and chopping firewood. And I'm dark."

Patti-Amma didn't comment. But she offered him more chai.

"No more chai, please. I should get going. I have to deliver firewood."

A crow, fluttering its black wings, glided down, sifted the dirt with its beak, and pecked at the vomit. Chenda picked up a stone and threw it at the crow. In the impact, the bird rolled over, hopped with its three-toed legs, and flew away. He tossed a lot more dirt on the vomit to hide it from birds and bugs.

CHENDA DIDN'T deliver firewood. And he went directly to the medical store and waited for Vijayan. Since his election, Vijayan had been coming late to the store. His new title as the MLA gave him the prerogative to set his own schedule. Besides, dancer Prabhu did his job by opening, dusting, and performing poojas at the store.

Vijayan didn't respond when Chenda greeted him, "Namaste, comrade." Instead, he looked at dancer Prabhu, gave a few instructions to him, and lit a Panama cigarette.

"Namaste, comrade," Chenda repeated.

With puckered eyebrows, he gestured at Chenda as if asking, "*What do you want?*"

"Could you please, please, help me go to America?"

Vijayan looked at him condescendingly. "You don't have a real name. All you have is a nickname, Chenda. With such a name, the Indian government won't issue a passport."

"Comrade Vijayan, I have a real name now. And I have my own address and a horoscope," Chenda said. "Our Guru saar made me a horoscope and gave me a name. Good name: Narayanan. Guru saar also said I could use his address in my passport and visa applications."

Vijayan laughed. "That's a fake name and horoscope. The astrologer cannot simply make names up and cook up horoscopes. You need a birth certificate to apply for a passport, and I cannot do anything without your birth certificate. You need a real birthday," he said, emphasizing the word "real.*"*

Chenda became quiet and walked away from the medical store like a child teased with orange candy, only to be taken it away from him.

He went to Patti-Amma's back porch, put on the white shirt she had given him for Onam, and set out for the five-mile walk to the United States Information Agency in Palayam.

The white two-story building sat majestically at the Spencer Junction near Trivandrum University College. Indian and American flags were hoisted on the building. The imposing entrance was guarded by a bearded man wearing white trousers and a colorful turban.

The security guard stared at Chenda and appeared to enjoy making him nervous. Beads of sweat formed on

Chenda's shoulder and armpit. Then, he walked across the street toward the red-brick Trivandrum University College campus. Outside the campus, boys and girls were waiting for local green buses. The boys ogled at the girls, and the girls giggled.

As if going for a job interview, Chenda had rehearsed these lines: *How do I get a U.S. visa? How much will it cost? How much is the plane fare?* He took a deep breath and crossed the road. When he neared the building, he was surprised to notice the security guard was not an American but a tall light-skinned Punjabi, draped in a pair of white trousers, a white coat, and a red-and-blue turban. He seemed amused by Chenda's walking up and down the street. Chenda's mind raced, pondering whether to walk away or go inside the USIA building. As Chenda neared the steps, the security guard, still wearing a poker face, stopped him and asked for the purpose of his visit.

"How do I get a U.S. visa? How much will it cost? How much is the plane fare?" he asked these three questions in one breath.

"Do you have a passport?" the security guard asked in a booming voice. Either he had the booming voice, or he made it up to make Chenda more nervous.

"No, saar," Chenda said. The "saar" part was due to fear or respect, or a combination of both, created by the security guard's intimidating posture and the well-pressed clean, white uniform and the red-and-blue turban.

"The first step is to get an Indian passport. Then come back," the security guard instructed as if he had the authority to issue U.S. visas. "Where do you work?"

"In Alumaram Village. I deliver and chop firewood and play the *chenda*."

The security guard's eyes twinkled, and his eyebrows knitted in amusement. "Want to go to America, eh? Are you sure?"

"Yes, saar."

"Speak with one of the officers. They will give you the details," the security guard said, and motioned Chenda toward the lobby.

Inside the lobby was a section for newspapers. Prominently displayed were The New York Times, The Washington Post, and The Wall Street Journal. Another section featured National Geographic, Newsweek, TIME, and other magazines. Next to the magazines was a shelf with neatly arranged glossy U.S. travel brochures. The USIA building also had a library. *So many books. You won't finish reading half of them in your lifetime,* Chenda thought. He saw two men sporting neckties, shiny shoes, and suits speaking in hushed tones as if discussing classified information. The lobby's floor was impeccably clean, unlike the dusty wooden floor of the medical store.

He took a large, thick, bound book containing maps and pictures. He wiped his hands on his mundu so maps wouldn't get dirty. He turned the pages one by one and read the names of the state by stringing together the alphabet Mashe had taught him.

"May I help you?"

Chenda turned around. Standing behind him was a middle-aged woman who wore a yellow chiffon sari with flower designs. She had a large, mini-moon size red dot on her forehead. A metal tag with her name and USIS in large letters was meticulously pinned to her blouse like a brooch.

"May I help you?" the woman repeated.

It was the first time anyone spoke to him in English, though in a thick Kerala accent. Until then, he didn't know that USIA had hired Indians except for the security guard. Chenda froze at the thought of replying in English. All he could do was shake sideways as if saying *no*.

Much to his relief, the woman said in Malayalam, "You can sit in one of these chairs and read. No need to stand."

Chenda didn't sit. He was eager to leave the opulent building. But he hung around a bit more so the woman wouldn't think he was a nervous wreck.

This is how Americans lived. Security guards, servants, tall buildings, fancy chairs, and books. A lot of thick books.

19

ALUMARAM Village saw several changes in a few months. Mashe had grown a flowing white beard, and he rarely came out of his house. Whenever he did, it was only to buy groceries and visit Mani near the marshland. And his breath and sweat emitted a strong smell of arrack in the morning, afternoon, and night. He spoke in monosyllables, and his wife stopped worshipping at the Amman Devi temple. She frequently argued with her daughters, Gauri and Paru. Mashe's conversations with Guru became curt and obtuse.

There were no political discussions at the medical store.

A conspicuous but never talked about change was that Muslims stopped eating at Kuttan's Brahminal Hotel and Hindus stopped patronizing Kader's Military Hotel.

The boys who played cricket on M.G. Road had formed two groups. The Hindu team, made up of good batters, played near the Amman Devi temple. The Muslim team, consisting of fast bowlers, played near Juma Masjid.

The wounds of the religious conflict continued to seethe under the sweltering, sticky humid summer.

Another significant development was that Comrade Doctor Vijayan had moved to a spacious office with tall white walls, a ceiling fan, and a peon at the Secretariat in Trivandrum City. He got engaged to Proprietor Krishnan's daughter and received a large dowry in advance. With that money, he found a husband for his sister. Both Vijayan's and his sister's weddings were held on the same day in a giant tent at his house in Marakana Village. A horde of politicians had brought gifts in shiny, gaudy wrappers. Appu, Guru, dancer Prabhu, Gopi, and Stephen were invited to both weddings. Mashe politely declined the invitation.

Chenda shimmered the kettledrum with a coating of coconut oil, tuned it, and rehearsed new notes to play at the weddings. But the invitation never came.

THERE ARE unexpected benefits when you deliver and chop firewood to homes. Gossips and rumors spread from house to house like the curry aroma. Chenda would hear them all.

"Did you hear that the Amman Devi temple cow went missing?" a housewife asked Chenda.

"Are you talking about the stray cow that hung around the temple?

"Yes. That white cow. The temple cow. Some say the Muslims stole it in the night and slaughtered it for its meat."

Chenda was skeptical. "I don't think they would do it. There are many stray cows and buffalos here. Why would anyone steal the temple cow? I saw it four days ago on the way to the river."

At five feet tall, with a milk-white complexion and a small U-shaped horn, the cow exuded elegance. People would bow in front of the cow, apply sandal paste and red kumkumam powder on its forehead, put a garland of flowers around its neck, offer bananas, and worship it. They never shooed the animal away even when it stood in the middle of the road, blocking bicyclists and handcarts. On the contrary, pedestrians and bicyclists gave way to the cow. It never occurred to anyone to inquire whether the cow was a Hindu, Muslim, Christian, Brahmin, or a parayan.

"Maybe you were the last to see it," the housewife told Chenda. "I don't think anyone saw it in the past few days."

Chenda simply listened.

The woman continued, "The temple priest and Cane-Swami are asking people to search for the cow. He says it is an unforgivable sin to kill the cow, the Amman Devi temple's gatekeeper! That, too, a white one!"

"Oh, oh!" Chenda reacted. "Cane-Swami is going to create a big problem."

Chenda had heard Cane-Swami telling people that his mission was to prove to the world that "Hinduism is better than other religions."

Cane-Swami would frequently quote Sanskrit verses. Though people had no clue what those words meant, they were mesmerized by his ability to spew Sanskrit phrases with a unique inflection. The temple priest and the management had ignored his arguments for Hindu superiority. If they criticized him, he would recite more Sanskrit verses and make them look ignorant. "You people are stupid. You shouldn't be managing the temple," he would admonish them. He also complained the temple committee members and the priest were filching money from the temple coffers. Or, he might allege a particular committee member was not a Brahmin.

LATE AT night, Chenda was besieged with restlessness. He tossed and turned to the left, right, on his stomach, then on his back to get a comfortable posture to lull him to sleep. He sat, leaning on the wall to rest, but to no avail. He took the kettledrum, went to the junction, and sat at the foot of the banyan tree. The village was eerily quiet. The humid summer air stood still. "*Something doesn't feel right,*" Chenda thought. On a hunch, he walked toward the Amman Devi temple. From far away, he saw Cane-Swami huddled with about thirty people. They held bamboo sticks, bicycle chains, knives, scythes, and torch lights.

"Eye for an Eye. This is India. Hindustan. It belongs to Hindus," Cane-Swami told them and whipped his cane in the air. *Swish. Swish. Swish.* "We should drive the Muslims and Christians out of this country. They should learn to recite the Bhagavad Gita, not the Koran or the Bible. Either they leave Hindustan or become Hindus. Cows are God's divine creation. Lord Siva's sentry. They should worship our cows, not eat them." *Swish. Swish. Swish.*

Cane-Swami and his Hindu fundamentalist followers walked stealthily to the mosque, which sat at the center of a predominantly Muslim neighborhood. There were no whispers and no sound of their footsteps.

Chenda ran to Juma Masjid and screamed, "run...run...escape," and banged the kettledrum as loud as he could. Tada...tada...tat...ta...It didn't sing. There was no rhythm or melody, just a cry for help. The mob, led by Cane-Swami, took a few shortcuts and covered the half-mile distance to the mosque within five minutes. They avoided the M.G. Road and took the less traversed side street.

Seeing Chenda, a burly man yelled, "Get out of here with your kettledrum before I kill you!" The man, whom Chenda had not seen before, snatched the drum sticks and flung them in the air. For a second, he thought of tackling the man who was at least six inches taller and about twenty kilos heavier than him. Undaunted, Chenda fervently pounded the kettledrum with his hands. It produced a muffled noise. Still, he banged the instrument and screamed as loud as possible, "Run…run…escape." Surprised by Chenda's tenacity, the burly man pushed Chenda, who lost balance and fell on top of the kettledrum. He got up and resolutely banged the kettledrum again.

The mob separated into two groups; one targeted Juma Masjid, and the other aimed at the nearby Islamic Elementary Madrasa. Their goal was simple: inflict as much suffering as possible on Muslims so they would never touch cows.

The burly man, part of the first group, had brought a bottle of kerosene, poured it on the side of the mosque's two-tiered thatched roof, and struck a match stick. The match stick didn't ignite. He took another match stick, which also didn't produce sparks. He took a third match stick, rubbed the matchbox on his shirt to remove moisture, and struck again.

"I got it! It worked this time," the man said, showing off the inflamed match stick. Then, he took a piece of paper from the garbage, lit and tossed it on the thatched roof. The flame spread in small waves on the first tier of the roof, then climbed to the top deck and quickly grew into a massive ball of orange blaze.

Meanwhile, the group at the Islamic Elementary Madrasa was infuriated by the Arabic letters above the Malayalam letters on the school's sign. "They are getting money from Persia. That's why the school's sign has a big Arabic sign and a small Malayalam sign at the bottom. It's an insult to the language of our land," Cane-Swami said. "The Malayalam letters should be on top and bigger, not the Arabic letters."

Two men in the group hit the metal sign with long sticks, knocked it down with a clang, and stomped on it. One of the rioters gathered the hand-woven, green prayer mats from the corner for students and set them on fire. The teacher's desk, chair, and the students' benches were tossed as a bonfire. Instantly, the fire reached the school's thatched roof and quickly spread. The Islamic Elementary Madrasa was wholly engulfed in flame.

The masjid's and the madrasa's fires leaped as if trying to touch the sky in a competition. The thick dry wooden beams of the mosque's roof ruptured like the explosion of firecrackers, shot off flames, and hurled cinders onto the tops of the neighboring homes. Their thatched roofs, too, were parched and combustible. The billowing smoke was chased by the blaze, jumping from one roof to the next, and the next, and to the next. The raging flames climbed from the west of the mosque and quickly crawled to the nearby homes. Both blazes converged into a giant cone-shaped inferno. Whipped up by the wind, from a distance, it resembled a massive funeral pyre.

"Let's go. This will do," Cane-Swami repeated. *Swish. Swish. Swish.* The Cane-Swami was still swishing his cane in the air when the mob returned victorious to his house. "Didn't we teach those rascals a lesson?" he asked.

"Yes, we did," the burly man replied. "We really destroyed their mosque and the school. I think a few homes also were on fire. This should be a strong warning for them not to mess with us."

"Good! No one will open his mouth about this. Not even to your wives. Is that clear?" Cane-Swami instructed.

The burly man hesitated and said, "The man with the kettledrum saw us. That rascal tried to stop me, and I gave him a couple of blows."

Cane-Swami stroked his beard and said, "Don't worry about him. He is a CIA spy. He is a parayan, and no one will believe him. You people go home and be with your family. If the police come to question you, tell them you know nothing and inform me immediately. The new MLA is on our side," he said. *Swish. Swish. Swish.*

CHENDA KNOCKED on homes around Juma Masjid and the Islamic Elementary Madrasa. More than his shouting and banging, they were woken up from their tired slumber by the heat wave, the din of crackling cinders, and the burned bits and pieces of the roof that rained like sparklers. The flames were so bright and blinding as if hundreds of thousands of lights were turned on by the Kerala State Electricity Board.

Sheikh Ali, the mullah of Juma Masjid came, screaming "Allahu Akbar."

Others ran out of their homes, screaming in horror. Tears streamed on their face at the sight of the mosque and the elementary school being devoured by fire.

"Who in the world would do such a thing to us?" Sheikh Ali shouted. One man responded, "It could be those Hindu bastards!"

Old women covered their nostrils with their hands and wept. Old men coughed and pushed the cinders away with their wooden walking sticks. A woman ran out with her two children—one in each hand—and men ran to their back-yard wells to draw water. Two young boys dragged their bleating goats and sheep from their small front yard. Chicken and ducks, let out of their wooden cages, hopped helter-skelter, and stray dogs howled at the billowing acrid smoke. And teenage boys and girls felt the seed of hatred for Hindus stir in their hearts.

Chenda rushed to Hassan's house, which sat at the west corner of the row of homes. Hassan was already drawing water from a well as fast as he could, filling plastic buckets and throwing the water at the burning homes. Chenda grabbed another plastic bucket that Hassan filled and did the same. As soon as he doused a flare, another popped up.

Exhausted, Hassan felt cramps in his hands and slowed down. Without hesitation, Chenda drew water from the well. Pulleys in deep wells squeaked non-stop. It was a losing battle. The well water didn't quench the thirst of the blaze. Tired and weak, the residents decided to save what was left of the water in the well and haplessly watched their homes gutted down, roof by roof, brick by brick, by the ravaging blaze.

When dawn broke out, the wind stood still, sucking the oxygen out of the inferno. Chenda joined the residents who carefully sifted through the smoldering ruins, salvaging broken utensils, clothes, soot-covered jewelry, half-burned family photos, and the remnants of hope.

"I'm sorry, Hassan," Chenda said. Hassan, gaunt and tired, slumped on the steps of his house and wept. His house narrowly escaped the blaze. Destroyed were his father's and uncle's homes and trust in people.

Leaders of the local Muslim League had gathered at Sheikh Ali's house, which escaped unscathed from the fire.

It was time for the morning aadhan. People kneeled on the ground, wiped their faces with their hands, and chanted "Allahu Akbar" three times. After the prayers, they gathered at Sheikh Ali's house. They looked at the charred skeletal remains of the mosque, the elementary school, and their homes.

By the time the rest of the village woke up, one fire engine and a water tanker arrived with their sirens blaring. Firemen hooked a hose to the water tank and sprayed water onto the flaming cinders. Within minutes, the water was used up, and the tanker drove off to replenish. The firemen tried to pump water from the wells. It was futile because the debris from the blaze in the wells clogged the hose. And there were no fire hydrants in the village. The firemen walked around, assessing the damage and empathizing with the victims.

"I've never seen such an enormous fire in my lifetime," the fire chief said. "This is huge."

The Muslim League leaders lamented the slow response. "If it were a Hindu neighborhood, I can guarantee you would come quickly."

"No saar, it is not true," the fire chief defended his department. "We only came to know about the fire this morning until someone telephoned us. There is nothing we could have done, even if we had come earlier. The water tanker can hold only so much water. We need at least fifty tanks of water. This appears to be arson."

On hearing the fire chief's statement, Chenda wanted to tell him that Cane-Swami was behind it. *"This would immediately set off an immediate revenge attack,"* he thought. *"Comrade Vijayan wouldn't believe me, and he would only support Cane-Swami. A snake."*

He was overwhelmed with a wave of yearning to tell someone about what he saw at night. The first person he could think of was Appu, whose house was nearby and only four streets away from the junction. Waken by Chenda's knocking on the door, Appu came out asking, "What's it?"

In one breath, he narrated what he saw. "How can we stop these Hindu-Muslim riots?"

"There is nothing we can do about it," Appu said. "Once you poison people's minds, you cannot clean it with Dettol. It will never go away. Like the boiling water in the tea kettle, the hatred will percolate, looking for a chance to strike back. History books are full of them. It is the downfall of humankind."

"Appu Chettan, we've got to save our village right now. Cane-Swami and Comrade Vijayan are in this together. I think I created a monster: Comrade Vijayan. I never imagined he would play games, pitting one group against the other."

"How are you going to do that?"

"I don't know. I should tell everyone in the village what he had been doing."

"Don't bother," Appu said. "It's your word against his. People will believe him. He is an MLA now. A big shot. Other MLAs are behind him."

"Appu Chettan," Chenda begged, "We must stop this nonsense."

"If you tried to expose them," Appu continued, "you will be in trouble. You'll never go to America."

"My American trip can wait. Somehow, we've got to save the village. Stop this Hindu-Muslim hatred. This is urgent," Chenda said and looked at Appu helplessly like a student beseeching his teacher's guidance.

"Right now, we cannot do anything," Appu said. "Let's wait till this madness dies down."

FIVE JEEPS screeched to a halt near Juma Masjid. Sitting crammed like mackerels in each Jeep were the driver, a Sub-Inspector, and six constables. This time, constables were led by Sub-Inspectors. One carried a bullhorn and announced the state government had declared a curfew. No one was allowed to leave his home from dawn to dusk.

"Bandh. Total bandh," a Sub-Inspector shouted on the bullhorn.

Chenda was standing, holding the kettledrum, near the banyan tree at the junction when one of the constables told him to leave. The constable raised his lathi, ready to hit him if he didn't obey his command. To please him, Chenda moved to the south of the junction and watched the goings-on.

One Jeep was strategically stationed near the banyan tree, one near the Islamic Elementary Madrasa, another near the Brahminal Hotel, and another near the Military Hotel. The fifth one went around the village, broadcasting the curfew. "Don't leave your home until seven in the morning. Anyone who violates the curfew will be shot at sight," he announced. "Let me repeat, anyone breaking the curfew will be shot at sight."

Vijayan arrived with the IG in an olive-green Jeep a few minutes later. The first thing Vijayan did was check out the medical store. It was safe. Then, Vijayan and the IG drove to the madrasa. They covered their mouth and nostrils with handkerchiefs to prevent the acrid smoke from drifting into their lungs.

Sheikh Ali and the victims, mostly men, surrounded them and demanded protection from Hindu extremists.

"We know who did this?" Sheikh Ali said. "You should put them in jail."

Before the IG could answer, Vijayan interjected, "Sheikh, we will launch a full and thorough investigation. We need at least one eyewitness. Do you have any suspects? Please let us know. This is horrible."

Vijayan saw Chenda staring at him from a distance. He hoped Chenda wouldn't talk to the IG and complicate matters. But he had a ready-made answer if Chenda came forward. "*He is a parayan. A fraud. He just made up a fake name to get an Indian passport and an American visa.*" Much to Vijayan's relief, Chenda stayed away. His eyes were red with sleeplessness, fatigue, and anger.

He heard the loud shouting of a Muslim League leader to the IG and Vijayan. "We won't sit silent when our homes are being burned down. We'll do whatever is necessary to punish those goondas. Muslims Zindabad."

Others raised their fists and repeated loudly, "Muslims Zindabad."

The IG listened to them patiently and told Sheikh Ali and the slogan-shouting Muslims, "We'll do everything possible to arrest the culprits. We will hunt them down. If you retaliate, it would only make matters worse for us."

To comfort them, Vijayan said the Chief Minister had requested the Central Government to send the military to restore law and order. "You will be safe. The military will stay here until the situation is brought under control and the curfew is lifted. All schools in Alumaram, Marakana, and nearby villagers will be closed. The villagers can leave their homes for work or purchase groceries and other essential items. The morning and evening KSRTC bus trips will be escorted by Jeeps, one in front and one behind."

The Alumaram Village was enveloped in fear and uncertainty as if in twilight during a solar eclipse. Teenagers didn't play cricket, Cross-toed Ammu and her niece Kamala did not sell vegetables, and both eateries were closed. The medical store, Appu's barber shop, Gopi's Fashion Tailors, and Stephen's Lucky Sounds and Lights were shuttered. Mani did not show up to sell the arrack. And the M.G. Road was deserted and ominously silent.

Mahatma Gandhi, in whose honor the road was named, had gone on hunger strikes to force a truce between warring Hindus and Muslims and succeeded. Under the present political climate, the Mahatma would have died of starvation.

SOLDIERS in military camouflage took up positions on every street. The rumor of military deployment became true. In the middle of the night, the strange rumblings Chenda heard came from the green military trucks that brought in soldiers from Pangodu Cantonment.

He rushed out to join the Muslims who had converged near Juma Masjid to pray. There were more soldiers than residents at the Juma Masjid and the Islamic Elementary Madrasa, the Amman Devi temple, the Military Hotel, the Brahminal Hotel, and the Brahmin's cluster. Military vehicles squeezed through the narrow streets and lanes, announcing, "Stay home until further orders. If you violate the curfew, we will shoot you."

Children peeked through the half-closed windows to glance at the soldiers with green steel helmets and rifles with long shiny steel bayonets.

"Don't go out," one mother warned her son. "Don't talk to those jawans. Those soldiers will kill you. See the sharp knives on their rifles? That's for stabbing the enemy."

One by one, reporters and photojournalists arrived in a caravan of taxis. They were stopped by police and told about the curfew and the shoot-at-sight order.

"It is not safe for you to visit the village. We'll escort you," a Sub-Inspector told the journalists. "But you must wait till the Chief Minister and the IG arrive. They are on their way here."

"Can't we speak to the victims until they come?" one reporter asked.

"No. Sorry."

However, photographers aimed their wide-angle lenses and took pictures of the burned shells of the mosque, the madrasa, and homes.

Chenda heard a reporter, agitated over the restriction of his movement, protesting to the Sub-Inspector, "This is censorship."

The Sub-Inspector replied, "Please have patience. Once the CM leaves, we will take you wherever you want, and you can speak to whoever you want. The situation is very volatile, and it is not safe for you to walk around alone."

Like clockwork, a convoy of Jeeps and two Ambassador cars with state flags on their hoods arrived. In the first Ambassador car were the Chief Minister of Kerala and his secretary. In the other Ambassador car were Vijayan and two other MLAs.

The Chief Minister wore a white handloom mundu and a juba—a visual proof that he was an ardent disciple of Mahatma Gandhi. During the freedom struggle, Gandhi exhorted Indians to make handloom clothes and boycott British-made garments.

The IG, the Sub-Inspectors, and the constables saluted the Chief Minister. The soldiers stood at attention at the command of their platoon leader. The Chief Minister looked at the devastation, and his jaw dropped in disbelief.

"The press is already here," the IG said. He motioned to the reporters and photographers that the Chief Minister was available for interviews and photos. The Chief Minister spoke loudly with Sheikh Ali and the fire victims so the reporters could jot down every word of the conversation.

Addressing the journalists, the Chief Minister deplored the arson and promised to launch a thorough investigation.

"We will not tolerate such cowardly acts of violence," the Chief Minister said. "Kerala is God's Own Country. We cannot let goondas shatter our peaceful coexistence." In an emotional cracking voice, he announced that he would form a task force, including Muslim and Hindu leaders, to investigate the fire and foster communal harmony. "My government will provide temporary financial relief to the victims. All victims."

Sheikh Ali heaved a sigh of relief at the Chief Minister's declaration. Chenda saw Vijayan cringe at the announcement. He had been outwitted by the Chief Minister, whose party, Vijayan feared, would gain Muslims' support.

Chenda chuckled at the Chief Minister's maneuver. *Brilliant,* he thought. *The CM stole Vijayan's thunder.*

The next to address the reporters was Sheikh Ali.

"We thank the CM for his support," he said and looked impassively at the Chief Minister. "We call upon his government to launch a comprehensive investigation immediately. We, Muslims, cannot live in fear. This government, your government, should act immediately before the situation gets out of control. We deplore such cowardly acts. Whoever did this at night, when innocent people— mothers, fathers, sons, and daughters—were sleeping, are cowards." Sheikh Ali gave a piece of paper to the Chief Minister. It was a petition signed by him and the victims of the fire.

Then Vijayan stepped forward to address the journalists. Chenda's ears perked up, and he heard every word uttered by Vijayan.

"I'm shocked by these events," Vijayan said. "This has been a peaceful community. A paragon, a role model not only for the State of Kerala but also for the entire country. These are hard-working, God-fearing people."

Vijayan raised his voice, "This is the doing of religious fanatics. This dastardly act was committed by miscreants from outside the village. There is no room for extremism in Kerala. I'll bring the two groups, Hindus and Muslims, together. But, I won't sit quietly until peace prevails."

All three of them uttered almost similar phrases. "*There must be a handbook on making political statements for different situations,*" Chenda thought.

After their chest-thumping speech, the Chief Minister, Sheikh Ali, and Vijayan posed for a group photo. Once the camera clicks stopped, the Chief Minister, accompanied by the IG and a Jeep of constables, drove around the junction and a few streets and left.

The Sub-Inspector kept his word to the reporters and assigned constables to accompany them. They interviewed sobbing residents, teenagers who attended the Islamic

Elementary Madrasa, and Sheikh Ali. And the reporters filled their short-hand books with long-hand scribbling.

Vijayan accidentally made eye contact with Chenda and quickly turned his face toward the journalists.

"Hindus, Muslims and Christians lived here in peace and harmony for ages," he told journalists. "We have all religious denominations. There's no discrimination. That's why this state is called God's Own Country. I'm proud to represent this great village. They elected me with an overwhelming majority to the assembly. I'll leave no stone unturned to bring peace to this community. By the way, please mention in your report that the compensation for the fire victims is my suggestion."

Chenda spent the rest of the day helping the victims salvage whatever the fire couldn't devour.

The villagers obeyed the military's curfew order out of fear than out of respect. In the evening, the Military Hotel and the Brahminal Hotel opened partially for business. They were ready to close on the slightest sign of trouble. Most customers were the soldiers who were stationed there to protect them. The soldiers ate vada and drank chai and smoked cigarettes or beedis. Occasionally, Kuttan and Kader gave them free chai.

Word on the street was that the police had arrested two Hindu fundamentalists responsible for the arson. It was confirmed by the next day's newspapers that ran a photo of two men, their faces covered with a white towel, on the front page. Next to it were the photos of the gutted mosque and the elementary madrasa. The headline read, "*Mosque, madrasa, 21 homes razed by fire, sparks religious strife; police arrests 2 goondas.*" The story and the photo caption didn't have the suspects' names, ages, or the details of their residences. The photo was supplied by the police public relations officer to the media, with a two-sentence news release stating the "investigation is under way."

The news of the arrests, real or fake, brought a sense of safety to the tense villagers.

"Finally, the government is clamping down on religious fanatics," Sheikh Ali said. "I hope they arrest all unscrupulous people."

CHENDA DIDN'T hear "shoot-at-sight" announcements the next day. The camouflaged military vans didn't patrol the streets. They were stationed near the banyan tree at the junction, which turned out to be a bad move because the vehicles' roofs were peppered with bat and crow droppings.

"The military is leaving," Chenda told Hassan, who was cleaning his flower cart.

"I hope they are not pulling out completely," he commented.

"I think they are doing it in different stages."

"That's much better."

The soldiers who stood like sentries at the eateries and drank free chai were gone. But there were soldiers near the mosque, the madrasa, and the Amman Devi temple. After two days, they, too, were gone.

Two days later, the Jeeps that patrolled the streets and lanes left at midnight.

Appu, Hassan, and Gopi cautiously half-opened their stores. But the medical store resumed selling rasayanam in full swing. Mani moved back his arrack business from the far end of the marshland to the original location in the narrow lane. And Chenda dusted and polished the kettledrum with coconut oil.

"Allahu Akbar." The aadhan prayers heralded sadly five times a day from Stephen's green loudspeaker, which was tied to a temporary mosque that stood on long, four bamboo legs.

The Amman Devi temple bells chimed wearily as devotees returned to attend poojas. And Cane-Swami 'swished' his cane and continued to berate the Hindu priest and the temple committee members for their religious tolerance.

During one of those evening visits to the temple atrium, he was distracted by a commotion on the street.

"The cow...the cow," he heard boys yelling on the street.

"Muslims are stealing another cow?" he asked and stretched his neck to see the cause of the commotion. He couldn't believe what he saw: The white cow, its face glowing, ambled toward the temple, oblivious to the devastation caused by its absence due to its search for romance.

Cane Swami blanched.

Swish. Swish. Swish.

20

ON HIS WAY to deliver firewood, Chenda noticed unusual activities at the Military Hotel. A stranger on a bicycle was whispering to Kader. A few seconds later, Kader hand-signaled his workers to leave. They took the cooking utensils, pans, the big brass tea kettle, and glasses and rushed through the back door. The customers in the eatery also left in haste, and he closed the business abruptly.

"Kader Chettan, you're closing the hotel early. Why?" Chenda asked.

He answered Chenda's question with another question, "Where are you going?"

"To the Brahmin's enclave. I have to deliver firewood to two homes near the temple," Chenda answered, holding the handcart filled with firewood and the kettledrum fastened on top of it.

"Don't go there now. It is not safe," Kader said and left in a hurry. From the street corner, he saw a group of men armed with sticks, bicycle chains, scythes, and machetes charging toward the enclave with rows of homes on either side on the far north of the Amman Devi temple. That was all the signs Chenda needed to pull over the handcart and run to the Brahmin's enclave.

There was no time to knock on every door and warn the residents. So, Chenda banged the kettledrum ferociously, hoping the residents would hear his warning, "Leave. Please run." Chenda's strategy worked. Alerted by the panic-filled drumbeat, some people came to see what was happening. Noticing the gang with sickles, some ran outside the homes. They were chased and beaten.

And some residents locked the doors and hid inside. They were not that lucky.

The Muslim mob had formed two groups: one broke through the door with an ax and lathis while the other ran through the side street and entered the back porches.

Trapped and taken by surprise, women and children screamed "Rama...Rama" as bamboo sticks landed on their heads, shoulders, and legs. Men, who tried to defend themselves, let out strange earth-shattering noises as the sharp edge of knives and machetes slashed through their arms, legs, and torso. The attackers chanted "Allahu Akbar" as they beat men, women, and children, thrashed their beds, chairs, and tables, and flung their utensils far from the kitchen onto the street.

Cane-Swami was nowhere to be found. But his bed was pummeled into bits, and the widow suffered large blue bruises on her face. She sat in a corner, hunched in a fetal position, and wept.

"Don't beat me. I'm innocent," the widow pleaded with the men.

"Where's that bastard? Fake swami?" one man hollered.

"He left early morning. I don't know where he went," the widow said, shielding her face from further injury.

Chenda ran to Patti-Amma's house and shouted, "We should get out of this place. Right now. Let me carry your Mister."

Patti-Amma didn't mind that Chenda had entered her bedroom.

"Please hurry. Please. I'll carry Mister. We should leave before those Muslim thugs kill us."

"Where will we go?" Patti-Amma asked.

"I don't know. It is not safe. Those crazy Muslims have lathis, knives, and machetes."

"This is my house. I was married here. I'm not going anywhere else."

"Patti-Amma, please listen to me. It's not safe. We have to leave. Now!"

Hearing the approaching noise of the rucks, Patti-Amma's husband tapped on the wooden cot as if asking what's happening?

"They, the Muslims, are coming to kill us," Patti-Amma told her husband. "I knew something like this would happen. Crooked Cane-Swami! Crooked MLA!"

"Patti-Amma, there's no time to argue. Let's go. I'll take both of you to a safe place."

"We are not leaving my house. If we die, we die here. In this house. In my house." Patti-Amma was obstinate and fervently prayed, "Rama, Rama. Lord Rama, please save us."

Chenda, Patti-Amma, and her husband were shaken up by loud booms, one after another, that reverberated from the Amman Devi temple.

"Sounds like bombs," Chenda said.

"Are you sure?" Patti-Amma asked in shock.

"What else could it be? Let me check." Chenda, his heart pounding louder than the kettledrum, looked out and said, "They had bombed the temple."

A hundred footsteps darted off like a herd of wild buffalos stomping from the temple to the junction. They sprinted through a side street, passing Patti-Amma's house. Her house and the adjoining houses were spared. And Chenda heaved a sigh of nervous relief. At least for now.

"Stay put here, please," he urged Patti-Amma. "Don't go out, come what may. I'll be back soon. Go inside and lock the doors. Both front and back doors. Don't open them."

Chenda ran from Patti-Amma's house to the Amman Devi temple and abruptly stopped at first sight of its structure. The temple's dome was blown up as though someone had chopped off its head. The blasts also tore an enormous hole in the tall red-and-white-striped compound wall. Large chunks of concrete were strewn on the inner sanctum-sanctorum, and a large amount of debris had been scattered outside the temple's wall. The temple looked like a battered, bruised lady.

The residents were too petrified to come out of their homes.

Chenda ran back to the junction, sweating and gasping, without realizing that the hoodlums could beat him to pulp. Hiding behind the banyan tree, he searched for recognizable faces among the ravaging mob. There was no Kader. No Basheer. No Hassan. No Essa. No Ismail. All were strange faces. Hired hoodlums.

One man with a bamboo stick saw Chenda and yelled at him to come out of hiding. Chenda didn't budge, and the man charged at him and raised the bamboo stick that landed forcibly with a whack on his shoulder. Screaming and trembling, Chenda fell on the ground. Another man kicked him in the rib, sending him rolling on the side of M.G. Road.

Yelling "Death to Hindus" and "Allahu Akbar," the mob spread out in two groups and unleashed terror. One group targeted the Brahminal Hotel. Kuttan locked the front door from inside and told his customers and workers to run out through the backdoor. The front door was a ceremonial piece of wood, and one of the men could easily kick it wide open. Kuttan took a few blows before he fell unconscious, and a bench with food on banana leaves fell on him. Within minutes, the eatery was obliterated for the second time, beyond recognition.

Appu shouted a warning to tailor Gopi, Stephen, dancer Prabhu and other store owners, "Close your shops. They are coming after us."

They shuttered their stores and ran to the safety of the urine-reeked bushes behind their establishments.

Arul locked the gate to his coconut oil mill from inside and told his workers to grab pickaxes, spades, garden forks, and other farming tools. There were six workers. "If they break the gate and enter, kill those motherfuckers. No mercy," Arul instructed them.

His house was spared. It didn't suffer any severe damage except a scattering of stones on the roof.

They also slammed the medical store's closed doors, causing as much damage as possible. The Brighten Your Teeth With Monkey Brand Tooth Powder and the Build Your Muscles With Black Monkey Vitality Jelly signs remained intact at the store. The store owners and workers who didn't hide from them in time took the brunt of it. The hoodlums ransacked these stores. They tossed out soda bottles, glass candy jars, betel leaves, cigarette packets, and everything within their reach. The goods fell on the road with a shattering noise. The bananas and plantains hung in the stores became piñatas. The vendors who tried to run away were chased, beaten, or stabbed.

"Please don't kill me," one man pleaded. "This is not my paan shop. I work here. Please have mercy. I'm the only breadwinner in my family." Mob fury has no mercy. It didn't matter to them whether the victim was the breadwinner or not. Long sticks landed on his hands and chest. "Oh, my hand. Oh, my hand," he cried, holding the two fingers that were partly cut off when he tried to block a sharp knife. He tightly held the bloodied fingers with the other hand. He cried in utter shock than in pain, "Amme, amme."

The hooligans, satisfied with the havoc they had inflicted, fled on foot and on the bicycles they had hidden behind the Military Hotel. The junction was littered with stones, bricks, wood and glass pieces.

Soon after the rucks had subsided, Appu, Hassan, Gopi, Stephen, dancer Prabhu, and other store owners slowly came out of hiding.

"Ayyo! What's happening to our village?" screamed Hassan. "They destroyed this place."

"Unbelievable," commented Appu and walked toward Chenda, who was helping the man who had lost two fingers. He tore his hand towel and tied the man's fingers with it to contain the bleeding. The bandage first showed a red dot. It gradually mushroomed into a large blotch and soaked the bandage with blood.

"Muslim extremists attacked us," Chenda said. "I saw them coming and I hid behind the banyan tree. It lasted less than ten minutes but felt like two hours."

"I thought it would never end," Appu said and helped a man whose shoulder was severely bruised.

Mani came riding on a bicycle and told the man with the bleeding fingers, "Come. Sit on the handle bar. I'll take you to the Medical Hospital. You need to see a doctor."

Then, he asked Chenda, "You want me to take anyone else? One can sit on the luggage stand."

"Take him," Chenda said, motioning toward a man who tried to stop the bleeding in his head by pressing it with his hands. Mani rode his bicycle as fast as he could with two bloodied passengers.

Arul opened his Oil Mill Factory's gate, and his workers brought pails of well-water and gave them to the thirsty victims of the assault. His workers held on to the pickaxes, sickles, and knives.

Guru, hearing the screaming and seeing people run through the street, came out of his house cautiously, checked both sides of the street, and peered toward the junction. He saw a store clerk squatting on the street and blood oozing out of his neck. Without any hesitancy, Guru took his hand towel and wrapped it around the man's shoulder to stop the bleeding.

Women came looking for their husbands, fathers, brothers, or loved ones. One woman was accompanied by her two children, who trembled with fear and clung to their mother's sari. Another woman covered her young daughter's eyes so she wouldn't see blobs of blood, broken tiles, glasses, and stones scattered at the junction.

"Please go home," Chenda told them. "It is not safe. Those thugs might come back. Please go home."

Chenda, with a piece of coconut husk, scrubbed a pool of blood at the foot of Mahatma Gandhi's statue at the junction. He poured water and scrubbed forcefully, but the blood had coalesced and stuck like red chewing gum. After several attempts, he gave up and covered it with dirt.

Arul telephoned Vijayan, who alerted the IG and the Chief Minister.

The news of the attack spread quickly to other villages, the Secretariat, the government offices, and the businesses in the city. Immediately, men left their work and came in taxis to protect their families.

Mashe stayed home. "We don't know what the world has come to," he told his wife. She didn't respond. But they didn't stop their youngest daughter, Gauri, who made vadas and took them to the neighbor's terrified six-year-old son. The boy was trembling and crying after hearing about the riots from his mother.

BY LATE afternoon, Chenda saw the usual drill. First, three Jeeps with Sub-Inspectors and constables arrived. They were followed by a convoy of green military trucks with soldiers. Some carried long bamboo lathis, and some carried rifles with polished glittering bayonets. They took positions as they did in the past in the areas prone to violence. This time, a platoon of soldiers was stationed at various points in Brahmin's enclave. Sub-Inspectors drove around in their Jeeps and announced the government had declared a state of emergency in Alumaram Village. It also included another shoot-at-sight order and a dawn to dusk curfew.

"No one is allowed to leave his home unless it is an emergency," a Sub-Inspector reminded people through a bullhorn.

By now, it had become a routine, sort of, for the IG, the Chief Minister, Vijayan, and a horde of journalists who had come to the village during the past two communal riots. They surveyed the junction, spoke to a few anxious people, and drove straight to the Amman Devi temple. Chenda, the kettledrum still hanging from his shoulder, followed them from a distance.

The Chief Minister surveyed the temple, looked at the reporters, and thundered, "Horrific! This is the work of outsiders. I'm sure they were terrorists sent by Pakistan. We won't tolerate our enemies. We'll leave no stone unturned until we arrest the perpetrators and bring them to book." The reporters jotted down every word, and the lensmen took photos of the Chief Minister in front of the damaged temple.

Vijayan rehashed the speech he made during the attack on the mosque and the madrasa. This time, it was for attacking the temple.

"This is an unprovoked vicious attack," Vijayan said, his voice rising. "We won't let those cowards go scot-free. We'll catch and punish them."

In his long-winded flowery speech, Vijayan vowed to give "compensation for the victims—peace-loving, hard-working Hindus of Alumaram Village." He had already made copies of his speech and distributed them to reporters.

The temple priest, emboldened by the presence of police, the Chief Minister, and Vijayan, came to the temple. He was a puny, light-skinned man. He wore the ceremonial sacred thread that loosely hung diagonally from his left shoulder to under his right arm. He had drawn yellow fingerprints with sandal paste on his forehead, shoulders, and chest. He stared at the sanctum sanctorum and broke down, "Devi. Amman Devi. I never dreamed people would commit such a sacrilege."

The Chief Minister and Vijayan approached him, followed by the horde of reporters and photographers.

"I'm glad you are safe, poojari," the Chief Minister comforted him. "I'm relieved no one died."

The priest nodded and urged them to accompany him to the inner sanctum to assess the damage. The deity was covered in a heap of debris and dust. He removed the debris and wiped the dust off the deity with his hand towel. Then, he outstretched his hands and raised his voice, "Devi! You are intact. Not even a scratch on you. It's a miracle. I know no one can touch you. Devi, you are the protector of the village. The protector of the world."

He protracted full length with his arms outstretched and held them together as if saying namaste. He laid in that position perhaps for about five minutes. His body trembled as he sobbed. The Chief Minister and Vijayan imitated him by clasping their arms in prayers. So did the reporters and the photographers.

One of the reporters asked the priest, "How do you feel?"

"Terrible," he answered. "I never thought someone, anyone, would touch our temple. Our Devi."

"What will happen to the temple?"

"We will resume our poojas tomorrow morning. As usual."

The Chief Minister interjected. "I promise you, poojari," he said within the earshot of journalists. "We will repair the temple and make it bigger and better. It will have a taller dome."

Vijayan jumped in. "I'll work with the Chief Minister. The PPP—People's Power Party—in cooperation with other parties, to come up with government funding for the temple. We'll prove to them that we won't be intimidated."

Meanwhile, Chenda entered the temple's atrium, leading to the sanctum sanctorum. Seeing him, the priest whispered to Vijayan, who transmitted the message to the Sub-Inspector. The Sub-Inspector gestured for Chenda to stop, walked toward him, and said, "Sorry, you cannot enter the temple."

Chenda looked at him quizzically.

"Parayans are not allowed to enter the inner sanctum. You must leave."

"OK," Chenda said and stepped out of the atrium. His head drooping and face sallow, he went to the junction.

THE NEWSPAPERS' front pages carried a three-column photo of the Amman Devi temple that stood like a headless saint. Next to it was a photo of three men whose faces were covered with towels. The headline read, "3 men arrested for temple blast." The news story didn't include their names, ages, and whereabouts. The information and the photo, passed on by the police public relations officer, stated that their identities were not revealed because the incident was still under investigation.

Vijayan hung the front pages with his photos prominently in his office at the Secretariat as if they were his reelection banners.

An MLA from another party stopped by his office, saying, "Congratulations!"

"For what?" Vijayan asked and offered a Panama cigarette. The MLA took the cigarette, lit it, and laughed, "So, you pocketed the vote bank again, eh?"

"What are you talking about?"

"The temple attack is good news for you. Now, the Hindus will support you. You promised them money and whatnot."

"They deserve the money," Vijayan said and smiled.

DESPITE THE CURFEW, Mani quietly sold the arrack. The military personnel and police looked the other way as long as he conducted his business from far inside the side street near the marshland without drawing much attention. The law enforcement officials were interested in restoring normalcy— any form of normalcy—even if it meant tacitly allowing Mani to sell illicit liquor. Mani's presence, like a landmark, in that corner was a part of the village's norm.

The military's presence had a calming effect. Cane-Swami and his supporters of Hindu nationalists didn't retaliate. There were signs of an uneasy truce among the warring factions.

The military withdrew in stages after a week. But, two constables were stationed at the temple. They smoked beedis, chewed paan, and drank free chai from Brahminal Hotel and Military Hotel. A few days later, the police had called off patrolling the village and returned to the East Fort station.

THAT EVENING, Mani, at the end of his liquor business, sent Chenda to buy chicken curry and parotta. They sat on a dry patch under a coconut tree, poured two glasses of arrack, and began to enjoy their dinner. Chenda gulped down his drink in one swig, belched, and said, "See what Comrade Vijayan is doing—tearing apart our village. We must save the village and bring it back to its lost glory. Then only I can think of going to America."

Mani, his mouth full of food, replied, "Don't worry about the village. What will be, will be. You must pursue your dream. Get out of here and play your music in New York."

Chenda poured himself another drink from the jar without asking or waiting for Mani to finish his drink. Mani rarely got drunk. He wanted to stay sober so he wouldn't forget who drank on credit and how much. No one disputed his mental ledger. Being sober during the business had another advantage: He could run fast and escape through the narrow streets along marshland and the nearby orchards if the Flying Squad members came to raid his business.

He gulped down his drink and extended the glass for another round.

"Eda, go slow," Mani said and replenished his glass. When they finished eating the chicken curry and parotta, Chenda stared at his empty glass.

"Are you thinking of America?" Mani asked and curled his mustache.

"No," Chenda said. "I cannot think of America now. We've to stop these Hindu-Muslim riots. This shouldn't be happening here. In our village. This village is my home. This is the only home I know." His eyes became moist. And Mani filled Chenda's glass. "Drink slowly, in small sips. This one is for the road. No more arrack for you."

Chenda took a small gulp and wiped his tears.

"Are you crying?" Mani asked.

He didn't reply, and caressed the kettledrum as if comforting an inconsolable sibling and asked Mani, "Do you think we will celebrate Onam as we used to do? As one community?"

Mani moved closer to Chenda. Like a big brother comforting his distraught little brother, he explained. "The caste and the religion stuff are a big joke. Do you know who all come here to drink? High caste. Low caste. Hindus. Muslims. Christians. They all drink from the same glass and eat spicy mango pickles with their fingers from the same bottle. Tell me, where is discrimination? Ha! There is no caste and religion when it comes to liquor. Ha... ha... ha! If I stopped my business for a week, they would feel miserable. Did you know that?"

Chenda smirked at the irony of it.

"I got them by their balls," Mani said, and curled his mustache with pride and laughed. "I can squeeze their balls and make them suffer by denying them arrack. If everyone drank, the entire world would be one big, happy family."

"You are joking?"

"No. I'm not."

He looked at Mani quizzically and, after a pause, extended his glass for another drink.

"You had enough," Mani said and refused to give him another drink. But Chenda offered to pay for it.

"Don't insult me," Mani admonished Chenda. "Have I ever demanded money from you? You can hardly stand up. What's wrong with you?"

Chenda extended the glass again as if begging for more liquor, forcing a wicked smile.

Mani shook his head mockingly, poured a half glass of arrack, and said, "Eda, Chenda. The whole world is screwed up. You cannot change it. Drink slowly. Very slowly."

Chenda took a sip and asked, "Do you think there will be the tiger dance, music, and the Onam play? You know, Stephen's uncle with a big belly always played Mahabali. The Brahmin boy with a long ponytail was the Vamanan. Hassan loved to recite the story of Mahabali's visit. I would play the *chenda*, that too, solo on the stage. People always clapped at the end. How nice?"

"Now, you are blabbering. That's what drunks do. Talk. Talk. Talk gibberish."

Mosquitoes buzzed around them, and frogs croaked mating calls.

"Eda, let us go," Mani said. "It is too late. I'll take you to Patti-Amma's house."

"Mani Chettan, I don't need your help. I can walk."

Chenda struggled to stand up, and Mani held him by his hip so he wouldn't fall.

"I'll take you home. Don't make a big scene; cops are there…at that corner."

They walked through a side street to Patti-Amma's back porch. And Chenda hummed:

"Ulagae Maayam, Vaazhve Maayam."

"The world is an illusion, Life is an Illusion."

21

CHENDA CHOPPED the firewood with an unusual vigor as if he had eaten the gooey substance featured in the "Build Your Muscles With Black Monkey Vitality Jelly" advertisement at the medical store. He raised the ax above his shoulder, stretched his body as long as he could, and brought the ax down with a heavy force, ostensibly taking his frustration on the firewood.

"I shouldn't have told Vijayan to run for office," Chenda muttered. "I created a monster."

Each chop of the ax was like a stab at his guilt. Usually, after about fifteen minutes of intense labor, Chenda would take a brief break to smile at the curious children. But today, he was on a wood-chopping spree, like a machine without a break. Chop…chop…chop!

Halfway through chopping, he stopped abruptly, dusted his chest and shoulder with the towel he had wrapped around his head, and told the lady of the house that he would be back later to complete the job. "You've got enough firewood for the next couple of days," he told her.

He returned the handcart and the ax to the lumber yard and set out to confront Vijayan. He went to Patti-Amma's back porch and took the white long-sleeved shirt and his only white mundu from the rusty metal trunk. He put them on, wrapped the checkered towel around his head, and walked to the Secretariat. He timed that he could reach the Secretariat within forty minutes.

Chenda wiped the sweat on his face a few times with the towel and hurried to the Statue area where the Secretariat was located. The rumble in his stomach reminded him that he didn't eat lunch. It was as if hundreds of red fire ants gnawing his stomach, begging aloud, *Feed us...feed us*. He felt the hunger that slowly pushed more blood into his brain and messed up his thoughts. That explains why people struggle to think clearly when they are hungry. Hunger was not new to Chenda, and he searched for a municipal street water pipe tap on the way.

"Is there any water pipe?" he asked a man.

"You see, the Sree Murugan temple there? Up the hill? There's a water pipe," the man said.

Chenda didn't mind the detour as long as he could find the water tap. He folded his mundu, bent under the water tap with an S-shaped hand pump, pushed the pump with one hand, cupped the other hand to catch water, and filled his stomach. He let out a loud belch, washed his face, and said he was not hungry anymore. At least for now.

The main gate to the Secretariat, where laws were made and broken, was adorned with posters and placards. There were makeshift tarpaulin tents set up by perennial protesters. For them, it was a temporary job with free meals. Inside the tents were straw mats for party workers to sit or nap when they got tired after shouting slogans. Hanging above one tent was a wide banner that read, "Fast unto death to stop government corruption and nepotism."

None of the strikers had died of hunger because they rarely skipped meals. When the fast-unto-death leader felt hungry, he would wink at his supporters. Soon, one of them would sit in his place as a decoy so the leader could slip to his room in MLA Quarters and feast on chicken curry and appam or biriyani catered to his room. The rumor has it that one leader gained weight during his fast-unto-death strike.

There was another gimmick. If a leader literally went on a fast-unto-death strike and his health deteriorated, his supporters would issue statements that the government had agreed to meet their demands. Then the leader would end the hunger strike by drinking lemonade in front of reporters, followed by a rousing victory speech.

Always there were protests in front of the Secretariat: Demands for higher wages, bigger Onam bonuses, promotion, equality, and justice. Even the ruling party's supporters would stage a rally for a cause before other opposition parties could seize that opportunity.

The Secretariat is huge. It can hold at least one hundred mud huts. The front lawn is large enough to house another fifty huts, Chenda thought. The white structure was beautified and pampered as if it was the queen building of Kerala. It was either to intimidate people or inspire awe, and garner respect for the bastion of power.

He passed through the Secretariat's tall wrought-iron gate, admiring the sprawling, well-manicured front lawn. Bushes were trimmed to the images of fawns, peacocks, and ducks to make the lawn a special tourist attraction. It was like the spruced-up facade of a brothel.

"Where is Comrade Doctor MLA Vijayan's office?" Chenda asked a gardener who was wearing an oversized khaki shirt and a lungi. The gardener pointed out to the eastern wing of the building.

Chenda removed his towel wrapped around his head and put it on his shoulder out of respect for the house of lawmakers.

He waited on the well-manicured lawn, despite the high humidity and scorching sun, wondering whether he should confront the comrade or leave it to the villagers to question him. *Why should I be the one to take the MLA to the task? How should I tell him to stop the brutal game? Yell at him? Should I look serious? Smile? Should I wish him namaste?*

The gardener stopped spraying water from a long black hose tied with strips of clothes in several spots to block leaks. Again, he motioned with his hand at Chenda in the direction of the MLA offices. He thought the gardener's gesture was a good omen and walked toward Vijayan's office.

The Secretariat's hallway with a high ceiling was intimidating—the same nervousness he experienced at the United States Information Agency. He stopped in front of an office with a hanging metal sign: MLA Vijayan, People's Power Party. Like a security guard, a peon was sitting on a wooden stool and reading a newspaper near the door. He looked at Chenda and puckered his forehead as if asking, *What do you want?* And buried his head in the newspaper's headlines.

"I want to speak with Comrade Doctor MLA Vijayan."

"About what?" the peon asked.

"It is personal," Chenda said.

"The MLA may want to know," the peon said, raising his head slightly above the newspaper to look at him.

Chenda stared at the peon who had the body language and the arrogance of a politician in the making.

"I'll explain it to the MLA, not you," Chenda asserted.

The peon was taken aback by Chenda's curt response. Unlike other visitors who came to curry favors, Chenda was resolute and not submissive. No more questions. His muscular physique might have something to do with the peon's change of heart. He informed the comrade was on lunch break for a siesta in the MLA Quarters. He gave the directions to the building, which was about a ten-minute walk from the Secretariat. Chenda left without heeding the peon's warning that the MLA shouldn't be disturbed during his siesta.

The MLA Quarters, an old house modified into a men's hostel with several single bedrooms, sat like an unseemly abode for power-wielding, flamboyant politicians. A ceiling fan whirred in the red-tiled rectangular lobby. There were three doors: One led to the office room, another to the MLAs' rooms, and the third to the dining hall where the elected officials ate subsidized breakfast, lunch, and dinner. There were a dozen hand-woven straw chairs for visitors.

The curry smell from the kitchen wafted into the lobby, blending with the lingering whiff of beedi and cigarette. The mix of those two different smells made Chenda cough.

"Do you have an appointment with comrade?" asked the receptionist, a middle-aged man who sported neatly combed oily hair, a thin mustache, and no beard.

"No. I don't have an appointment."

"Then you've to wait. We have clear instructions not to wake up MLAs."

"This is urgent," Chenda replied.

"I've heard this a hundred times. I cannot disturb the MLA. Sorry."

It was not a long wait. Vijayan, wearing a banyan and a lungi, was going to the dining hall for chai and vadas when he saw Chenda.

"What a surprise! It's nice to see you," Vijayan said. His hair was disheveled, and his banyan was crumpled. He gestured with his hand to Chenda to the dining hall.

"Come, come. Let's have chai," Vijayan said, and showed two fingers to the server. "What brings you here?"

For a moment, Chenda was carried away by Vijayan's friendliness and hospitality. Chenda's smile vanished as soon as he realized that Vijayan was acting dumb.

"I'm not hungry," he said.

"Eda, don't be ashamed to eat. They make good vadas here. Eat a couple."

Chenda didn't reply. His hungry stomach said "yes" and eat as many vadas as he could. But his brain said "no" and prevailed.

"I want to talk about the riots in the village," Chenda said, his voice stern and furious.

"The Muslim-Hindu conflict?" Vijayan asked. "It is all a big conspiracy by the CIA and other parties. Our opponents, you know. They want to blame our PPP, destroy us."

"I don't believe you."

"Trust me when I say the CIA is involved in it," Vijayan said. "They pay black money to party leaders to create mayhem in our country. Americans won't let us prosper. I learned a lot about the CIA after becoming an MLA."

The server brought two plates of vadas and two cups of chai in two steel tumblers.

"Eat," Vijayan urged. "I thought you came to remind me about your Indian passport and the U.S. visa. I didn't forget it."

"Not interested in the passport and visa."

"What?"

"Right now, we have to save our village. Too much Hindu-Muslim enmity," Chenda blurted out in a loud voice. "My American trip can wait."

"OK. Why are you angry at me?"

"You… you are destroying the village. You're tearing apart the community."

"Calm down, calm down," Vijayan said. "You don't have to raise your voice. What you're talking about?"

Tears trickled down Chenda's face, which he wiped with the towel. His lips quivered. Words were jumbled up in his brain like the mixed vegetables in aviyal curry. "I know you and the snake Cane-Swami are pitting one group against another."

"What nonsense?"

Chenda took a long breath and, in a stern, measured voice, said, "I know that you set Muslims against Hindus, and then Hindus against Muslims. You told the Cane-Swami to attack the madrasa. Comrade, you have changed."

"It's all a big nonsense," Vijayan yelled. "Eda, don't spread lies."

"These are not lies, Comrade Doctor Vijayan. I saw you give money to Cane-Swami. I was delivering firewood to his neighbor. I saw the whole thing."

Vijayan turned red, stood up, folded his lungi up to the knee, pointed his finger at Chenda, and yelled, "Shut up! Enough! You… rascal… you will pay for this. No one talks to me like this. Do you know who I am?" He answered his own question. "I'm an MLA. Member of the Legislative Assembly. Not a parayan handcart puller, like you. How dare you... you... a wayward low caste man to accuse me of this? I've done a lot for the village."

Neither of them spoke for the next few tense moments. They stared at each other in disgust.

After a pause, Vijayan said, "Eda! The money was a loan for him. He will reimburse me with interest."

Chenda didn't respond.

Vijayan continued, "Alumaram residents know the good things I've done for them. I'm building a hospital for them. Did you know that? The whole area will see a huge development. It will look entirely different in a few years. It is going to look like Trivandrum City. You will be surprised."

Chenda replied, "We know it. The hospital development is next to your dowry property in Marakana, not in Alumaram Village. Your property value will go up at least one hundred times."

Furious that Chenda knew much about his personal affairs, Vijayan moved closer to Chenda within striking reach. Vijayan's cigarette-laced breath made Chenda cough.

"That is a lie," Vijayan retorted. "You are good at spreading rumors. You are too dangerous. No wonder the *chenda* groups don't want to include you."

Chenda wiped the sweat on his face with the towel and hesitatingly said, "I'm not the only one to know this. Our Appu, Guru, Gopi, and Mani know this. They talk behind you. They don't have the guts to tell to your face."

"So, you... a parayan... think you have the guts. We will kick you out of this place," Vijayan screamed. Hearing the ruckus, a server rushed toward Chenda, raised his hand, and was poised to hit him.

"Get out of this place. Right now. You are a mother-fucking parayan. Get out before I kick you out," Vijayan barked at Chenda and gestured at the server. On cue, the server pushed him. Chenda lost balance and tried to hold on to a table and then to a chair. He fell on the floor with a thud like a jackfruit falling from a tree.

"Get out…get out. Now!" the server screamed at Chenda.

The server pushed Chenda toward the door with a warning, "Eda, never set foot here. We'll break your legs. Don't ever mess with MLAs."

DAZED, CHENDA stepped outside the MLA Quarters. He dusted off his shirt and mundu with the towel. He massaged his right shoulder to alleviate a piercing pain—the result of the bruise suffered from the fall. The afternoon humidity was merciless. Drops of sweat formed on his forehead, chest, and his back. Two mosquitos flew around his forehead, trying to quench their thirst with his blood. He swatted them with his hand towel, wiped the sweat again, and wandered as if pulled by the strings of powerlessness.

Helpless, like a zombie, Chenda wandered awhile. He realized he had reached Shankhumugham Beach when he felt the chill of the Arabian Sea breeze. The waves frolicked in gentle ripples, humming the song of love and peace. Young boys and girls collected seashells of different sizes and textures as souvenirs from the pristine beach with white sand resembling granulated wheat. Long stretches of tall coconut trees, vying to tower over each other, swayed. Far away on the horizon, the sun gradually descended into the Arabian Sea:

First shedding its blistering rays for a soothing hue of orange rays, then adding a coating of red and a golden glow, putting up a show as it slid down to the serenity in the abyss of the ocean. Claude Monet would have been in rapture with his canvas and brush.

Agitated over the sun's retreat for the day, the waves threw a temper tantrum—rolling and pounding and mercilessly whipping the shoreline. In the twilight, the waves gained strength. They became boisterous and vicious, fighting like rowdy teenagers to display their destructive force. An anomaly, not far from the beach, serenely sat the Trivandrum Aerodrome.

How does one fly from here to America? The plane has to stop at several big cities to fill petrol, Chenda thought and rubbed his face with his hands as he stood near the fence around the runway. About a dozen tourists peered through the fence, looking for signs of an airplane or any activity. A big white mansion with two floors served as the aerodrome's terminal. Perched on top of the building was a glass box—the air traffic control room. A wide concave antenna slowly circled three-hundred and sixty degrees on the roof. The humongous aircraft he had seen during his previous visits was not there. Instead, a small plane with two seats and a propeller that resembled a giant ceiling fan attached to its nose was taxied near the hangar.

The onlookers perked up when a man in a pair of white trousers, a white long-sleeved shirt, and a necktie boarded the aircraft. Soon the giant fan whirred, and the plane began to move on the runway, took off, and flew up…up…in the sky.

"Wonderful!" Chenda said to no one in particular.

But a boy, who wore eyeglasses and a watch, was not impressed. "This is a small plane," he complained to his father.

"Yes, son. This plane belongs to the Royal Flying Club of Trivandrum. I don't know when the big plane comes."

Chenda interrupted their conversation, "The big plane had already left. It comes at eleven in the morning and leaves at four in the afternoon. It has eight windows on both sides and two huge fans."

The boy stared at Chenda as if questioning his knowledge.

"I know it. I come here often to watch the big plane land and take off. It's fascinating," Chenda said and made a hand motion of the plane landing and taking off.

"How big is it?" the boy asked.

"Very big. It can carry two elephants."

"Why is the aerodrome near the beach?"

The boy's father interjected, "Son, it is easy to land and take off. No buildings to hamper the flight."

"Oh, I see."

Still, Chenda, the boy, and others peered through the long fence around the aerodrome erected to prevent dogs, cows, and buffalos from straying into the runway. However, a dog would sneak through the fence, strut around the runway with its head up, and pee at the pole with a long, fluttering windsock painted with black and white horizontal circles. The balloon's movement indicated the wind's direction to the air traffic controller. The tourists looked at the runaway again, hoping an errant plane would land.

Please take me out of here on the big plane. Chenda prayed silently to all Gods of all religions, as he had done several times before. *I'll do anything to go to New York. Play the music at Carnegie Hall. I'll beg the pilot to take me with him whenever the plane comes. I would promise to cook for him and clean his house and the airplane. I'll play the chenda for free for passengers.*

There was no sign of the drone of the big airplane.

Balloon vendors, peanut hawkers, and visitors left, carrying their tired children on their shoulders to the KSRTC bus stop. A mosquito bite reminded Chenda that it was time to leave the beach.

22

WHEN YOU don't have a home, you might wander around to escape from loneliness until you get tired. That's exactly what Chenda did. From the airport, his feet took him to Veli, then to the city via the renowned Sree Padmanabhaswami Temple. The West Fort, one of the four built around the parameters of the four directions of the temple, was a harbinger of the renowned Hindu house of worship. The fifteen-foot tall fort would receive a facelift in preparation for the Arattu procession. Within days after Arattu, the fort would be defaced with new movie posters and political slogans.

Chenda passed West Fort and reached East Fort, facing the city. He stood spellbound by the intricate sculptures in the stunning temple tower. He unfolded his mundu, prostrated on the dirt floor, outstretched his arms, and silently prayed to Sree Padmanabhaswami for peace and prosperity in the village. Not for an Indian passport and a U.S. visa. He appeared to be a speck from the tip of the two-hundred-and-ten-foot tall temple tower ornate with exquisite sculptures of Hindu themes. Reportedly built in the eighth century, the temple was the anchor around which the City of Trivandrum grew, just as the Alumaram Village evolved around the banyan tree.

Chenda's lips moved as he prayed, "Lord Padmanabha, please bring peace to the village." His eyes swelled with a roller-coaster of emotions.

The hustle and bustle in East Fort tapered and became desolate at this hour, except for the bats on the nearby trees and a few KSRTC's local green buses waiting to take late-night commuters home. A mile-long Chala Bazaar across East Fort, which buzzed with merchants and customers haggling over prices, was getting ready to shutter the stores and retire for the day. Homeless men waited impatiently for these stores to close so they could sleep on the stores' long concrete steps.

Chenda found himself walking to the Central Railway Station, not far from East Fort. He snuck into the railway station through a broken fence to avoid buying a platform ticket. Unlike the vacant airport, the railway station was busy with passengers and their relatives and friends who had come to send them off. There was only one platform but long enough to accommodate two trains—on the western end stood the departing train, and on the eastern end stood the train that had just arrived.

And the Madras Mail was preparing for departure.

In red shirts and towels wrapped around their heads, Porters carried suitcases, metal trunks, and gunny bags for passengers. Once you set foot in the railway station with a piece of luggage, you had to hire a porter despite its small size and weight.

Curious teenagers checked out the wooden seats and dark fans with spider webs in the train's compartments; grown-up relatives offered unsolicited safety tips to passengers. Adding to the hullabaloo were vada, idli, tamarind rice, chai, and coffee vendors. Two boys, in knickers and no shirts, slapped their skinny stomachs as if they were percussions and sang heart-breaking two-liners from movies. Their favorite was the song from the 1951 Tamil movie *Samsaram:*

"*Amma pasikuthe, Thaye pasikuthe.*"

"Mother, (I'm) hungry. Momma, (I'm) hungry."

Some passengers would give five or ten paise to silence their annoying music. And some, weary of their own sad songs, would look away.

The steam engine, a black monster tube heavier than Balan's elephant, let out an ear-shattering hissing and whistle. It gave new meaning to the phrase "let out the steam." A laborer in khaki pants and a red bandana shoveled coal into the flaming hot pit inside the engine. The assistant engineer smoked a cigarette and checked the engine's wheels. A black towel was tucked into the waist band of his navy-blue pants. The train's Chief Engineer, a six-foot, burly man with bushy whiskers, watched the activities on the platform. All three had tanned faces from constant coal flames and traces of soot on their necks. Like VIPs, they seemed to enjoy the attention of onlookers. The Chief Engineer said something in English to the assistant engineer. These conversations were a new experience for the curious onlookers. They had learned to read and write English in school, but their English-speaking skills were limited to reciting the memorized line: "*To be, or not to be: that is the question.*"

He wanted to ask the Chief Engineer whether the train would go to America. But he lacked the courage. He didn't want to be laughed at by the Anglo-Indian Chief Engineer.

CHENDA WAS fascinated to see a young woman clinging to her husband's hand at the railway station. The husband was sitting near the window of a train compartment. Both were on the verge of crying. Others stood a few feet away so the newlyweds could spend intimate moments before the Madras Mail chugged away with the husband.

"Please send a telegram as soon as you reach Madras," the woman kept reminding him. The man said "yes" and assured her he would whisk her to Madras once he rented a house. "I promise it will be soon. I promise." She quickly took his hand and slyly planted a kiss on it. Others pretended as if they didn't notice the public display of affection.

The station master blew a long whistle—a signal to the Chief Engineer to fire up the engine. The Chief Engineer climbed on the engine's operating cubicle and waved at the station master, who blew the whistle again. The Chief Engineer responded by blowing the train's whistle. It was the time-keeper for the neighboring homes without clocks.

The station master waved a green flag, and the engine moved forward with a chug. Then another chug. And another. The enormous wheels of the machine effortlessly chugged the compartments, followed by another whistle. Teary-eyed, the woman waved at her husband.

Chenda sat on a wooden bench and watched the train vanish under a bridge.

The visitors and vendors had left the platform. The porters disappeared. And the long platform became empty. No hustle, no bustle, and depressingly quiet. He felt a familiar feeling creeping in—a blend of melancholy and loneliness. There would be no one to send him off to America or receive his telegram about his safe landing in the strange country.

He leaned on the bench, tired and forlorn. He didn't realize that he had fallen asleep until he was awakened by two packs of stray dogs barking at each other to claim the rail yard. With tails raised, the packs' leaders snarled and gnashed their sharp, yellow teeth at each other. The more ferocious group pushed back the other pack. The retreating pack regrouped and launched an offensive. Loud barking and gnashing ensued. The back-and-forth see-saw attack and retreat abruptly ended when the leader of one pack bit its opponent's face. The injured leader growled, whimpered, and strode away with its followers in tow. The same brutal scenes would be played out the next night as both packs fought to dominate the territory as had been happening in the village.

A GIANT CLOCK with Roman numerals at the railway station chimed twelve times. Chenda's stomach growled again. *Feed me. Feed me.* He dusted off his shirt with the towel, drank water from the city pipe on the platform, and walked out of the railway station. The railway station and the adjacent long-distance red-bus terminal were well-lit but were empty. The paan, fruit, chai, and juice vendors had closed their tin-roofed shops and had already gone to their thatched homes. The red buses, after their marathon run in and out of the city from dawn to dusk, were parked helter-skelter. The drivers knew exactly where they had parked the buses. It was a well-organized disorganization.

Half-heartedly, Chenda braced for the six-mile walk back to Alumaram Village. The road further down was swathed in darkness. It would be at least one mile before the Kerala State Electricity Board's light appeared. A lone, long wooden lamp post emitted tired yellow light from a sixty-watt bulb. Flies and mosquitos flew around the yellow light as if enjoying a midnight rendezvous. In villages, only the main junctions had electric lamp posts—a sign of human inhabitation. Chenda, guided by mud huts that were sporadically located on the street as landmarks, trod cautiously on the gravel road to Alumaram Village.

His legs were slow—no need to hurry. No one was waiting for him. None to ask why he was late, laugh, or cry with him. "Why? I'm a parayan. A black. I'm a mother-fucking black parayan!" Startled by his scream, frogs leaped from one ditch to another in the rice fields, followed by a rustle.

"I don't care if Comrade Doctor MLA Vijayan kills me," he screamed again. "He is a crook. A rotten crook. Why did I tell him to run for office? God, forgive me." Exhausted, he sank down on the road, held his hands on his face, and wept bitterly. When there were no more tears to shed, he wiped the dry tear marks on his face with the hand towel and walked wherever his feet took him.

Strangely, you can somehow find your way even in the pitch dark. You develop a sixth sense and a feel for the direction you have frequently traversed.

Chenda spotted the yellow streetlight at the junction, thanks to the Electric Engineer who plugged the porcelain socket into the lamp post in the evening. Despite the frequent flickering, the light in the lamppost was like a beacon, guiding the village's location to pedestrians and handcart pullers.

He walked the unpaved path on the steep hill past a few mud houses with thatched roofs. Some homes' frontage had been converted into make-shift stores and were closed with wooden planks. And men slept on the wooden counter that jetted out of the store. Some slept on bare coir-cots outside their homes. Old newspapers became bedsheets. And the checkered lungi they wore in the day became the blanket to protect them from the early morning dew and dust. They rested their heads on their hands and breathed through their tired mouths. It was then he heard the noise he had heard often. A rumble. It took a couple of seconds for him to realize the source of the rumble was his empty stomach. The rumble became louder. And frequent.

A patch of green on a narrow lane between two homes had the remedy to pacify his stomach. The area was protected by a crudely-made wire fence with sharp edges. He tip-toed toward the fenced-in area, kneeled and carefully slipped his hand, and pulled a tapioca plant. He was not alone in stealing food. A bandicoot darted from among the plants, startled by the rustle created by Chenda when he pulled out a tapioca plant. With one tapioca in hand, he quickly left the narrow lane, broke its crunchy root-vegetable in one snap, peeled its rind, and took a bite. And another bite to quiet the rumble. He licked the sweet taste of the tapioca on his lips. It felt sweeter. *Stolen food tastes better than the food you bought at hotels.*

CHENDA stood in front of Patti-Amma's back porch, not eager to go inside. He knew Patti-Amma didn't sleep much, and she would be awake. He sat on the steps, looked at the stars, and felt sorry for them. The sun and the moon can escape from east to west, but the stars don't. They had to sit in the same spot in the sky night after night and watch people kill each other.

He didn't want to bother Patti-Amma. A glass of arrack would be good now. *Just a glass of arrack would do,* he thought. He entered the back porch, took his kettledrum, and walked through the narrow lane to the marshland. The moon peeped between thick clouds to see what was happening below. That's all the light Chenda needed to locate the snakeskins Mani had sprinkled—a clue to where the arrack bottles were hidden. Chenda bent his knees and dropped his hand into the swamp to feel the jars. He pulled out one jar, wiped its mouth with the towel, and took a long swig.

He sat down and took another swig. He didn't need the spicy mango pickle in the thick glass with yellow round stains. With every swig, he could feel the acrid potion going down his mouth like hot, red lava spewed by a furious volcano. He didn't know how long he sat there drinking until he almost finished the jar and felt an urge to throw up.

He tried to get up, but felt his head spinning like a cartwheel. He held on to the kettledrum but lost balance and fell. After three or four tries, he got up again using the kettledrum for support, staggered, and fell again. He lay there for a while and slowly leaned on the mud wall near the marshland. He stretched his hand to pull out another jar, but his hands had become limp like a wilted leaf. He struggled to stand up. He put the kettledrum on the ground and sat on it as if it was a make-shift stool. He heard footsteps and slowly turned to look at the noise. All he could see were two blurred images. He rubbed his eyes and screwed them up for a better look despite the darkness and intoxication.

"Mani Chettan, is it you?"

No response.

"Who are you?" he yelled. His voice was slurred. "What do you want?"

Two men, partly obscured in the dark, emerged. One of them kicked the kettledrum, which slid, dislodging Chenda, who landed with a thud. The kettledrum rolled over, and Chenda stretched his hand to grab it. But the man kicked it again with such a force it went airborne and tumbled and rolled over and landed in the marshland, splashing water. In the impact, the kettledrum's leather head was torn open, leaving a gaping hole. "Oh, my *chenda*," he cried.

"Get up," the man ordered him. "Get up, you motherfucker."

With both hands planted on the dirt, his face thrust forward, shoulders bent, Chenda got up.

"You… bloody peacemaker," the other man said. His voice spewed hatred, and he thrust a sharp object into Chenda's stomach. He pulled it out and jabbed it again. Two stabs in quick succession near the same spot.

"Ayyo, Dhyvame!" Chenda cried and held his stomach, blood oozing out of his stomach. It was sticky and warm on a cold night.

"Oh, yeah! God will help you. Keep praying. You stupid parayan," the man shouted.

Chenda made a strange noise and breathed heavily. He gagged and coughed. His stomach made a loud rumble triggered by the arrack whirling in his stomach. He leaned on a nearby mud wall, held the bleeding wound with one hand, and covered his mouth with the other hand. It was too late. A putrid yellow fluid and bits of tapioca gushed out from his stomach like water spurting from the hand-pumped street pipe at the junction. "Aargh," he uttered. With each violent motion of vomiting, more blood spurted from the wound. Blood spread all over his mundu. He tried to stop the bleeding with his hand towel, which quickly was soaked in blood. Then he heard another surge in the stomach like the non-stop thrashing waves at the beach. "Aargh." He didn't realize how many times he threw up. Finally, the vomiting stopped, but the motion of throwing up, followed by a loud growling noise, continued. Holding the stab wound with one hand, Chenda searched for the kettledrum with the other hand as if performing a high-wire act. He lost his balance and fell, hitting his head on the gravel near the marshland. He heard the men laughing and the rustling of the leaves.

"Who are you? Why did you stab me?" he yelled. There was no fear in his voice, only confusion.

There was no reply. There was only the silence of the village trying to sleep, interrupted by croaking frogs, buzzing mosquitos, and the howling wind. They sounded like the wailing and shrieking of frightened villagers escaping from the marauding Muslims and Hindus.

Chenda looked around. In the dark, no one was visible. He lurched and hit the ground as if someone had pushed him again. He got up and stepped forward by moving his body sideways for balance and then another step like a child learning to walk. He looked around and yelled, "Who are you?" The blurred two images quickly vanished, and the sound of their footsteps faded into darkness. Fireflies played hide-and-seek among the tall coconut and banana trees that stood as silent spectators.

"Are you trying to kill me?" he yelled again. No answers. Soon, he was zigzagging without realizing that his legs were taking him to the Alumaram River. With a slur, cupping his bleeding wound with a hand, he sang incoherently:

"Ulagae Maayam, Vaazhve Maayam."

"The world is an illusion, Life is an Illusion."

23

APPU, ON HIS WAY from the police station to the Secretariat to inform Vijayan about Chenda's death, realized that pushing the bicycle's pedal, especially with elephantiasis on one leg, was as hard as pulling a handcart. He panted while climbing the steep road to the Post Office Junction near his destination. The summer heat and humidity didn't make the ride easier. Appu sweated profusely, and his shirt clung to his body, which had become sticky.

Even though he had passed by the Secretariat umpteen times, this was his first visit inside the complex. He was enamored by the stately elegance of the sprawling white structure.

Many visitors unfolded their mundus and stood up in reverence whenever they saw an MLA or a former MLA, who was dethroned by the new brand of Young Turks.

Appu walked through a long row of offices with swing doors, looking for Vijayan as if searching for a designated seat on a train. The peon was reading a Malayalam magazine. Seeing Appu, he peered over the magazine and asked, "What do you want?" Politeness was, and is, crossed out of the political lexicon.

"I want to speak with Comrade Vijayan."

"He is busy. Who are you?"

"I'm Appu. Tell him barber Appu from Alumaram Village is here to see him."

"Why?" the peon asked and stared at Appu's bulging right leg.

"Someone important died, and I want Vijayan to know it."

"Comrade Doctor MLA Vijayan," the peon corrected him.

"Yes, Comrade Doctor MLA Vijayan!"

"Who died?"

"Someone important."

"The MLA is in a meeting, and he may want to know who died. He doesn't want to be disturbed because some beggar died." Even the government peon, watchman, gardener, and ground sweeper exuded an aura of superiority they developed over the years by breathing the political power of the Secretariat.

"He is not a beggar," Appu was curt as if the peon had insulted a family member. There was no time to waste. Chenda's body might decompose. Flies had already begun to swirl around the body when Appu left the Alumaram River. Losing patience, Appu raised his voice, "His name is Chenda. Please tell the comrade that Appu is here. It's urgent."

"Oh! I think he was here yesterday. Please wait here," the peon said and gestured Appu to sit on a bench next to his wooden stool. "The MLA is attending a committee meeting. I will inform him right now."

Appu looked around the Secretariat: The rooms had high ceilings, large windows, fans, and electric lights. Men patiently waited to seek favors from elected officials, and peons fetched chai, coffee, and vadas for their bosses. Appu couldn't help recalling how quickly Vijayan's fortune had changed after his election.

APPU STOOD up out of respect as soon as he saw Vijayan, who had developed the swagger of a seasoned politician. While walking, he held the tip of his handloom mundu and swayed the other hand. His white handloom shirt failed to hide his new paunch, and his eyes sparkled with the confidence he had gained after the election. The peon, who followed him, carried a brown leather briefcase and a stack of files fastened with rubber bands.

"Come in, come in," Vijayan said as he pushed the swing doors to his office and signaled the peon to bring two cups of chai. "Long time, no see," he said and lit a Panama cigarette, an upgrade from smoking beedis.

He took another puff from his Panama cigarette, looked at the photos in his office, and complained, "Career politicians from other parties are ruining this country. Those rascals are destroying our lovely village."

Appu was astounded to hear such foul language coming out of Vijayan. Finally, he made eye contact with Appu and asked, "Good to see you. Who died?"

"Chenda."

Vijayan deadpanned, became quiet, and slumped in his mahogany chair behind a long teak desk. He stroked his chin while Appu sat straight in a straw chair in front of the table. There were three more chairs for guests. More chairs for guests meant the more prominent you are. Chairs are the status symbols like the medals on a military uniform.

Behind Vijayan's chair on the wall were the photos of him with the Chief Minister of Kerala and other MLAs. Stacked on a corner were his election posters of the blue rocket and placards, "People's Power Party Zindabad" and "V for Victory." Chenda's fingerprints were clearly visible on these posters and signs.

Appu waited for some reaction from Vijayan. There was pin-drop silence. The silence of shock? The silence of grief? The silence was disrupted by the squeak of the swing door by the peon, who brought chai in two stainless steel tumblers.

"Drink, please," Vijayan said. "How did he die?"

"I don't know. It looks like he was stabbed. There are big gashes in his stomach. And a few cuts and bumps in his head."

"He gets into trouble unnecessarily," Vijayan said, his voice echoing frustration. "I don't know why he poked his nose in Hindus' and Muslims' affairs. I guess he wanted to be a peace-maker. Those bloody Muslims might have done it. Or Christians. They get tons of black money from Persia and the Pope to convert Hindus. There are a lot of fanatics, you know. Chenda could have married a parayan girl, settled in one of the hamlets, and be a happy family man."

Appu was quiet and massaged his right leg to alleviate the pain induced by the long bicycle ride.

Vijayan sighed and asked, "When did he die?"

"We don't know. Cross-toed Ammu found the body under the bridge this morning."

"This morning?"

"Yes. The body is still under the bridge. We didn't touch it."

Again, a pause. Vijayan lit another Panama and said, "He came to see me yesterday, you know. He wanted me to help him go to America. I told him I would try my best and asked him to see me after a week. Poor boy! Always dreaming big!"

For the first time, Appu noticed a tinge of sadness in Vijayan's voice, and his eyes became moist. He was about to continue the conversation, then stopped as if searching for words. After another try, Vijayan said slowly, "Did anyone inform his parents?"

Appu explained that he didn't know any of Chenda's relatives. "I thought you might know them, and you were good friends. He started the People's Power Party and worked tirelessly for your campaign."

Vijayan took several puffs, one after the other, from the cigarette and smoked away his mortification of being corrected by Appu. Vijayan sat straight, raised his finger, jabbed the table with fingers for emphasis, and said, "He has nothing to do with the PPP. The party was my idea. I have always wanted to be a political leader and serve people. I don't know much about him. He was always at the store begging for free rasayanam, an Indian passport, and an American visa."

Appu turned gaunt. He wanted to shout, Y*ou, ungrateful bastard! You're a hotshot MLA because of him*. But to avoid an argument, Appu sat tight-lipped like an obedient wife.

"Please drink chai," Vijayan said to pacify Appu and continued, "Come to think of it, he didn't have a birth certificate when I asked for it."

Vijayan explained that Chenda vaguely remembered being called Kunju Mon, Baby Boy. "The fact is that he really didn't even know his own name," Vijayan said. Again, there was a pause. The only sound punctuating the air was the honking of taxis, green buses, and red buses as if they were in a noise pollution contest. Adding to the din were the slogans shouted by strikers at the Secretariat's gate.

Appu told Vijayan that he had already reported the incident to the police. "I'm coming directly from the station," he said. "If you put in a kind word, they will act quickly."

"OK. I'll telephone the IG right now," Vijayan said. "Meanwhile, check with Mani and Patti-Amma. Patti-Amma may be related to him." Vijayan speculated that since Patti-Amma's husband was bedridden, she and Chenda could be romantic partners. "Something is going on between them. Patti-Amma is a lonely woman, you know," he said and chuckled.

Appu didn't laugh and held his hands tight, so he wouldn't be tempted to slap the MLA, drag him out of his office and kick his fat belly. Instead, he took a deep breath and said, "Comrade Vijayan, you shouldn't say such things. I'm shocked you said this. You are not the same man I knew. Patti-Amma is old enough to be his grandmother. She is brave to offer him shelter on her back porch."

Vijayan stared at Appu. No one would dare correct an elected official, especially an MLA. That, too, twice. Vijayan's initial sorrow was short-lived, and now he appeared relieved by Chenda's death. *No one other than me could claim to be the founder of the PPP*, Vijayan thought. He changed the topic by asking whether the lumber yard owner might know Chenda's relatives.

Appu nodded, finished the chai, and left the Secretariat for the lumber yard at the junction.

24

THE LUMBER YARD owner was getting ready to close the shop when Appu approached.

"I'm going to the river to see Chenda's body," the lumber yard owner said, choking with emotion. "Is it true he was stabbed?"

"True," Appu said. "I didn't know he had enemies."

The lumber yard owner coughed, then shook his head. "He has no enemies, Appu. But he meddled in the religious rift. Why? Those fanatics won't listen to him. I told him to stay away from the riots and not upset Comrade Vijayan until he gets him an Indian passport and an American visa," the lumber yard owner said. He took a deep breath and lit a beedi. The smoke, thick with sorrow, jetted out of his nostrils and mouth. "You know what he said?" the lumber yard owner asked and replied to his own question. "Chenda said his American trip could wait. He wanted to restore peace in the village." He took a few puffs, one after another, from the beedi.

Appu, his voice ringing exhaustion, asked him whether he knew Chenda's parents.

"Why?"

"They have to claim the body."

"I have no clue about his parents. He never talked about them or his native village."

"He worked for you, delivering and chopping firewood. You must have known something about him."

"True, he worked here. But he never said anything personal. It is a long story of how he ended up here," the lumber yard owner recalled. "He was a little boy when I first met him. I found him sleeping in front of this lumber yard one morning long, long ago. First, I thought he was a runaway. I woke him up and told him to go home. I've got to open it for business, you know. He went to the alumaram tree and sat at its foot. Then, I saw him drinking water from the hand-pumped pipe, the one at that corner, and going back to the alumaram tree. I knew something was wrong. I asked him where was home was. Appu, do you know what he said?"

"What?"

"He said this village was his home," the lumber yard owner said, wiping his moist eyes with a towel. "The boy won't say anything else. If I asked about his parents, he would change the subject. I gave him twenty-five paise and told him to buy something to eat. He wouldn't take the money. So, I told him to stack the lumber in small pieces in that corner. I made him work for an hour and then gave him the money. He took it. He brought dosas from the Brahminal's Hotel, ate one dosa, and saved the other to eat later."

Appu looked at the lumber yard. Stacks of parched lumber of various sizes and shapes were facing the mud wall of the shop. Scattered inside the shop were half-chopped firewood, two sharp-edged axes, and the handcart that Chenda had used.

"The boy hung around the shop till I closed it. I told him to sleep inside, and he cleaned the corner near the door. I gave him an old gunny bag to sleep on. Do you see the sawdust here? It's not healthy to inhale it. You will get TB very easily," the lumber yard owner said. "Then, one day during a heavy monsoon, he told me the Brahmin lady had asked him to stay on her back porch."

"You mean, Patti-Amma?"

"Yes. A kind woman. It was generous of her. At least it's a home. A Brahmin letting a parayan live on her back porch! Unbelievable nowadays," the lumber yard owner said, taking another puff from the beedi. "He did errands for me. When he grew older, I asked him to deliver and chop firewood. At first, he didn't collect money for chopping the firewood from people. I had to remind him to charge customers at least fifty paise for his labor. I let him use my handcart for free, but the other man has to pay one rupee per day."

The lumber yard owner took a deep breath and cupped his hand over his mouth to suppress a cough. The cough sneaked out through his fingers into a muffled grating noise. Another cough quickly followed before he could cover his mouth, followed by another. Appu took a few steps back and said, "You shouldn't be smoking. It's not good for your health."

The lumber yard owner wiped the sweat caused by coughing on his neck and his skinny chest with gray hair. "It is not the tobacco; it is the sawdust here. All the sawdust and mites make you cough," he explained. "Patty-Amma's back porch is safe for the boy."

"Yes. It was a good decision," Appu said. "Do you know who taught him to play the *chenda*?"

"Oh," the lumber yard owner said. "The Revolutionary Namboothiri taught him. You know the Namboothiri who lived in that big house with Alphonso mango trees on Lal Lane? This was before you opened your barbershop."

"I think I might have heard about him: The one who taught at the Music Academy?"

"Yes. He was a professional *chenda* player. He was an artist and didn't care about religion or caste. That is why people called him Revolutionary Namboothiri. Often, he spoke about the need for a major revolution in India. I guess he was preaching for a revolution in people's thinking. Instead, many people want chaos."

The lumber yard owner continued, "One day, Namboothiri was practicing the kettledrum at home. He saw the boy standing outside his house, fully immersed in the music and tapping his fingers. Namboothiri called him inside his house, I mean the front porch, gave him an old kettledrum and a pair of drum sticks, and told him to play just for fun. Even though the boy didn't have any training, he played the instrument like a pro. Better than Namboothiri's students," the lumber yard owner said and laughed. "Chenda told me that Namboothiri trained him in the evenings. First, he had to practice on a stone slab, which, I think, he did pretty well. Then, he played on a wooden plank before Namboothiri gave him a kettledrum. Did you know that Namboothiri made the kettledrum specifically for our Chenda?"

"Really?"

"Yes. Usually, when the kettledrum's surface becomes soggy and loses its tension, it should be replaced with a new buffalo skin from Madras. Guess what? Chenda's instrument never had that problem. It always sounded new. It is a miracle. Namboothiri knew that Chenda was gifted. A natural! He could play any note, just like that," the lumber yard owner said, and snapped his fingers for emphasis. "There's something special about him, Appu. Something noble. Divine. Pure."

The lumber yard owner recalled how Chenda enchanted the crowd with his music at Namboothiri's funeral. "He died of a heart attack. It was a sad day. The boy was inconsolable. He cried and cried. Then, he started playing the *chenda* as a tribute to his mentor. It was ugran! You know that Namboothiri's students had formed music groups, but they won't include Chenda. They think they would lose business because of him. What a shame!" The lumber yard owner paused, looked at Appu, and continued, "Can I tell you something? No one knows this."

"What's it?" Appu asked, and raised his eyebrows.

"You know Chenda has been saving money to go to America. His dream trip. He gave me his daily earnings for safekeeping. I kept a record of his money, which came to about three thousand rupees. He asked for his savings and spent it all."

"Spent?"

"Yes, Appu. He spent every paisa on Vijayan's election. He spent his own money on posters and signs at the hamlets."

"I thought Chenda collected donations from those hamlets," Appu said.

"Hamlets? People in the hamlets are dead poor, Appu. All they eat is the fish they catch from the stream and tapioca. And rice, once in a while."

"Does Vijayan know this?"

"No. Chenda never told anyone. I'm the only one to know this."

25

APPU'S NEXT stop was Patti-Amma's house in the Brahmin's cluster. The Brahmins' homes had tiled roofs and attics converted into storage rooms or bedrooms. They were built in a long vertical, narrow design to allow smooth airflow to and from the back porch to the front verandah like a tunnel. These homes were stacked side by side like a row of match boxes. If you stood close to the wall, you could hear the neighbor's every sneeze, cough, and the moan of love-making. They all had brick steps from the street to their verandah, and an open sewer ran under the steps. Every morning and evening, women swept these steps and decorated them with intricate designs made of red and white powder. There were two rows of homes facing each other. In the middle was an unpaved street traversed by pedestrians, bicyclists, handcarts, and vendors. An automobile could hardly squeeze through the street. Teenage boys played badminton with plastic shuttlecocks.

In the afternoon, a municipal water tanker with a long-perforated pipe sprinkled water on the street to settle the dust. Children ran after the tanker to catch the water with bare hands from its sprinkler, shouting. "Cold. Cold water. Ah!"

The hot breeze whipped up the dust once the water dried, which usually happened quickly. Soon after the tanker had left, the boys resumed their game. And girls gathered on their verandahs and giggled at the boys or talked about popular Malayalam, Tamil, and Hindi movie actors such as Sathyan, Sivaji Ganesan, Raj Kapoor, and Padmini.

Every house had a well on the back porch with an entrance from the back alley, so their servants, mostly light-skinned Nairs, didn't have to come through the front door. "You don't want them to bring germs to the house. Do you?" they would explain if you asked why the servants' movements were restricted. Brahmins women spoke Tamil, whereas their Nair servants spoke Malayalam.

Appu had never been to Patti-Amma's house, though he had an inkling of where she had lived. Being one of the longtime residents, she was well known in the Brahmin's cluster. Her homemade papadams were popular among residents and the stores at the junction.

At Patti-Amma's house, located in the middle of the right-side row, Appu rang the bicycle's bell as if it was the doorbell. Patti-Amma peered out the door, and seeing Appu, she ambled to the verandah. "Who are you?"

"I'm Appu, the barber. Namaste, Patti-Amma. Sorry to bother you."

"Oh, barber Appu! I've heard about you. All good things," Patti-Amma said in Tamil, which was adulterated with Malayalam words. "Come in…come in. My Mister cannot get up. He had a stroke. What do you want?"

"Patti-Amma, you know the handcart puller? The *chenda* player?"

"Yes, yes. He sleeps on my back porch," Patti-Amma said. "Is he drunk again?"

"No, Patti-Amma. He is dead. His body is under the bridge."

Patti-Amma stood still as if she had been frozen to a pale, ivory statue. Appu didn't know whether to enter the verandah, shake Patti-Amma or call a neighbor for help.

A stream of tears flowed down her wrinkled cheeks, which she wiped with the tip of her sari. "Was it his body found under the bridge?"

"Yes. Who told you?"

"The boys in the next house told me there was a pretam in the river, and they ran to see it. I didn't know it was our Chenda. Is it true he was murdered?" she asked and wiped the tears again.

"Looks like it."

"Hare Rama. Rama. What this country has come to. Please, don't stand outside. Come. Sit," Patti-Amma said and pointed toward a straw chair on the verandah.

"No, Patti-Amma. I'll wait here," Appu said, standing on the brick steps. He was reluctant to go inside a Brahmin's house.

"Paravayillai. Don't worry, this is my house. Come in. Sit in this chair. You look tired. I'll bring chai." Patti-Amma's firm voice assured Appu that she meant what she said. Then he heard a strange noise that he hadn't heard before. She was wailing, "Oh, my God! Oh, my God! Rama! Rama!" Then, he heard Patti-Amma telling her bedridden husband, "He's gone! That poor *chenda* player is gone. Somebody killed him."

Her husband might have been confused because she repeated the sad news a couple of times, "You know the boy who played the *chenda* and slept on our back porch? He is dead. They found his pretam under the bridge." Appu wanted to look inside the house and find out what was happening, but he was afraid and nervous that others might think he was trying to steal from her home.

Patti-Amma's eyes were red and moist when she returned with chai in a steel tumbler. Her hand slightly quivered, either from the weight of the bad news or the weight of the tumbler.

"Please put the tumbler on the floor. I'll pick it up," Appu said, hesitant to take it from her hands.

"It's alright, don't worry. You can take the chai from my hands," she said, extending the tumbler to him. Appu looked again at Patti-Amma to make sure she realized what she had just told him and gently took the tumbler from her hands. It was a strange experience for him because Brahmins deliberately avoided physical contact with non-Brahmins while giving or receiving things.

"Did he ever say getting into a fight or argument with anyone?" Appu asked.

"No, he wouldn't even swat a fly. Such a nice boy," Patti-Amma said.

"I know. That's why we are shocked," Appu said and sipped the hot chai. "Is Chenda related to you?"

She shook her head, said 'no,' and wiped the tears again "Is he related to your husband?"

"No, he is not related to my Mister either," Patti-Amma said. "The boy never talked about his mother, father, or anyone else. He didn't know them. I asked him once. He said his father brought him to the village when he was little, dropped him off at the junction, and left. That's it. Paavam. Poor soul."

Appu explained that he had been trying to locate his parents, siblings, or close or distant relatives and had not been successful.

"How did he end up here? On your back porch?"

"One day, after chopping firewood for me, he was resting on these steps," Patti-Amma recalled. "He must be tired. I gave him idlis, the leftover from my Mister's breakfast. He relished every bit of them as if he had not eaten idlis with sambar. He was like a starving child. He said he couldn't remember eating any homemade food. You should have seen him. He literally licked his fingers and didn't waste even a drop of sambar. I felt sorry for him. Poor soul! He said he slept in the lumber yard, so I told him to sleep on my back porch. It is safe here. The sawdust in the lumber yard would give you TB. Did you know that? It'll be terrible. He was a good boy. Often, he talked about playing the *chenda* in America. I thought he was crazy. But then, people have wild dreams and hopes. That's what keeps us alive," Patti-Amma continued. "Did you know that he would play the *chenda* in his sleep? At night, while going to the bathroom, I could hear the music. He must be sleeping. I think the instrument sings on its own. It is strange. But strange things happen in the world."

Appu looked at her, wondering whether she had occasional delusions. Unperturbed by his quizzical look, Patti-Amma continued, "He did errands for me. He delivered papadams to stores and collected money. Very punctual. He never stole even a paisa from me. Never! I can trust him with one thousand rupees. You know, my Mister couldn't work after the stroke. His pension is very minimal. That's what happens if you retire early. So, I started to make papadams. Different kinds of papadams. Another boy used to deliver them to stores. He was not trustworthy. Stole money from me. Then, this boy volunteered to deliver them and collect money every week. It was a great help. I'm seventy-six, and I get tired pretty easily. I can't leave my Mister home alone to sell papadams. I go out only to the temple for the morning pooja and quickly return home."

"Where are your children?"

"I have a son. Parameswaran. You might have cut his hair."

Appu patted his forehead as if trying to jog his memory. "If I see him, I'll remember him."

"It was a long ago," she continued. "My son lives in Bombay... in Maharashtra... with his wife and three children. It takes four days by train to come here. They must catch a train to Madras first and then catch another train. Why go through all this trouble? He sends money once in a while. It's not enough to pay for our expenses. He had changed after his marriage. I think his wife had brainwashed him. He was a good son. I wish God had given me more than one child. At least one of them would have taken care of us."

Appu found the chai rich and filling. Patti-Amma had sprinkled a pinch of cardamom for flavor and used plenty of milk. Appu needed that nourishment. Even on a hot, humid day, a cup of hot chai bolstered his tired spirit and brought comfort. But he had never sat in a Brahmin's house before, drinking chai, which made him a nervous wreck. He folded his hands, then unfolded, carefully put the cup on the floor, took the cup, and put it again on the floor.

Patti-Amma looked at Appu pensively and said, "We are all God's children. Hmm! Isn't it what Sree Narayana Guru said? Sree Narayana Guru didn't have big degrees, but he had wisdom."

There was a brief, grief-filled lull before Patti-Amma continued to reminisce about Chenda.

CHENDA HAD brought prosperity to her and her neighbors, she narrated.

"One heavy monsoon day, I told him to sleep near the kitchen inside the house. Otherwise, he would be soaked by rain. There was blinding lightning and thunder. Deafening thunder. It was not safe to sleep on the porch. It was the first day of the month. That evening he brought in more money from papadam sales than ever. I couldn't believe it. I made one week's sales in one day. He brought me luck."

That day, Patti-Amma recalled, she had urged him to sit on the front veranda for five minutes every morning on the first day of the month. The arrangement worked this way: She would give him fifty paise the previous evening—twenty-five paise to be given to her in the morning and the rest for him as a token of appreciation. Money should flow in and not out on the first transaction on the first day of the month. "Trust me, Appu. I sold a lot of papadams and made more money than ever. My sales went up every month. Isn't it strange?"

Patti-Amma said she had shared her little secret with her neighbors. "Guess what? They, too, wanted him to be their good luck charm."

The only difference was that, unlike Patti-Amma, they didn't accept the money from Chenda's hand. They would leave a small steel saucer where Chenda would place their twenty-five-paise morning income. He had built a clandestine clientele of seven Brahmin houses. His routine was to come early in the morning, sit on their verandahs for five-ten minutes, and put twenty-five paise on the steel saucer, and leave secretly like a paramour after an early morning tryst.

There was another caveat: He should take a bath before entering their homes. To satisfy them, Chenda would take a dip in the Alumaram River early morning and rush to their homes. On their verandas, small steel saucers eagerly waited to receive the first currency of the household's monthly income.

"Sometimes, I gave him food. He never complained or asked for more. Hmm. Paavam. Poor soul!" Patti-Amma said. "Who found the body?"

"Cross-toed Ammu," Appu replied.

"Oh, the vegetable woman? She brings me fresh vegetables every day after the market closes," Patti-Amma said and narrated how she once tried to hook up Kamala with Chenda. "Every day, at noon, the vegetable woman and her niece would come here. I would give them hot rice porridge. Poor souls. That's their lunch. One day, I asked Kamala why she was not married. First, she said she feared her husband would leave her after a few years as her aunt's husband did. Then, she said she was poor and ugly, and no one would like her. Have you seen her? She's so pretty, like our movie star Padmini. Nowadays, young people lack self-esteem. They think they are ugly. Anyway, I told her she was beautiful, and any man would fall for her, even a blind one. Then I mentioned to her about Chenda. He is such a good boy and handsome. I knew he needed a family. Everyone needs a family, even if it's an unhappy one. You know what Kamala said? She was not desperate to marry a parayan, and he was black. Can you believe it? She wants to marry a light-skinned man like our Maharaja. Is Chenda really a parayan?" Patti-Amma asked.

"I don't know, Patti-Amma. But people think he is a parayan," Appu replied.

"Maybe because he is black," she said and wiped her face again with the tip of her sari.

"Patti-Amma, we all feel sad. We are shocked and confused," Appu said and looked outside so she wouldn't see his teary eyes. At the same time, he wanted to save her from the embarrassment of being seen weeping.

"He has been drinking a lot lately. He comes home drunk and talks to himself. Says too many bad words," she continued. "I didn't know where he learned to talk like that. Oh, Rama…Rama…If he was my son, I would have made him wash his mouth with Lifebuoy soap. I think he was angry at the medical store manager, the MLA."

Appu listened attentively to Patti-Amma and sipped chai.

"Chenda… the boy… knew that man's secrets. He is not a real doctor. Did you know that?" Patti-Amma asked. "Do you think he killed the boy?"

"I don't think so," Appu replied.

Patti-Amma was visibly exhausted after narrating Chenda's story and leaned on the wall for support.

"I would have claimed the body and cremated it," Patti-Amma said. "I'm too old, and my Mister can't walk."

Appu told her not to worry about Chenda's body. "We will manage."

"Good. God bless you," Patti-Amma said. After a brief pause, she asked, "Do you know any boy, trustworthy, to sell my papadams?"

"I cannot think of anyone right now."

"How about Hassan? The flower shop boy?"

Appu was surprised that she mentioned Hassan's name. "Patti-Amma, he is a Muslim. Do you want a Muslim to work for you?"

"What's wrong with that? He sells flowers to everyone. Hindus, Muslims, and Christians buy flowers from him, don't they?"

"But this is different. He has to come to your house to pick up papadams and give you the money. He's a Muslim, Patti-Amma. Other Brahmins would create problems for you and him."

"What the world has come to? Look at the crows," Patty-Amma said and gestured with hands to the birds pecking on the street. "Do you know their religion? Or caste? People are madayans. Fools! They become wiser when they get old."

However, Appu told her he would send Hassan to discuss her business proposition.

"Tell him," she said, "if he is afraid, he can come through the back porch. All he has to do is pick up the papadams, deliver them to stores, and collect money once a week. I'll give him a fifteen percent commission."

"I'll ask him."

Appu tried to take a glimpse of Patti-Amma's husband again. All he could see was a bed and a skeletal figure in the dark room. "Who cuts his hair?"

"I do," Patti-Amma replied. "Our maid helps me to make him sit and clean the hair."

"I'll come after a week and cut his hair."

Patti-Amma looked at him intently.

"If you don't want me to come inside the house, I'll understand," Appu said. "It's free."

"You can come inside the house. Anytime to visit my Mister," Patti-Amma said, gestured with her hands to him to wait, and went inside.

A few minutes later, Appu heard the whoosh of Patti-Amma's sari, resembling the rustle of the leaves in the banyan tree. "Give this to your wife," Patti-Amma said, handing a package wrapped in a piece of newspaper.

"Can I see?"

"Sure!"

Inside the package were about fifty papadams. Surprised, Appu looked at her and smiled. "Thank you."

"No problem. It is from us," she said. After a pause, she asked, "Where will you find the boy's relatives? Someone has to claim his body."

"I'll check with Mani."

"The arrack vendor? He may know something about the boy. He gets the boy drunk. Let me know what you find out about the boy. His belongings are still on my back porch."

All along, a middle-aged woman from across the street had been staring at Appu. It made him uncomfortable that he was being spied on. Clearly, she was not happy about a non-Brahmin's presence in the cluster.

As soon as Appu left, she scowled at Patti-Amma, "Tell your servant maid to clean the veranda and the steps with water. Sweep the steps with a broom and mop your verandah with a wet cloth. You also should sprinkle water mixed with cow dung on the steps and your verandah. You've to purify your house."

Patti-Amma replied as loud as she could, "He is Appu. The barber. A good man."

"So what?" the woman shouted from her verandah. "They are shudrans. First, you let the parayan boy live on your back porch. Now, you let a barber inside your house. You don't know what diseases they have. They may have leprosy."

Patti-Amma dismissed the neighbor's complaints with a wave of her hands. The neighbor was in no mood to let it go. "It's old farts like you who destroy Brahmins' high status in society. Karmam, karmam! No wonder you are cursed, and your husband is bedridden," she said. Then she brought a pail of water and sprinkled it on her doorsteps as if to ward off evil spirits that might spread to her house from Patti-Amma's verandah.

26

WHILE NEARING the marshland, Appu saw Mani sitting under a coconut tree with his hands tightly held on his head. Next to him was a half-empty glass of arrack. Seeing Appu, Mani broke down.

"I swear, I'll find out his killer and strangle him," Mani said, made a fist, and pumped it in the air as if smashing someone's head. His eyes were bloodshot. The smell of arrack, beedi, and rage gushed from Mani's mouth. "He doesn't deserve this, Appu? Such a nice man. What did he do wrong?"

Appu placed the bicycle near the coconut tree and leaned on it, quietly seeking comfort in each other's company.

In between sobs, Mani said, "When I went to the river for a bath, I was told there was a pretam. I didn't know who it was. I was shocked to find out it was our Chenda. Guru showed me the stab wounds on him. I couldn't believe it." Mani's lips quivered. His usually booming voice turned soft, like a cyclone tapered into a breeze. There was no intimidation or steely stare in his eyes; they were brimmed with sorrow. And he didn't curl his mustache with his fingers. There was not even an iota of the fearless thug's image he had projected over the years to protect his illegal liquor business. Until now, Appu didn't realize that such a strong man could be fragile at heart and weep like a child. Grief has a strange way of bringing out emotions you didn't know ever existed.

Mani took a sip from the glass and wept, "I can't handle seeing him in the river… so helpless…so innocent like a little lamb. I don't have the strength to see him like that, Appu." After a pause, he said, "I think he was stabbed here."

He described to Appu the scene he saw at the marshland: The leaves covering the hidden arrack jars were in disarray, and Chenda's kettledrum was lying, bobbling its head, among lotus leaves and weed. Its head was torn, its body had cracked at several places, and its tension cord snapped and mangled.

"I knew immediately that something was wrong. I'm sure Chenda was definitely assaulted or stabbed here. Look…look at the blood on the wall," he said, pointing out to the area of the wall. Appu recoiled at the sight of the blood, splattered like crude strokes of red paint on the mud wall.

Then, Mani looked affectionately at the kettledrum and continued, "I pulled it out of the marshland. It was entangled in the weed. It was completely broken. He took care of the kettledrum as if it was a divine gift from God."

Appu looked at the kettledrum and flailed his hands as he did when he saw Chenda's body.

Mani, cracking with emotion, asserted, "I think someone else was here. Maybe one or two men. I don't know what happened. But it was horrible."

Appu wanted to stay with Mani and comfort him, but first, he needed to find out whether Mani was related to Chenda. "You know… someone has to claim the body and cremate or bury it. It should be done quickly. We cannot leave it there," Appu said. During a lull in his sobs, Mani asked Appu whether he knew Chenda's relatives.

Surprised by the question, Appu responded, "I thought you two were related."

"No... no. I'm not related to him," Mani said. After a pause, he continued, "I wanted to ask him to live with me, you know, on the other side of the river. But my cousins objected. We were brewing arrack in my shack. They didn't want too many people there. It might draw unnecessary attention of the Flying Squad."

"I understand," Appu said. "Do you know Chenda's parents?"

"We never talked about them. Did you check with that crook? The fake doctor MLA?"

"Vijayan doesn't have any clue. I met with him at the Secretariat earlier today."

Mani took the half-empty glass he had hidden near the culvert, took a gulp, and offered Appu a drink. Appu politely declined, saying he didn't want to smell alcohol while trying to locate Chenda's folks.

"Do you know his religion? At least that would give us some direction."

"He never told me anything about his religion, even when he got punch drunk. People spill their secrets when they are drunk. They blabber a lot about their family, but he never did. He either played the *chenda* or talked about America. Of late, he was sad. Very sad and brooded about the riots."

Mani took another drink and tried to stand up. He stumbled, sat down, and continued talking.

LIKE MANY others, Mani couldn't remember when he first met Chenda and how they became friends. But he relied on Chenda for help to transfer arrack from big jars to small bottles, hiding those jars and bottles in the swamp, and being on the lookout for police and snitches.

"He was the only person, besides me, to know the location of the jars in the marshland," Mani told Appu and gestured with his face to the swath of marshland. They were covered with lotus that bloomed in summer. Under the gorgeous lotus flowers were schools of tiny fish, tadpoles, and frogs—meals for hungry snakes.

"Often, Chenda and I ate together," Mani continued. "I would send him to buy parotta, mutton, or chicken curry from the Military Hotel. We would sit here, under this tree, and drink and eat. Then, I would ask him to describe America."

Chenda would vividly describe the architectural marvel of the Empire State Building, the stately ambiance and interior of the Carnegie Hall, and the ever-cheerful Mickey Mouse. A journey to a fascinating world some ten thousand miles away. There was no need for a passport, a visa, or an expensive plane ticket to travel with Chenda to his dreamland.

"I have heard about America a hundred times and was never tired of listening to them another hundred times. The way Chenda describes it never gets bored."

APPU'S FOREHEAD twitched, amazed by the strong bond between Mani and Chenda. He remembered how Mani taught a lesson to a Brahmin boy who harassed Chenda. The Brahmin boy taunted Chenda by demanding that he perform oral sex on him. He wanted to prove to his friends that he was a tough guy. "You... fucking parayan, suck my kunna. You'll enjoy it. If you don't do it, I'll kick your black ass and drive you out of the village," the boy yelled at Chenda. Mani, who overheard this, quietly sneaked behind the boy, grabbed him by his neck, lifted him with his left hand, and gave a hard knock on his head with his right hand. Then he pinned the boy's head against the wall, slapped him, and threatened to slash his throat with a sickle. The boy trembled with fear and cried. All his macho showmanship had evaporated. He apologized profusely to Mani and Chenda while his friends ran to a safe distance from where they saw their friend being humiliated.

"I'm sorry Mani-Chettan. I'm so sorry. They forced me to say these mean things," the boy pleaded. Then, he looked at Chenda, showed respect by prefixing the Chettan title to his name, and addressed him, Chenda-Chettan. Chenda, the big brother! "Chenda-Chettan, please tell Mani-Chettan to stop hitting me. Please!"

After that episode, no boys—Brahmins and non-Brahmins—made fun of him and addressed Chenda Chettan.

MANI TOOK a swig from his glass and reminisced.

"Appu, what I'm going to say is strictly confidential," he said, then hesitated. But the liquor in his stomach began to unlock deep secrets. The slur in his speech became more pronounced, and Appu had to perk up his ears. "He went to jail in my place. Who else will do that for me? I wish he was my brother."

"This is an interesting story. It is true," Mani continued. A new Sub-Inspector, who didn't know about Mani's deals with old guards at the station, raided his liquor business. The Sub-Inspector, accompanied by two constables, managed to catch him. In the evening, Chenda, with a large bag, went to the police station to meet Mani. In the bag were parottas, mutton curry, chili chicken wrapped in banana leaves, and three bottles of arrack.

Friendship with law enforcement officials had special perks. Mani had briefly talked with the Sub-Inspector in charge of the evening shift and gave him the bag. Without fuss, Chenda volunteered to stay in the six-feet by six-feet square cell until he was discharged the next day. By late evening, Mani was back at the marshland pouring arrack to his customers and offering spicy mango pickles. The regulars came, one by one, drank arrack and ate the pickles with their fingers. It was like the three monkeys: See nothing. Hear nothing. Say nothing.

At the police station the following morning, the new Sub-Inspector was baffled to see a dramatic change in Mani's appearance: Overnight, Mani had become muscular, gained a large belly, and didn't curl the mustache with his fingers.

"Your name is…hmm… Mani, right?" he asked. "Yes, saar," Chenda mumbled, looking at the floor to avoid eye contact. The senior Sub-Inspector called the new Sub-Inspector aside and asked: "Do you have any eyewitnesses to the arrack sale? No? Then, there's no case. We'll keep him till noon, then release him." The new Sub-Inspector got the message: Shut up and don't mess with Mani.

"Here's another secret," Mani said. Once, a rookie constable wanted to impress his superiors. So, he hauled Chenda to the station and asked him to be a witness to Mani's liquor business. It turned out to be a hard lesson for the newbie. His supervisor told him to stay out of the village, and Chenda was released the same evening.

Mani looked at the marshland, then at Appu, and cried, "My best friend is gone. I'll kill the motherfuckers who did this to him."

"We all feel the same," Appu said and got on his bicycle.

"Where are you going?"

"To the church. The priest there may know something about him."

"Let me check with him."

27

A WATCHMAN opened the door to the rectory of the Church of the Sacred Heart of Jesus when Appu knocked.

"Please wait here, in the lobby," he told Appu. "I'll tell Father Thomachan that he has a visitor."

The watchman was clean-shaven and sported a crew haircut like the boys in the orphanage in the church compound.

Appu looked around. A long wooden crucifix welcomed visitors to the lobby. Next to it was a green vase with a bouquet of sunflowers, marigolds, and roses. On the walls were several photos of smiling former orphans who had become successful in life, got married, and returned to adopt an orphan or two.

He stood up in reverence as the Director, the Reverend Thomas Killippalam, came into the lobby. He was also the church pastor.

The parishioners and non-parishioners initially called him Reverend Thomas Achan, which, over time, shrunk to Thomachan.

The Director title was a misnomer. It created an image of a man in his late forties with gray hair, a thick mustache, a paunch, neatly starched ironed clothes, and an officious appearance of an IAS bureaucrat. But Thomachan didn't have any of those pomposities. He appeared to be in his early thirties with an unkempt beard and disheveled hair. His white cassock was crumpled, and it needed washing and ironing. He looked like a laborer who had just returned from a night shift at the nearby brick factory.

"Would you like to adopt a child," he asked Appu. "There are many children here who need loving homes. Boys get adopted quickly, not girls unless they are light-skinned. No one wants dark-skinned girls."

"No, Father Thomachan, I'm not here to adopt a child. I already have a child. A boy," Appu said sheepishly, showing a tinge of guilt because he didn't come to provide a new life to an orphan.

Appu explained the purpose of his visit. "I thought at least you would have information about Chenda."

Thomachan took a deep breath and made the sign of the cross. His eyes swelled like Patti-Amma's. Then, he covered his face with his hands and wiped the tears. "I'm sorry to hear about his horrendous death. What a tragic fate! I know Chenda is in heaven. In our Lord's house. He used to help us chop firewood. Come to think of it, I have spoken to him several times without knowing his real name. Everyone here called him Chenda. So did I. I'm embarrassed that it never occurred to me to ask Chenda about his family."

The watchman brought a glass of lemonade mixed with salt for Appu. "Drink this. It's very humid out there," Thomachan said. "I'll say a Mass for him. May his soul rest in peace. I hope the police arrest those who hurt him. I heard that he tried to intervene in the Hindu-Muslim conflict. Do you think the Hindus or the Muslims killed him?"

"I don't know, Thomachan."

"What'll happen to his body?"

"I'm not sure. We cannot leave the body there. Someone has to claim it and do the final rites."

Thomachan mulled over the situation and said, "In that case, I'll claim the body. We've got to give him a decent burial. He was a good Christian. A good Catholic. He never missed the Christmas parade and other church festivals. He had a mental calendar and showed up on time without fail."

He recalled that Chenda loved to accompany Santa Claus and the carol singers. "Have you seen our Christmas procession?"

"Yes, I have."

"Good! Then you should know he played the *chenda* at the procession."

Appu listened patiently as Thomachan described the procession: Women carried oil lamps; the children from the orphanage twirled colorful ribbons; and Chenda played superb music, preceded by Santa Claus sitting on Balan's elephant and waving at people.

Thomachan continued: "He did chores here at the orphanage. I've seen him joking with the children there. And he would let them practice on his kettledrum. He was like an elder brother to them. They are very fond of him. A kind man. What a tragedy!"

"Did he grow up here?" Appu asked and suggested it was worth checking the registry of orphans.

Thomachan was flummoxed. Appu realized his blunder when Thomachan replied, "I could check our records if only we knew his real name. Let's go to the orphanage and ask the children. He might have told them about his parents. One more thing, I don't want the children to know that Chenda is no more. They will be sad."

"OK."

THE ORPHANAGE was made up of a warden's room, a kitchen, and two long halls—one for boys and another for girls. Each boy and each girl had designated sleeping places on the cement floor.

They slept on straw mattresses that were rolled toward the wall during the day. Discolored small pillows, which were sparkling white once, were placed on top of each mattress as if they were paperweights.

Seeing Appu and Thomachan, they stopped chit-chatting and stood up. They looked at Appu, wondering whether he had come to adopt them. They were between the ages of five and twelve. Older children were sent to orphanages for "big boys and girls," Thomachan explained. He turned toward the children and asked, "Does anyone know our Chenda's real name? Did he say anything about his mother? Father?"

"Our Chenda Chettan? We thought Chenda was his real name," a boy replied.

"Did he say where he was born? His parents?"

"No," the boy said, looking at his fellow orphans.

"Then what did he talk about?"

"America," a girl interjected. "He told us that there are no poor people in America. The roads are so clean that you could sleep on them. Americans drink a lot of beer. Beer is cheaper than water. And everyone has a car. Huge cars! Big cars! Americans live in big mansions. So big that our two mud huts will fit inside an American home."

The girl recalled that Chenda would draw a picture of an American house on the ground with a twig. A tall chimney jetted out of the roof and stretched its neck to admire the neighborhood. The girl continued: "On Saturdays and

Sundays, Americans will have picnics under big umbrellas on the beach. The beaches are clean and beautiful. Compared to those beaches, our Kovalam and Shankhumugham beaches are small. Very small."

"What else did he say?" Thomachan asked.

"He wanted to open a *chenda* music school in New York," the boy said. "He has a name for his music school. It is the Kerala *Chenda* Music Academy of New York." The boy repeated, "The Kerala *Chenda* Music Academy of New York. KCMANY."

The girl was eager to chirp in. "Chenda Chettan promised to take us to America. Once he buys a big car and a big house with a chimney, he will take all of us to America. It was a promise."

Appu knew that after Chenda's visits, the orphans would sleep, dreaming about large cars, Mickey Mouse school bags, a house with a chimney, and not agonizing over why their parents had abandoned them.

The boy interjected, "Why are you asking so many questions?"

Appu replied that he was trying to contact Chenda's relatives because he was ill.

"Oh, my God," the girl said and looked at her friends. "In our evening prayers, we must pray for him. We should say a special novena."

"Let's all pray," Thomachan said.

They nodded in agreement.

The watchman, who listened to the conversation, added that Chenda loved the cake baked by the cook as a treat for children on Sundays. The cook always gave a large slice to Chenda. Instead of eating the cake, he would save it.

"This is for Patti-Amma's Mister, he would explain," the watchman said. "Mister Iyer had a stroke. The egg in the cake would give him strength. They wouldn't know that you have used an egg in the cake. They are Brahmins. Vegetarians."

28

AFTER THANKING Thomachan for his efforts, Appu went to Juma Masjid, hoping Sheikh Ali might shed some light. The one-mile bicycle ride to the mosque, located north between the church and Alumaram Village, could have been less tiresome except for the sweltering heat, humidity, and the heavy right leg.

Sheikh Ali, the mullah of Juma Masjid, was supervising the workers who were tearing down the burned remnants of the mosque and the Islamic Elementary Madrasa. He wore an impeccably clean white skull cap with golden embroidery, a long-sleeved white shirt, and a checkered blue lungi. A fresh white towel with a green border hung loosely on his shoulder.

Appu greeted Sheikh Ali with namaste and said he was sorry about the riots and the arson.

"I never expected this," Sheikh Ali said and looked at the burned walls—the only remains of the mosque, the madrasa, and the Muslim homes. "We're building a bigger mosque with concrete walls, a concrete dome, and four tall minarets. There will be two loudspeakers for our aadhan calls. The mosque will be a replica of a small Taj Mahal. We are also building a first-class, state-of-the-art elementary school. It will have more classrooms, brick walls, and a concrete terrace. We are also helping the residents to repair their homes."

Appu couldn't come up with appropriate words to cheer up Sheikh Ali. However, he apologized as if the attacks on the mosque, school, and Muslim homes were his fault. "I'm sorry, Sheikh. I don't know what to tell you."

Sheikh Ali stroked his gray beard and commented, "It's not your fault. What can you do? Nothing much. It is a miracle that no one died in these horrific arson. Thank Allah for that."

Appu repeated, "Thank God" and explained about Chenda.

Puzzled, Sheikh Ali stared at Appu. "You mean, our Chenda? The man who always carried the kettledrum? Dead? Was it his body under the bridge?"

"Yes."

"He was here the other day, helping people escape from their burning homes. I can't believe this," Sheikh Ali said and wiped his face with both hands.

Appu waited for Sheikh Ali to regain his composure.

"How did he die?" Sheikh Ali asked.

Appu's answer was the same: "There were stab wounds on his stomach and cuts in his head."

"I'm so sorry. I'm really sorry, Appu," Sheikh Ali said and bowed his head as if praying. Then, he asked, "Was it the Hindus who did it to him? Or the Christians?"

"I don't know," Appu said.

Sheikh Ali invited Appu to his house with a tiled roof and a long verandah near the mosque. They sat on a bench on the verandah, and Sheikh Ali instructed a servant to make chai. Out of respect for Sheikh Ali, Appu agreed to drink chai even though he was not thirsty or hungry. After a few seconds of silence, Appu asked, "Do you know his real name?" Appu said. "You are my last resort, Sheikh."

"I always called him Chenda. I never asked him for his good name. Let me ask the workers," Sheikh Ali said, looked at the laborers, and asked, "Anyone knows Chenda's real name?"

The workers looked at each other and shook their heads to indicate "no."

"His relatives? His home?" Sheikh Ali raised his voice.

Again, the workers shook their heads negatively and resumed their task of removing burned wooden beams, twisted metal pieces, debris, and piles of ash.

In a voice echoing emotion, Sheikh Ali said, "Chenda asked me after the fire why Hindus and Muslims couldn't get along. I said it was not true. We all got along well until that bastard Comrade Doctor Vijayan poisoned the air. Now things are out of hand. I saw him weeping as if his house had been burned down."

There was an uneasy pause. Then Sheikh Ali asked, "How's your business? Did the riots affect you?"

"Not much. People need haircuts, you know. But young people come once in three or months. They want to be hippies."

The servant brought chai in two small glasses. Appu took a sip and said he couldn't find even a thread of information about Chenda's relatives.

Sheikh Ali removed his skull cap, passed his fingers through his hair, and asked, "What will happen to his body?"

"No idea."

"Was he circumcised?"

"I don't know."

"I'm sure he is a Muslim," Sheikh Ali said. "I'll take care of the body. He comes to the mosque often. He had celebrated Ramzan and Eid with us."

29

APPU RETURNED to the river bank like an explorer after a failed expedition. Guru, Hassan, Stephen, Gopi, and Mashe were guarding Chenda's body. Mashe came out of his self-imposed hermit-like confinement to the river bank.

A few feet away, Cross-toed Ammu and Kamala stood in front of the crowd.

"I went all over the place," Appu told Guru. "No one knows his real name, his parents, his relatives, or his birthplace. Strange!"

Soon Cane-Swami, Sheikh Ali, and Father Thomachan came. They rushed to see the body.

A few minutes later, a white Ambassador pulled up. Vijayan got out of the car and told the driver to wait. He didn't say namaste or bow his head to the crowd as he did during the campaign. Instead, he went straight to the riverbank, folded his handloom mundu up to his knee, rolled up the sleeves of his handloom juba, and stood closer to the body lay. He looked intently at Chenda's wounds and then at his face, still half-submerged in the river. Chenda seemed to have a genial smile—the same smile when he told Vijayan, "Doctor Vijayan, you should become an MLA."

Memories have a strange way of stirring up nostalgia. They could dig deep into the abyss, pull back the past strand by strand, and hurl emotions in your heart and face. The scenes of Chenda painting the signs "Vote for Comrade Doctor Vijayan" and playing the kettledrum at the first campaign speech at the junction flashed before his eyes. Vijayan's lips quivered, his eyes swelled, and he covered his face with the cotton towel he had on his shoulder. Once he regained composure, Vijayan told Appu, "Chenda yearned to go to America. Now, look. Look at him. Dead! In the river bank with stab wounds."

Appu remained stoic and let the MLA spout the words of grief and guilt.

"I thought the police would be already here," Vijayan said. "We cannot leave Chenda like this."

Appu looked at the body again and gasped as it slightly swayed sideways in a ripple created by the breeze. Instantly, the crowd reacted. Some stood up for a better view, and others stretched their necks to see it.

"He is moving," Appu said.

They looked at the body, confused, not knowing what to do. Their confusion was exacerbated by the *Chenda* music that sailed softly from a distance. "Dum... tada... tada... tatatada... dum." Gradually, the music grew louder. And louder and near. 'Dum... tada... tada... tatatada... dum.' Vijayan, Appu, Guru, and Hassan looked at each other in astonishment.

"Who is playing the *chenda*?" Appu asked. No one answered. He looked in the direction of the source of the music. It came from the other side of the river. He didn't see any musician with a kettledrum. All he could see was the rustling of leaves in the jungle of trees—banana, jackfruit, and tall crooked coconut trees. Suddenly, the chime of the cymbal and the cadence of the kombu wind instrument emerged and blended with the *chenda* beat. With the of fusion cymbal and kombu, the *chenda* music grew louder and louder. It reached a crescendo as if Chenda was playing his kettledrum—his two drum sticks transforming into four, to six, to eight, and to twelve and a flock of birds fluttering on the kettledrum's tanned leather surface. It was as if the music was blasting from Stephen's long, green loudspeaker.

Appu, Guru, and Vijayan covered their ears with their hands. Petrified, Stephen and Hassan ran to a safer distance, stopped, and stared at the trees across the river. Cross-toed Ammu and Kamala held each other's hands and stood close for a sense of safety.

Gradually, the cymbal and the kombu music subsided, followed by the *chenda* music the way it emerged from the bank across the river. Soon, thick dark clouds formed in the sky. Clouds at that time of the year were unusual. A long streak of lightning crisscrossed, tearing through the cloud, portending the deafening thunder that followed. Teardrops trickled from the cloud. Mahabali, the King of Kings of God's Own Country, must be weeping.

Pushed by the rising water, Chenda's body swayed again.

"Let's pull him out of the river and cremate him," said Cane-Swami, the first to claim the body.

"How do you know he is a Hindu?" shouted Sheikh Ali, questioning his ownership of the body. "He is a Muslim. He had come to the mosque and prayed with us. We should bury him according to our rites."

"Don't even think about it," Cane-Swami screamed. "Chenda is a Hindu. I know it. He worshipped at the temple. He lived at Patti-Amma's house. In the Brahmin's cluster."

Thomachan told them to calm down. He claimed that Chenda was a Christian. "You've seen him at Christmas processions with Father Christmas, haven't you? What more proof do you need? We will give him a decent Christian burial."

Ignoring him, Cane-Swami folded his saffron mundu, swished his cane, and asked the Hindus in the crowd to help him carry the body out of the water.

"Don't you dare touch it," Sheikh Ali shouted. Surprised, Appu and Guru looked at each other because Sheikh Ali always spoke in a measured, calm tone. It was different this time. "I'm warning you, Cane-Swami! He is a Muslim. If you take him, you'll pay for it." He motioned the Muslims in the crowd to help him carry the body. About a dozen Muslims came forward.

Cane-Swami was determined not to let Sheikh Ali and his supporters win. If Muslims won, it would cause his swift downfall as a Hindu leader. He would be publicly humiliated by Brahmins and non-Brahmins. No one would call him Swami. No namaste. No free milk. And the widow would kick him out of her house.

Hindus in the crowd outnumbered Muslims, which emboldened him to rush toward Chenda's body. Spontaneously, Sheikh Ali ran and passed Cane-Swami, turned around, and blocked him. The only way for Cane-Swami to reach the body was to push away Sheikh Ali. They scowled at each other like the two packs of dogs at the railway station. Cane-Swami's and Sheikh Ali's chests swelled with ego; their eyes flared with disdain for each other. Their lips twisted with fury, and they stood so close that they could smell each other's stale breath and sweat.

Sheikh Ali raised his hand to wipe the raindrops from his face. A huge mistake. Cane-Swami thought Sheikh Ali was about to hit him. That's all the misunderstanding needed to trigger a full-blown battle. Soon Sheikh Ali and Cane-Swami were trading punches and pushing each other. Their supporters joined the fray. Long bamboo sticks and bicycle chains they had hidden behind the bushes appeared. Those who didn't have weapons battled with bare hands, and kicks flew.

Scared, the women and young boys ran for safety. Thomachan stood confused, not knowing how to bring the situation under control when a man pushed him. He turned around and pushed the man back. In the melee, Thomachan took a few blows in the shoulder.

"Calm down. All of you, calm down," Vijayan yelled at the top of his lungs. His pleading was drowned in the din of the factional fight. Vijayan raised his hands to draw the attention of the warring factions, but he was knocked down by a stone thrown by someone. Thick, warm blood dripped from his head. He sat dazed and pressed the wound with his towel to stop the bleeding.

"What have I done?" he asked Appu and extended his hand so Appu could pull him up and move to safety behind the large pillar of the bridge. "I should have listened to Chenda about the tennis ball incident. I didn't know things would get this ugly."

Appu looked at Vijayan sympathetically and said, "You created this mess; now you fix it," as if telling a student to redo a test.

Chenda's body swayed in the water again. His face and legs were now fully immersed in the water as if he was ashamed of the pandemonium on the land.

"Ayyo! The river is taking Chenda," Vijayan shouted and got into the river to pull the body. When Vijayan thought he got hold of his leg, the undercurrent gained speed and moved the body further. They formed a human chain under the knee-deep water and struggled to grab Chenda's leg, hand, or head. But the Alumaram River wouldn't let him go. The river teased them by moving the body a little deeper.

It was too late when Sheikh Ali, Cane-Swami, and Thomachan realized what had happened. They signaled their supporters to stop fighting. With bloodied faces, holding bamboo sticks and bicycle chains and sharp-edged machetes in hand, they watched the Alumaram River thumb its nose at them.

Like a thief, the river, with its soft hands, gently pulled Chenda a few more feet away from Vijayan, who stood chest-deep in the water holding on to Appu, who was holding on to Guru, who held on to Hassan and Stephen. At the end of the human chain was Mashe, who planted his feet firmly on the ground, his body leaning backward. He held Stephen's waist with his frail, outstretched hands. Seeing their struggle, Cane-Swami, Sheikh Ali, and Father Thomachan joined the human chain behind Mashe.

By then, the river had moved Chenda further deep into the safety of its bosom at the epicenter of the undercurrent. The body moved faster, then flipped upward, facing the sky. If he could, Chenda would be looking for an airplane flying to America.

Chenda's head bobbed as if saying goodbye to God's Own Country, and the fast flow of the Alumaram River carried him to the tranquility of the Arabian Sea.

30

FIFTY YEARS LATER.

Police have closed Chenda's file, put it in a cardboard box with other First Information Reports, and tossed it in a storage room.

Chenda's FIR reads:

Date:16-4-1965.

Name of the complainant: *Barber Appu (Big leg)*.

Case: *The complainant reported finding a male's body under the Alumaram River Bridge*.

Address of the complainant: *"AV 23 Alumaram Village."*

Name of the deceased: *Chenda. (Real name: Unknown)*.

Address: *Alumaram Village*.

Age: *Twenty-six*.

Autopsy report: *None*.

Place of birth: *Unknown*.

Parents/relatives: *Unknown*.

Birthmarks: *Unavailable*.

Color: *Black*.

Religion/Caste: *Harijan/Parayan*.

Alumaram Village leaps into twenty-first century with the widening of M.G. Road to a two-way tar paved road. Ox- and handcarts give way to Maruti, Honda, Hyundai cars, and autorickshaws traverse bumper-to-bumper on the road.

Weaving through exhaust fumes-pumping vehicles is a steady stream of motorcycles driven by men, women, and reckless teenagers who don't believe in traffic lights. Drivers honk incessantly as if exercising their right to free speech.

Krishnan Good Health Herbal Medical Store has been replaced by Krishna Medicals and Pharmaceuticals LLC., which is run by Proprietor Krishnan's son, Govind. It sits on the ground floor of a two-story structure at the same spot. On the second floor are the offices of Advocate Padmanabhan Iyer, B.Com, LLB (Honors), Ph.D., and Vidya and Jay Chartered Accountants Ltd.

The store where Stephen's Sound System operated has become Sai Music and Electronics. You can buy Apple, Microsoft, Dell computers, cell phones, high-definition TVs, cameras, and other electronic items.

The Brahminal's Hotel has become a remodeled, spacious Lakshmi Vegetarian Bistro. The site of Kader's Military Hotel now features a huge golden arch: McDonald's.

With wheeling and dealing, Vijayan became the Chief Minister of Kerala. His tenure lasted only three years before his coalition government of PPP and other parties fell apart. His coalition partners jumped ship, lured by the opposition parties' promise of more lucrative portfolios and commitment not to investigate their personal finances.

During his short reign as an MLA and a Chief Minister, Vijayan has bought two Ambassador cars and one Mazda. He also built a bungalow and a thirty-bed private hospital in Marakana Village and has become the hospital's chairman and CEO. In hindsight, that turned out to be a prudent decision because a few months ago, he suffered a stroke. Now he is receiving treatment at the hospital's VIP suite. For free!

Through his political connection, Vijayan arranges an Indian passport and an American tourist visa for his brother-in-law. The latter overstays his visa and illegally works as a cook in an Indian restaurant in the Bronx. The word in the village is that he is the General Manager of a five-star hotel in Manhattan.

Vijayan's son, Ajayan, has become the president of PPP and the MLA of the specially carved constituency in his hometown of Marakana Village.

Alumaram Village has a new MLA: Comrade Prabhu. He is also the PPP's District Treasurer. People stopped calling him dancer Prabhu.

The political arena has a new party, the Bharatiya Janata Party. It has emerged as a key player by allegedly using a few pages from the PPP's playbook.

Hindu-Muslim riots still flare up—a sign that elections are around the corner. The villagers are impervious to such religious conflicts.

An Indian and Foreign Liquor Store operates near the marshland where Mani sold illicit arrack. When people collect their salary every first day of the month, a long queue forms at the store. Sub-Inspectors and constables don't have to stand in the queue. The liquor store has an iron gate, an iron bar counter, and an iron door to prevent break-ins. Owner Mani comes in the morning and leaves in the evening in a Maruti driven by a bearded man in Levi jeans.

An investment banker has purchased Patti-Amma's and her neighboring homes, tore them down, and built a three-story house with a roof garden and a two-car garage.

The once clean Alumaram River, where people took bath and washed clothes, has become a breeding ground for mosquitos. Algae have formed in many sections, giving a green coating to the water. It has been turned in to a conduit for garbage disposal. Empty plastic bottles, building debris, and leftover food are strewn, reducing the magnificent river into a floating landfill.

Alumaram and Marakana villages have electricity and the city water system.

There's no promised school in the hamlets. In fact, the huts and shacks have been demolished and the farmlands have been dug up to build upscale high-rise condos and a five-story mall. The once idyllic landscape now looks like an inconsolable rape victim.

There are no more thatched roofs and mud homes, thanks to the new generation that took up jobs in the Gulf countries to earn their fortunes.

Cane-Swami was kicked out of the house by the widow and her neighbors when they found out the woman he had brought into the house one night was not his niece, but a prostitute. No one knows where he went. *Swish. Swish. Swish.*

Hassan closes his flower shop, takes up a job as a sales clerk in Muscat, and is promoted to the store's General Manager. He has built a two-story house near the mosque. He is also building a four-star hotel where Arul's Coconut Oil Factory once operated. The four-star hotel is called Hotel Amal, named after Hassan's granddaughter. Arul lost his business and reputation when TV stations ran stories that he had been adulterating high-grade oil with low-grade oil.

The mosque has a giant dome encased in gold-plated copper sheets and four thirty-foot minarets that stand like sentries. The Amman Devi temple also saw a sea change. It has a tall stone tower carved with religious symbols and a thirty-foot flag post that, too, is covered in gold-plated copper sheets. Both houses of worship boast tall, concrete compound walls and a computerized sound system that blares pre-taped prayers.

A petrol pump operates where Vijayan made his political debut, and Prabhu shook up to Elvis' music. Next to the petrol pump are two large billboards with Malayalam and Hindi movie posters featuring male and female stars. All of them are gorgeous and light-skinned.

Blonde European teenagers are popular models for Indian jewelry and cosmetic businesses.

Newspapers and websites publish matrimonial advertisements. Two samples:

Parents of Brahmin, Vaikhansa, tall boy, 34, doctor, younger looking, settled in US., invite correspondence from Brahmin, Vaikhansa, girls or their parents, preferably a doctor, should be sophisticated and home-loving. Send a bio-data with a color photo to....

Suitable alliance for a Vellala girl, 28, pretty, well qualified, IT, employed in Bangalore, fair complexion, from Vellala boys with similar qualities. Email a bio-data with a color photo to....

Trivandrum Aerodrome, following a multi-million-dollar expansion, becomes Thiruvananthapuram International Airport. There are daily flights to and from the U.S. with stopovers in the Middle East or Europe.

The banyan tree still stands at the junction. The long branches that had jutted onto M.G. Road are missing. The tree looks like a diabetes patient with a few body parts amputated.

Not able to withstand the dust and the noise, the bats have migrated or died, leaving the tree forlorn and frazzled.

Guru's nephew took over the family's tradition by opening a computerized astrology business: AstrologyXpress. For a fee, a computer will spit out your horoscope and your future. All you need to do is punch your date of birth, the time of birth, and the year on the keyboard. If you are unhappy with the horoscope, you can punch another date, time, and the year of your birth. You can do so until AstrologyXpress predicts that you will be rich and famous.

Appu's son now runs the "Modern Hair Salon." It has three swivel chairs and two junior barbers. Appu and his son are the senior barbers. He stopped cutting hair when his son grew old enough to hold a pair of scissors and a comb. Age and carpal tunnel syndrome on his right hand made Appu hand over the shop to his son. But he still comes to the barber shop daily and occasionally cuts the hair of old-timers.

ON FRIDAYS, Appu and Guru, in their late eighties, meet at the junction to reminisce or enjoy each other's company. They never heard from Mashe since he sold his house and moved to Cochin to start a new life twenty years ago.

Appu has lost a few pounds, but not the elephantiasis. It has swelled massively as if his body fat has been lumped on his right leg. His shoulder is hunched, a gift from hovering over people's heads. His wrinkled face brightens upon seeing his old pal from a distance. Guru moves slowly and frequently stops between his house and the junction.

The same umbrella, its top patched with black scotch tape, is tucked under his armpit. The umbrella's bent handle has become pale and yellow like the banyan tree's branches with peeled barks. He uses the umbrella as his walking stick. He has tossed the brown gunny bag under his wooden cot.

Guru's face lights up on seeing Appu from far away.

"You need a haircut," Appu says when Guru nears the barbershop.

He has heard the all too familiar words many times.

"Can't I wait for another week?"

"No. It's very long. Come, I'll give you a haircut."

Guru spits the paan juice, which has lost its force and doesn't jet as it was until a few years ago. The paan juice drools over his chin. He wipes it with the hand towel and enters the Modern Hair Salon. Appu's son moves aside so his father can work on his favorite client.

Appu's scissors snip slow as if in no rush. During the haircut, Appu asks, "Why did you stop reading horoscopes?"

Guru replies. "After Leela's death, I don't have the motivation to do anything. I taught my nephew the basics of astrology, and he has developed it into a successful business. I get tired easily, Appu. Look, I've only two teeth. I've to crush the paan and chew it. They don't make strong, pure tobacco anymore. Everything is artificially flavored."

"Yes, they don't make things as they did before. Now everything is made in China," Appu says. "I wanted to ask you this for a long time."

"What's it?"

"How did you come up with the name Narayanan for Chenda?"

Guru is silent. Confused, Appu looks in the oblong mirror in front of the customers at the shop. It reflects Guru turning sallow. His head droops, and he coughs twice. Appu pauses and gently brushes the hair from the barber's black gown with pictures of scissors and combs.

"Are you alright?" he asks.

"Yes," Guru says. "Narayanan is the Lord's name. Lord Vishnu. The protector of the universe." Guru takes a deep breath, sighs, and continues, "When Leela was six months pregnant, we decided that if the baby was a girl, we would call her Narayani. If the baby was a boy, we would call him Narayanan. God who gives also takes it away. Leela had a miscarriage. God took away the baby too soon, Appu."

Appu becomes silent, taken aback by the weight of grief Guru has been masking over the years. He puts the comb and the scissors on the counter and wipes his face. He looks at Guru's reflection in the mirror. He can't figure out whether Guru is sobbing or coughing. He takes a bottle of water from a mini fridge in the shop, opens, and gives it to Guru.

After a pause, in a cracking voice, Appu says, "I'm so sorry, Guru. I didn't know this. I'm really sorry for you and your wife."

Guru sips water from the bottle, looks at Appu, and reflects, "Time flies, memories don't." After a pause, he continues, "I spotted a blip in the baby's horoscope and offered several poojas to Amman Devi and other Gods. Didn't work. It's my karmam. I might have done something terrible in my previous life."

"Please don't say such things, Guru," Appu admonishes. "It's providence. God's will. There's nothing we can do about it. Had you thought of trying for another child?"

"No. We did not. We were afraid the same thing would happen again. We couldn't handle another tragedy. Anyway, I thought I would give the name Narayanan to our Chenda. And Leela didn't object."

"It's a good name," Appu says. "It was perfect for him."

Guru's head droops again. Appu gently straightens it and resumes cutting his hair.

Their conversation turns to a familiar topic.

"Did Cane-Swami's people kill Chenda?" Appu whispers.

"I don't know," Guru says, his voice cracking with sorrow.

"Sheikh Ali's men? Did they kill him?"

"I don't know."

"Anyone from Thomachan's church?"

"I'm not sure."

"Was Vijayan behind it? He and Chenda had a falling out, you know."

"True, they didn't see eye-to-eye toward the end," Guru says. "But Vijayan cried like a baby when he saw Chenda's body."

"Guru, death rattles people's sense of immortality and brings out regret, guilt, and sorrow," Appu says, and sweeps the clipped hair on the floor with a broom.

"How many times have we discussed this? A thousand times?"

"Maybe, two thousand times. I still can't get a closure."

"I know. I feel the same. Chenda was a good man," Guru says. "Whoever did, they killed an innocent man and a great *chenda* player."

"Yes. He was the best," Appu replies. "Ugran *chenda* player. No one can match him. Did you see all these new *chenda* music schools? I don't know what they teach. No life in their music. They simply bang on the kettledrum."

"You are correct. Today's *chenda* groups play some strange kind of music. They call it fusion so people can dance. It is dance music. The new age music is set to the feet, not to the soul," Guru says and sighs.

Appu nods, brushes off the fallen gray hair from Guru's shoulders, and removes the barber's gown. Guru, after getting out of the chair, offers fifty rupees.

"Don't insult me, Guru. We are lifelong friends. We're family. Put the money back in your pocket. The haircut is free," Appu says.

"That is what you told me the last time," Guru says, dusting off the residues of hair on his mundu. "Please take the money."

"I said no. Pay me next time."

Guru shakes his head and slowly steps out of the Modern Hair Salon. Appu leaves the scissors on the counter and accompanies Guru. Appu, dragging his right leg, and Guru, holding the umbrella for support, walk toward the banyan tree. They sit on the newly built cement parapet around it.

"You know today is full moon night," Appu says.

"Yes, I know. I'll be waiting for our Chenda's music," Guru says.

ON FULL MOON nights, when tranquility sets in, Chenda's music floats like a gentle breeze from the foot of the banyan tree. "Dum... tada... tada... tatatada... dum." As the drumbeat grows louder and reaches a crescendo, the music is elevated with the rhythmic chime of the cymbals and the cadence of the kombu wind instrument. "Dum... tada... tada... tatatada... dum." The village is bathed in the splendor of Chenda's music.

Driven by curiosity and awe, Guru's nephew and his friends once checked out who plays the enchanting music. Like sleuths, they walked around the banyan tree, along the streets, and behind the bushes. They were dumbfounded and terrified when they couldn't find any musician.

Appu and Guru know that Chenda is playing the kettledrum with his eyes closed and is waltzing in abandon with the invisible angels of music. His two drum sticks would multiply to four, then to six, to eight, and to twelve as if a flock of birds fluttering on the kettledrum.

About the author

It took Cliff Anthony about seven years of writing, rewriting, tweaking, and a few pints of tequila to complete *Tears in God's Own Country.*

A native of Kerala, Cliff made America home in 1986.

To pay for his food and mortgage, Cliff teaches journalism and freelances in Cleveland, Ohio.

Please visit www.cliffanthony.com.

Jayge, Kerala